# Whispers in the Dark

## Dan Padavona

## Copyright Information

Published by Dan Padavona

Visit our website at www.danpadavona.com

# Whispers in the Dark

# CHAPTER ONE

When she was young, the playful screams of children delighted Darcy. Now they disorient the widowed mother of two and make her glance around the beach, fearing someone needs help.

A crowd of tourists and locals crowd the beach off Genoa Cove. As Darcy rubs sunscreen on her legs and scans the water for the kids, the sun beats on the sand and promises an endless, scorching summer. Hunter, her eighteen-year-old son, leaps through a wave and bumps into his girlfriend, Bethany Torres. Together, they topple into the froth. Darcy has never seen Hunter laugh and smile as much as he does when he's with Bethany. They're good for each other, both warring with internal demons but determined to survive.

A few waves away, Jennifer, Hunter's younger sister, turns and squeals when a breaker crashes against the backs of her thighs and threatens to knock her face-first onto the sand. Like Hunter and Bethany, Jennifer has lived a nightmare over the last year. It's a wonder any of them are here to enjoy this fine day, when it seems vacation will last forever.

Six months have passed since mass murderer Michael Rivers, the man Darcy Gellar shot and captured almost four years ago, escaped from a prison outside Buffalo, New York. Winter's breath froze the air over a cold Georgia town when the news broke, and Darcy felt certain the Full Moon Killer would come after her family just as he'd sent murderers Richard Chaney and Eric Stetson to kill Darcy. But it's June 28, the cold of winter long forgotten as a heat wave grips coastal North Carolina, and nobody talks about Michael Rivers anymore. The national media's voracious appetite for news about the escaped murderer seems to be waning. Rivers vanished in December, slipping through the nets cast by the FBI and New York State Police. Since then there have been no credible sightings of the madman.

But that doesn't stop Darcy from worrying. He's out there. Free. And he won't stop until he finds Darcy and kills her.

Darcy rolls onto her side and places the new Stephen King novel in her bag. Beside her, a family of four—two overweight parents watching over a pair of toddlers—build a sandcastle. They must be northerners judging by the pasty white flesh and New Jersey accents. A radio plays to the other side of Darcy's towel, a classic rock-and-roll song she danced to during college. All around her, families and couples ignore the heat and celebrate the hope and rebirth that's only witnessed at summer's onset. She wonders how they can smile without cares, but they haven't experienced the hell Michael Rivers put her family through.

It's quiet times like these when Darcy's mind wanders. Her bank account is almost drained of her husband's life insurance payout. Tyler died of an aneurysm when Jennifer was too young to remember her father, but Hunter remembers, and Darcy knows the wound cuts as deep into Hunter as it does into her. After she survived the Full Moon Killer's attack, Darcy retired from her position with the FBI's Behavior Analysis Unit. Since then, she's lived off the insurance payout and the middling salary she makes as a graphic design artist. She's considered a full-time career, even a return to the FBI, but she can't be away from her children for more than a few hours without her anxiety flaring that Michael Rivers or one of his henchmen will take them.

In the water, Hunter lifts Bethany onto his shoulders and wades through the waves, threatening to drop her into the ocean. She's bronze-skinned and perfect, her curly brunette hair drenched and dangling past her shoulders. One look at the girl's smile and Darcy would never know Aaron Torres, her brother, raped Bethany last year with the help of his football teammate, Sam Tatum. Aaron and Sam will go to prison for their crimes, but the legal system moves tortoise-slow in Genoa Cove. While Aaron and Sam await trial, they're out on bail. Since their release Darcy hasn't been able to stop looking over her shoulder. Both boys will hurt Hunter if they catch him, though doing so will lengthen their sentences.

Jennifer returns from the water and plops down on the towel beside Darcy. It's not yet July, and the girl's tan is in August form. Though the turquoise thong bikini leaves nothing to the imagination, Darcy won't fight Jennifer over her clothing choices. It's an argument neither can win, and Darcy is thankful her daughter still ventures into public after two abductions in the last seven months.

Over Jennifer's water-beaded back, past the serpentine shoreline, the distant cliffs rise over the cove and throw shadows over the water, turning the ocean black during the late afternoon and evening. This darkening of the offshore shallows earns Genoa Cove the nickname Darkwater Cove, a name which will forever be synonymous with last year's murders. The locals blame Darcy for bringing evil to their village. She agrees.

Closing her eyes, Darcy allows the sun to pull her back to her childhood. During summers, her parents took Darcy to Mid-Atlantic beaches for vacation, but her mother never let Darcy go near the water until she was twelve.

"The waves are too strong," her mother would say. They'd drag little Darcy out to sea. So while the other kids frolicked in the shallows, Darcy watched life play out from a towel thirty yards from the tide's reach.

"When are we eating?"

Darcy's eyes spring open at the sound of Jennifer's voice. Her daughter lies on her side, shoulder length brunette hair dripping on the sand. Darcy's stomach rumbles, and she realizes it's well past dinnertime. How long have they been at the beach?

"Are you ready to head back?"

Jennifer looks toward the water, where Hunter and Bethany dance through the breakers, hands held.

"Yeah, let's go."

Darcy hears the hurt in Jennifer's voice. Since their childhoods, Jennifer and Hunter have remained inseparable. Hunter taught Jennifer to swim and was the first to coax her into the ocean when she was barely old enough for grade school. Darcy knows Jennifer is happy for Hunter—he's found someone—but she's a third wheel now, a tag-along who doesn't fit in with her older brother and his girlfriend.

While Jennifer gathers their belongings and packs the beach bag, Darcy waves at Hunter. It takes half a minute for Hunter to notice. Then he waves back, but there's a dejected slump to his shoulders as he follows Bethany out of the water. Hunter doesn't want the day to end.

Jennifer almost has the bag packed when a scream pulls Darcy's head around. A throng of sunbathers leap up from their towels to see what the commotion is about. Darcy steps around the crowd for a better look. Her daughter clutches her arm when the lifeguard whistles across the water. The male lifeguard in red trunks jumps down from his perch and crashes through the waves. About twenty yards out in the water, a girl's head bobs in and out of the froth, her arms splashing with desperation as the tide drags her away from shore. A rip current.

A female lifeguard with long blonde hair follows on the male's heels. As Hunter and Bethany join Darcy and Jennifer at the shoreline, the lifeguards dive over waves and swim toward the girl. For an excruciating moment, the drowning girl's head dips beneath the waves and doesn't come up. Already she's several yards farther out to sea than she'd been when the whistles rang out.

More lifeguards race from their posts, and a college age male with zinc on his nose pushes the crowd back from the water. The two lifeguards reach the drowning girl. The male drags her back to the shore with the female's aid.

Is she breathing?

Concerned mutters drift the crowd, and somewhere a young boy cries. When they lie the girl on the sand, she coughs and spits out water. Thank God.

"Please," Jennifer says, tugging Darcy by the arm.

Darcy nods in understanding. Her daughter can't watch, not after witnessing Eric Stetson choke the life out of Sandy Young after Stetson abducted Sandy and Jennifer. Hunter opens his mouth to protest, wanting to ensure the teenage girl is okay. Then he understands and drapes an arm over Jennifer's shoulders, leading her up the beach.

Nobody speaks as they shuffle on sandy flip-flops over the steaming blacktop. Darcy points the key fob at the Prius and unlocks the doors, and the teens pile into the backseat, exhausted and withdrawn. She lowers the visor when the descending sun blinds her, then turns out of the parking lot and takes the coastal route back to her neighborhood.

Back to reality.

For a fleeting moment at the beach, she'd forgotten her neighbors. Now she senses their glares as the Prius rounds a curve and passes the well-manicured lawns and upper-class homes. Dr. Merritt washes his Jeep in the driveway. His eyes shoot up when the Prius approaches. Darcy waves, but the doctor looks away. When she pulls into the driveway, there's no one to greet her or wave hello from across the street. Doors close, shades are drawn. Somewhere two neighborhood dogs bark.

"Grab the bag," Darcy says to Hunter when the doors open.

She unlocks the house with the three teenagers standing behind her. The air conditioning is like a slap across her sunburned shoulders when she steps inside.

"I'll take Bethany home," Hunter offers as Darcy enters the alarm code into the keypad beside the door.

"You sure? You're welcome to stay for dinner, Bethany. I'm grilling burgers."

"No thank you," Bethany says, eyes heavy as she leans her head on Hunter's shoulder. "Mom is expecting me."

Bethany's parents separated by necessity. The father

rented an apartment across town so Aaron could stay with him. Though the Torres family tried to justify their son's sexual assault as a misunderstanding, they couldn't allow Aaron to live under the same roof as Bethany. At least not until the judge acquitted Aaron, which the Torres parents are confident will happen once the courts hear Aaron's side of the story.

Darcy hands the keys to Hunter. While Jennifer shuffles toward the bathroom to shower before dinner, Darcy slips out of her flip-flops and pads barefoot to the kitchen where she interrogates the refrigerator for barbecue sauce. With the jar empty, she'll have to make do with whatever is in the fridge and cupboards. The front door closes. Darcy hears Hunter and Bethany giggling in the driveway. Then the Prius pulls into the street, and the fear that something bad will happen to her child creeps up on Darcy and whispers in her ear. Already she counts the minutes until Hunter returns.

She places a small bowl on the counter and whips up a barbecue sauce for the hamburgers. As Darcy spoons out a sample and tastes the concoction, her eyes stop on the picture attached to the refrigerator. Amy Yang in black robes, the tassel on her cap marking her as a proud high school graduate. A girl with a bright future and her entire life ahead of her before the Full Moon Killer tried to abduct her. What were the chances she'd be alone in the parking lot when Michael Rivers came through? Like encountering a great white in waters that haven't seen a shark in decades. Though Amy escaped the budding serial killer that night, she never truly survived. The trauma from the experience crippled her and prompted her to quit college. Then, after she moved to nearby Smith Town, serial killer Richard Chaney finished the job Michael

Rivers started. Darcy blames herself for Amy's death. She'd invited the girl into her home, made her one of the family. But she hadn't kept her safe.

Grabbing the matches, Darcy unlocks the deck doors and fires up the grill. She keeps her head low, eyes focused on the growing flames. Yet she's aware of the setting sun and the dark seeping out of the horizon. She takes a deep breath and lets it out, letting go of her fears as she uses the process her therapist taught her. It doesn't work. She can feel the dark like a winter wind scraping at her flesh. The fire goes out. Her fingers tremble as she attempts to restart the fire, fumbling three matches before she gets the coals to catch. She cups her elbows with her hands and paces the deck. Curses herself for caving in to her anxieties.

The anti-anxiety medicine sits on her nightstand inside the bedroom. A quick walk down the hall. But she took a pill this morning. Another dose would start her down the road to addiction again, and she won't put her children through another nightmare.

Except she can't stop her hands from shaking. This is the worst episode she's had in months, and dusk hasn't yet set in. If only she could rely on a neighbor or had someone to talk to. But the people of Genoa Cove will celebrate the day she's six feet under.

# CHAPTER TWO

Voices inside the kitchen bring Darcy out of sleep.
Initially, she writes the voices off to the remnants of a
dream. Then the floor squeaks, and Darcy bolts upright,
heart thundering, hands gripping the blanket. Someone is
inside the house.

A girlish giggle sets Darcy at ease when she swings
her feet off the bed. Checking the clock, she sees it's eight-
thirty, later than she prefers to rise, but much too early for
her daughter. As a rule, Jennifer doesn't rise before ten
during vacation.

More laughter echoes down the hallway. Two girls.

Dragging a brush through her hair in the bathroom,
Darcy cleans up and brushes her teeth. In shorts and an
over-sized t-shirt, she looks presentable when she wanders
into the kitchen. The girl sitting across the table from
Jennifer is blonde and beautiful. She wears a impish grin
as though she's spent the morning conspiring with
Jennifer. The girl spots Darcy in the entryway and stands,
causing Jennifer to swivel her head.

"Oh, Mom. This is Lindsey Doler. We're trying out
together for varsity cheer in August."

Lindsey crosses the room and offers her hand to Darcy.

"I'm sorry if we woke you, Ms. Gellar."

Darcy likes Lindsey already. If this was Kaitlyn, Jennifer's best friend, the girl would have been twice as loud and wouldn't have apologized. Come to think of it, Kaitlyn acts like she runs the house when she visits.

"No, of course not," Darcy lies. Anything to foster Jennifer's new friendship. "Were you on the junior varsity team last year?"

"No, this will be my first year cheering. I played basketball last winter."

Judging by Lindsey's long, athletic legs and firm arms, she'll have no trouble making the varsity team as a first-year member. Darcy's eyes stop on Lindsey's bracelet. It looks like a replica of the one Jennifer purchased with her babysitting money—a sea-blue cord, clear glass beads, and a stainless steel charm with a shell emblazoned on one side.

"Are you wearing matching bracelets?"

Lindsey laughs.

"No, Jennifer let me borrow hers. It's pretty, isn't it? Makes me think of the beach."

Jennifer raises her wrist, a pale tan line marking the missing bracelet.

"Duh, Mom."

Darcy tuts.

"Hey, when I was your age, a lot of my friends wore the same bracelets."

"This sounds like a weird gang initiation thing."

The girls share a laugh.

"Yeah, right," Darcy says, opening the cupboard. "I guess it was kinda cliquey."

Darcy offers to make the girls breakfast, but Lindsey says she needs to meet her father downtown in a half-hour. The two girls hug and end their conversation with a promise to get together later.

"Can I give you a ride home?" Darcy asks.

"Thank you, but I rode my bike," Lindsey says, retrieving her helmet from beneath the table. "It was nice to meet you, Ms. Gellar."

"Nice to meet you too, Lindsey. Stop by anytime."

After the door closes, Darcy swings back to Jennifer and grins.

"I like her," Darcy says, hands on hips. "Why haven't you invited her over before?"

Jennifer shrugs and sets the eggs and milk on the counter beside the bread.

"We didn't talk much before this summer. It's not that I didn't like her, but she ran with the athletic girls, not the cheerleaders."

"Well, she's very polite." Not at all like Kaitlyn, Darcy thinks. Jennifer reads between the lines and groans. Darcy nods at the breakfast items on the counter. "Want me to make french toast this morning?"

"I'll make it," Jennifer says.

"Oh? What's the occasion?"

"Nothing special. Maybe I want to cook breakfast for my family for a change. You're always doing everything for us."

Darcy turns toward the cupboard to hide her smile. Yes, Lindsey is a good influence on her daughter. Standing on tiptoe, Darcy retrieves the maple syrup and sets it beside the bread.

"Better make a large batch. You know Hunter wolfs down french toast like he's coming off a hunger strike."

Darcy taps her nails against the counter. "Hey, what if I take you shopping after the breakfast dishes are put away?"

Jennifer lifts an eyebrow.

"Now it's my turn to ask what the special occasion is."

"If you're not interested, we can hit the beach when Hunter rolls out of bed."

"Who said I'm not interested?" Jennifer cracks the eggs into a bowl and mixes in the milk. "There's a new place called Donovan's at the edge of the village. They have the cutest skirts on the planet."

And they're twice as expensive as identical items at the mall. Darcy leaves the thought to herself. After everything Jennifer dealt with over the last year, she's owed a mother-daughter shopping trip with no strings attached.

Though Jennifer overcooks the french toast and burns the edges, breakfast tastes perfect to Darcy. She wishes every morning went as smoothly.

Hunter, half awake as he leans over the table, shovels the first bite of breakfast into his mouth. Jennifer, dressed in a floral sun dress and sandals, waits for Darcy beside the door.

"And don't open the door for anyone you don't know," Darcy tells Hunter, earning herself an eye roll. He waves her away with his fork.

The late morning temperature already blistering, Darcy holds the door to the Prius open until the heat rolls out. Inside, she cranks the air conditioning, but the interior doesn't reach a comfortable temperature until they're at the edge of downtown. During the ride she keeps one eye tuned to the security camera displayed on her phone.

Running the feed drains her battery, yet she won't relax unless she's certain Hunter is safe and no one is poking around the property, searching for a way inside.

Darcy parks in the municipal lot. Inside Donovan's, Jennifer models every dress on the rack, displaying each with a million-dollar smile. The search for the perfect dress takes forty-five minutes, but Darcy doesn't care. The shop is blissfully cool, though she doesn't appreciate the college age clerk ogling Jennifer.

After Jennifer settles on a jean miniskirt and top, Darcy buys them coffee in the center of the village. Thunder growls over the ocean, pulling Darcy's gaze toward the water. She glances again at the phone. The security cameras show an empty yard. Now and then, shadows dart across the yard when birds fly past.

"Relax, Mom. Hunter has it under control."

Darcy gives Jennifer a forced smile. Needing to get changed before she meets her friends later, Jennifer says she'd just as soon head home. Darcy doesn't argue. The thought of leaving one of her kids alone for another second eats a hole in her stomach, despite Hunter being a legal adult and capable of living on his own. And that makes Darcy think of college. Picturing Hunter's bedroom empty clenches her chest. With all that's happened to her family and the constant potential danger of someone watching them from the shadows, she's let it slip from her mind that Hunter is about to be a senior in high school. Had his elementary school not held Hunter back a year, he'd already have graduated.

As Jennifer pops the trunk and slides the bags inside, Darcy airs out the car again, wishing the distant thunderstorm would roll over downtown. Anything to break this heat. Yet when she props her phone in the cup holder, blank screens stare back at her. Her first reaction is her battery died. But the phone wouldn't display several windows outlined in white if the phone lost power. The screen would turn black. Which it hasn't. The cameras aren't working.

Or someone cut the signal.

Gunning the engine, Darcy cranks her head around when Jennifer takes too long arranging the shopping bags. After receiving the hint, her daughter frowns and slides into the seat.

"What's the rush? I thought we were having an enjoyable time."

Darcy turns the phone over, not wanting Jennifer to see the source of her panic. Glancing up at a black cloud blotting out the sun, Darcy points.

"The quicker we get going, the better chance we have of beating the storm."

Unconvinced, Jennifer slumps in the seat and fires off a text. Most likely Jennifer messages Kaitlyn. Darcy's mood swings are the most probable topic.

With Jennifer distracted, Darcy sets the phone in her lap and backs the Prius out of the parking spot. A sports car whips past, forcing her to slam her foot on the brake pedal. When the coast is clear, Darcy releases the brakes and inspects the backup camera.

On the coast road, Darcy pushes the Prius over seventy. She's fifteen mph over the limit. If there's a speed trap ahead, she'll return home with an expensive ticket. So far the rain is holding off. Occasional fat droplets splash the windshield, the humidity palpable even inside the car. She takes the turn into her neighborhood too quickly and almost rolls the Prius. Jennifer grips the door handle, her face pale.

By the time their little house at the end of the loop comes into view, the tires grind through three inches of water. Branches litter yards, and an enormous elm tree hangs askew over the road, a strong gust away from flattening the Prius. The elm's branches snag wires. Darcy doesn't breathe until the car clears the obstruction.

Lightning snakes down from the clouds and explodes over the cove, followed by a blast of thunder. Darcy races from the car to the door with Jennifer covering her head. She fits the key into the lock as the wind ripples her shirt and tries to drag her off the stoop. The door flies open and bangs against the foyer wall.

"Hunter? Are you here?"

Darcy enters the alarm code and listens for her son's answer. It's quiet inside the house. Her heart rate spikes. But when she throws open the bedroom door, Hunter lies on his side on the bed, his headphones on.

Jennifer peeks inside the room and shakes her head. Darcy sits on the edge of Hunter's bed and shakes his shoulder. Her son twitches and spins around, his eyes confused until he removes the headphones.

"Dammit, Hunter. How can you hear me calling you with your music turned up so loud? Do you always have to wear headphones?"

"Sorry. I just put them on a half-hour ago."

"You didn't answer my calls."

"Guess I didn't hear. Anyhow, I read you aren't supposed to use your phone during an electrical storm."

He's right. But that never stopped either of her children before. Darcy huffs and hurries to the kitchen. Though it's mid-afternoon, the house is as dark as dusk. A flick of the wall switch verifies the power is out and the cameras aren't working. The generator should have kicked on.

Darcy slides the bolt back on the deck door and steps onto the porch. The rain stopped, and the wind isn't as strong. A faraway rumble of thunder proves the storm moved on. Still, she's wary of lightning as she steps across the deck, the planks slick with water. The lawn feels like a swamp under her sneakers as she treads toward the slumbering generator. After checking the connecting cable, Darcy scratches her head. The generator fired up during two storms last month. It can't be out of gas. But when Darcy checks the fuel level, she finds the tank bone dry.

"You've got to be kidding me."

She leans against the generator and rubs her temples. Darcy swore she'd keep track of the generator fuel level and never risk losing power. How could she be so stupid?

With a curse, she ascends the deck and closes the door, sliding the bolt into place. First order of business this evening is to fill the generator. She can't face the dark again.

# CHAPTER THREE

The devil hides in the chat room. Darcy knows he's there, but the devil is silent. Careful. Always watching.

Morning light slips through a crease between the drawn curtains and paints a fiery stripe across the bedroom carpet. A door closes in the hallway while Darcy clicks through the serial killer fan website. The quiet footfalls leading down the hallway must be Jennifer's.

The sink runs in the kitchen, then the clink of a glass when Jennifer sets her drink on the counter. Hunter is still asleep with the clock approaching noon. He stayed up late playing shooter video games, and though his voice disrupted Darcy's sleep after midnight, she's happy he has friends. Not like last year. Hunter won few friends after they moved to Genoa Cove from Virginia. His classmates treated him like an outcast. Dating Bethany Torres raised kids' opinions of Hunter. A shallow reason. But after the bullying Hunter endured last year, Darcy feels thankful he has friends heading into his senior year.

Seated on the floor with her back against the wall, Darcy pushes the bedroom door shut with her foot. She searches the website for her name, then repeats the process for Jennifer and Hunter. The most recent thread devoted to the Gellar family dates back three months. The entire Internet knows they live in Genoa Cove again, so it doesn't worry Darcy that the post contains their address and a Google Maps link. It's old news, though if Darcy had her way, they'd live a few thousand miles from the cove and its memories. Darcy swore she'd never return to the North Carolina village after the Chaney murders, which the police attempted to pin on Hunter. But the house hasn't sold since she placed it on the market last November. Apparently, prospective buyers shy away from homes targeted by serial killers.

Forcing herself to stop searching, Darcy closes the browser and pulls up a view of the security cameras. The palm tree fronting the vacant house next door wilts under the sun, the wind calm as if it's too exhausted to blow the cooler ocean air inland. The front sidewalk lies empty, and the bordering grass sports gray patches despite recent thunderstorms. Three Adirondack deck chairs look out upon a wildflower meadow. All is quiet.

After Darcy brought her family back to Genoa Cove, the FBI maintained a vigil over the residence. They've since pulled their agents, though Eric Hensel, Darcy's former partner in the FBI's Behavior Analysis Unit, calls every day to ensure the Gellar family is safe. Now the Genoa Cove PD provides their only protection. The same officers who failed to take Darcy's warnings seriously before last autumn's murders. Darcy slides the laptop into its case and sips an iced tea. Condensation beads on the glass and leaves a puddle on the nightstand.

The phone rings. Darcy jumps as if the phone is a tarantula. When she answers, she hears a man breathing.

Michael Rivers.

She receives these calls every few days, always from a different number.

"Hello, Michael. Aren't you going to talk to me?"

No response. Just the murderer's breaths rasping. She ends the call and sets the phone down, waiting for it to ring again. When it doesn't, she copies the phone number and time into her notebook. Darcy shares the hand-printed log with the FBI and Genoa Cove PD per their requests, but she doubts the usefulness of the information. It's a burner phone. Always a burner. He's already tossed the phone into the garbage.

She can't stay here. Needs to get into the light and wash away the sickness bubbling in her stomach.

In the hallway, Darcy listens at Jennifer's door. Her daughter types at the keyboard. At Hunter's door, she knocks and pushes the door open a crack. Darkness rolls through the opening. Hunter snores with the covers dragged over his head as Darcy enters the room and tiptoes around the dirty clothes strewn across the floor. It takes two shakes to rouse Hunter up from sleep. He's stares at Darcy in blurry eyed confusion.

"I'm going out. Can you watch your sister?"

Hunter itches his head and raises himself up to his elbows.

"Yeah, sure. Where are you going?"

"Just out. Downtown, maybe. I don't know."

"Everything okay?"

No, nothing is okay, she wants to say. The serial killer who wants to gut our family just breathed at me over the phone.

"Everything is fine. I just need a little sun."

"Have fun," Hunter says, collapsing on the pillow and yanking the covers up to his chin.

Darcy drags the covers down to his shoulders.

"You charged your phone, right?"

He groans and lifts his phone off the nightstand. A quick swipe to check the battery life.

"Sixty percent."

"Good. Don't open the door for anyone."

"I know, Mom. We've been over this so many times."

"Hunter, listen. If anyone calls and you don't recognize the number—"

"I know, I know. Don't answer. Got it. Stranger danger."

"Don't turn this into a joke."

He slams his head onto the pillow and rips the blanket over his face.

"I didn't. I just want to sleep, okay?"

"The number for the police is on the refrigerator."

"Right," he says, drawing out the word like someone who's heard this speech too many times. "Or call 9-1-1 if anyone trespasses into our yard."

"And if you call the police, ask for Detective Ames or Officer Haines."

An irritated moan. Hunter rolls over and faces the window.

Leaving well enough alone, Darcy closes Hunter's door. Heat boils out of the Prius when she opens the door. She drives toward downtown with the windows rolled down until the air conditioning kicks on, looking straight ahead and avoiding the neighbors watching her pass.

Downtown Genoa Cove looks like an image plucked from a tourist pamphlet. The main strip is paved in red brick with an island in the center. Upscale clothing shops and restaurants line the thoroughfare. A jazz quartet plays a Charlie Parker song outside the Mediterranean restaurant across the street.

After failing to locate a parking spot on the street, Darcy parks in the public lot behind the library and follows the sidewalk toward the shopping district. A little browsing will set her mind at ease, reset her for the rest of the day. She grabs the door to Maria's Dress Shop when a familiar voice calls behind her. Turning, she sees Julian Haines crossing the street. The Genoa Cove policeman isn't in uniform. He wears white shorts and a green surf t-shirt, his sunglasses reflecting the storefronts in double images.

"Hey, aren't you working today?"

"Contrary to popular belief, I don't work everyday," he says, pushing the glasses up so they rest atop his head. "I see the kids let you out of the house."

"Well, contrary to popular belief, the town psycho takes a day off to shop now and then."

He creases his brow.

"Nobody calls you a psycho. Please don't say things like that."

"You don't know my neighbors. What brings you out on this fine morning?"

He shuffles his feet and stuffs his hands into his pocket.

"Bored. If I sit at home all day, I'll go through a bag of potato chips." Julian must exaggerate based on his slim waist and chiseled arms. "How about I buy you a cup of tea?"

Darcy gives Julian a playful grin.

"Is this a date, Officer Haines? People will talk."

"It's a cup of tea. Get over it." But when she giggles, pink tinges his cheeks. He tilts his head at a cafe at the end of the block. "Have you ever tried matcha? My niece says it will melt your face off if you drink it too fast."

Darcy grimaces.

"Is that the green powdered stuff I see my kids drinking?"

"Yep."

"Sure. What's the worst that could happen?"

"It might morph you into the Incredible Hulk."

"I'll take that risk."

Darcy steps off the curb. Julian's hand shoots out and grips her forearm. He yanks her onto the sidewalk as a red sports car speeds past with music blaring through its windows.

"You okay?"

"I'm fine," Darcy says, touching her hammering heart.

"Damn teens driving like they're the only ones on the road. That was too close. I should call in the license plate."

"No, don't," Darcy says, hooking her elbow with his. "Let's just get off the street."

Acoustic guitar plays through speakers inside the cafe. Julian and Darcy order lattes from a youthful woman with braided hair and multiple lip piercings. In his early thirties, Julian is a decade younger than Darcy. But even Julian looks like a crusty adult amongst the crowd of teens and twenty-somethings ordering teas. They choose the window table to get away from the crowd.

"So you never told me what you came downtown for," Julian says, wincing after he takes a sip. Green powder crusts his lips. Darcy smirks until he raises his eyebrows. "What?"

"Go like this," she says, running her tongue over her lips.

He follows her lead.

"Better?"

"Better."

"Good. I feel like I'm a parent spying on my kids in here."

Darcy swallows a chuckle. Julian doesn't have children and hasn't dated since Darcy moved to Genoa Cove a year ago.

"That should be my line," she says, dabbing the corner of her mouth with a napkin. Three sips into the latte, and Darcy rides the buzz of a full cup of coffee. "And since you asked, I came downtown to browse. I'm afraid my wallet isn't large enough for these stores."

He smiles and moves his eyes to the counter, where a teen boy in ripped blue jeans requests an application. The counter girl shoots the boy a petulant stare and hands him a pen.

"What do you think? Applying for his first job?"

Julian narrows his eyes in consideration.

"Based on the spiked hair, earrings, and skateboard outfit, I doubt he's banker material. What do you think? You're the former FBI profiler."

Darcy laughs and shushes him, worried someone will hear.

"That was four years ago."

"I bet you still have the gift."

Okay, he asked for it. Darcy can't turn off the internal profiler.

"He's at least seventeen. This isn't his first job. He didn't tear those jeans skateboarding. You pay extra for manufactured rips."

"Not like when I was a kid," he says, raising the mug to his lips. "We'd wear blue jeans and play tackle football in the lot behind the old middle school. You earned the rips back in the day. Okay, how about somebody else?"

Darcy lowers her head and hides her eyes behind her hand.

"You really want to embarrass me."

"I still owe you from that time you whooped my ass at the dojo."

Darcy falls back and laughs, but a warning rolls around in her head. Why did Julian volunteer for Bronson Severson's self-defense class? Severson, a former GCPD cop, took a bribe from Michael Rivers and tried to kidnap Darcy and her family. She'd trusted Severson because he used to work for the force and taught self-defense. Strange that Julian aligned himself with Severson.

"Please, I didn't whip anyone. I broke a rear choke hold, which by the way was totally illegal."

"Huh, I never realized there were rules in real life attacks. You should thank me for testing you."

"Well, thank you."

He sets his mug on the table and glances at the window, shaking his head. Darcy clears her throat to grab his attention.

"I still don't get it. The old guard knew Severson was a dirty cop. You volunteered at a serial killer's gym?"

"Hey, I'm sorry," he says, wiping at an imaginary spill on the table. "That was stupid of me."

Darcy looks away and chews her nail.

"Don't worry. I've survived a lot worse in my life than Bronson Severson. What I don't get is what a nice young cop who never trusted Severson was doing inside that dojo."

"I wasn't there for Severson, I'll tell you that much." When her eyes prompt him to elaborate, he shrugs his shoulders. "I joined the GCPD six years ago, fresh out of grad school. During my senior year, my roommate's girlfriend got raped walking back from the library after dark."

"That's terrible."

"Yeah. The students organized a march to protest violence against women. We all participated, but I couldn't help feeling we weren't doing enough. Then one girl in student government, I think Kayla was her name, got the bright idea to organize self-defense clinics. Now that made sense to me. It made a difference, and since I'd taken Taekwondo through high school, I volunteered to be one of the…test dummies."

"You mean all the girls got to beat you up."

"Something like that. Then when I joined the force, my captain suggested I teach self-defense to women. The high school lent us the practice gym on Sundays, but turnout was low. Too many people in church or having brunch with the family. Then Severson opened his gym and started charging a king's ransom for self-defense classes. I thought he was fleecing the town, but I figured I should volunteer."

Julian's explanation sets Darcy at ease. She twirls a lock of hair around her finger.

"You wanted to make a difference again."

"Sure, I think I did. But enough about me." He glares conspiratorially toward the back of the room. "How about that guy?"

"Who?"

"The pudgy guy with the glasses. Looks like he's the owner."

"We're still doing this profiling thing?"

"I'm interested."

She glares at Julian through the tops of her eyes.

"Okay, but this is the last time."

"I promise I won't ask again."

The middle age man sits alone at a table with papers spread in front of him.

"Yes, he's the owner."

"That's obvious," Julian says. "But what's his motivation?"

"He's desperate and in the midst of a midlife crisis. Look at the keys on the table. The emblem."

"What about it?"

"He's driving a Jaguar. Now look at his shirt. Sweat stains around the collar, food stains down the front. This is a guy who can't upgrade his wardrobe because he put all his money into a car."

"I like that theory. What else?"

"The way he shuffles through the papers tells me the shop is bleeding money. He's confused because it shouldn't be. Business is great, the place is packed, but he's out of his element. His customers are one-third his age, and as far as he's concerned, they speak an unfamiliar language. Notice how he scowls every time he looks at the girl working behind the counter. He's not frustrated with her work rate. She's barely keeping up with orders. But she's alien to him, a whole different species. The nose ring. The strange clothes. He can't relate."

The man organizes the papers and slaps them on the table.

"His business is going under," Darcy says, continuing. "Give it sixty days, and you'll see a for-sale sign in the window. Purchasing the tea shop, like buying the Jaguar, was impulsive. He's filling a void in his life. And from the white stripe around his finger, I'd say he recently removed a ring he'd worn for a few decades."

"He just got divorced."

"Exactly."

Julian smirks and points at her.

"You're good. They teach that at FBI school?"

"FBI school? That's not what they call it. And no, not unless you're angling toward profiling."

Darcy swings her head toward an elderly woman staring at her through the window. Mrs. Andrews, one of Darcy's neighbors. Darcy frequently sees Andrews speaking with Mr. Gibbons, and she can guess what they say about Darcy and her family. Andrews continues to stare until Julian turns to look. She raises her nose and stomps past the tea shop.

"What was that all about?"

"Another one of my loyal neighbors."

"Don't lump all of Genoa Cove together because of how a few neighbors act toward you."

"A few? It's everyone, not just Gibbons and Andrews. I don't get what they have against my family. The police found Hunter innocent, and yet the village still believes he's a killer."

"You'd be surprised by how much support you have inside the village."

"They must be the quiet majority because nobody has spoken on our behalf since last year's murders."

Darcy and Julian drink their teas and study the other patrons. An uncomfortable silence falls between them. Darcy breaks the silence after she orders a second mug.

"Now that you've put the former profiler under the microscope, I'd like to know why Julian Haines got into law enforcement. Smart, young guy like yourself could have gone into any career he wanted."

Julian looks down at his hands, weighing what he

wants to tell her.

"I didn't grow up here. I'm from Newark, New Jersey, if you can believe it."

"You ditched the accent."

"Moved when I was ten." He shrugs, then scratches the back of his neck. "My father was a cop. Walked the nasty side of Newark for most of his career. The things he saw...after a while, he couldn't take it anymore and wanted something better for his family. So he moved us here."

"Did you have a brother or sister?"

"An older sister. She's twelve years older than me and married. Her daughter starts college next year. Weird that my niece is going into her freshman year, and I feel like I just left college."

"Sounds like you followed in your dad's footsteps."

"I suppose I did."

"Do you like Genoa Cove?"

"I love it. Crime is low, the sun shines year round, and people care about each other." Darcy cocks an eyebrow. "Most of the people, that is. I take it you wish you never came here."

"It's weird. I spent most of my life wanting to live beside the ocean. When I pictured my future house, the village I lived in, it looked like Genoa Cove. Now all I want is to live on a hill somewhere far from this place."

"Why a hill?"

"Because you can see your enemies coming."

# CHAPTER FOUR

Hands buried inside his pockets, Julian watches Darcy's Prius until she turns off the main strip. When he can't see her anymore, he unlocks his car and slides behind the wheel. It takes a long time before he turns the key in the ignition, their conversation playing in his head on an infinite loop. What was that she said about living on a hill? It might have been a flippant statement, an exaggeration. He doesn't think so. She hates Genoa Cove, and he can hardly blame her. She's moving. He read it in her eyes, could almost picture her future home from the hopeful quirk of her lips when she mentioned it.

With nothing but an empty house awaiting him if he drives home, Julian turns the car toward the Genoa Cove Police Department. As he drives, he wrestles with indecision. Since Darcy moved back to Genoa Cove last winter, they'd become friends and grown close. Many times he felt certain she wanted to expand their relationship, perhaps become lovers. Yet she kept him at arm's length. Look, but don't touch. No, it was more than that. She could handle a physical relationship. But an emotional relationship? It's not her fault. She lost her husband to an aneurysm and is raising two teenagers alone. And she's been a serial killer's target for almost a year. If only Darcy let Julian in. He can protect her.

Darcy isn't being straight with him. He deserves no better, for he wasn't truthful when he expressed his love for Genoa Cove and its police force. For several months, he's considered moving on to a larger city where he can make a difference.

When he enters the bullpen area, the short-staffed department appears sparse this afternoon with most of the officers walking beats. Detective Ames blows through with a folder in his hand. At first, Ames seems preoccupied with whatever case he's working. But when Julian walks toward his desk, the detective calls his name and beckons him to his office.

Ames's office is cramped and overrun with toppling stacks of paper and disorganized files. His jacket hangs on a rack. A little more gray dots the detective's hair than last year, an artifact of the Darkwater Cove murders, as the media calls them. He's lost weight too. The sweat-stained shirt hangs off his body like he's shedding skin.

Ames slides into the chair behind his desk and motions for Julian to have a seat.

"Detective?"

Ames runs a hand through thinning hair and weighs his words.

"I understand you're spending a lot of time with Darcy Gellar."

Julian fights to sit still. Is someone watching him?

"Who told you that?"

"What you do on your own time is your business, and I'm not the chief, just a guy who's been around the block enough times to know when a fellow officer is taking the wrong path."

"Whatever you heard, I'm not in a relationship with Darcy Gellar. She's a friend, nothing more."

"You bought her lunch today."

Julian's spine stiffens.

"We had drinks, and yeah, I paid. Who gave you this information?"

"Don't jump to conclusions, Officer Haines. It's a tiny village. People gossip."

"Gossiping, I accept. But why would someone relay the information to you?" Julian points into the bullpen. "I trust every cop out there like he's my brother. You need to tell me if I shouldn't."

Ames taps a pencil on the desk before tossing it into the drawer.

"Darcy Gellar is trouble, Officer. Not by her own doing, I contend, but trouble nonetheless. Half the village wishes she never moved to Genoa Cove, and I dare say more than a few, if taking a lie detector test, wish Richard Chaney finished what he started last year."

"Is that the way you feel, Detective?"

"Of course not. I've bent over backwards to keep the Gellar family safe." Ames goes silent and stares blankly at the wall. Resetting his thoughts, he rubs his face and settles back in his chair. "When I see Julian Haines, I see unlimited potential. You're the sharpest officer on the force. You could be a detective in less than a year and chief before the end of the decade."

"What does this have to do with Darcy Gellar?"

"You don't rise to Chief of Police without a lot of handshaking. Look at me. I'm not a politician, and I've reached my ceiling. But not you. The mayor already knows your name from your work on the Darkwater Cove murders. He sees big things for you."

"But he doesn't want Darcy Gellar in his village, and he can't stand her sullying the image of one of his future detectives." Julian scoffs and sends Ames a disappointed glance. "Is our motto to *protect and serve*, or protect our image so we can get ahead?"

Ames shows Julian his palms.

"I'm not justifying it. But that's the way things are. Do yourself a favor, Officer Haines. Whatever it is you have with Darcy Gellar, end it. Today. It's not worth the effort, anyway. She'll be gone by autumn."

"Wait, are you saying she's leaving Genoa Cove?"

"It's for the best."

"How could you know this?"

"Darcy Gellar contacted Kudlow Realty a month ago about another property."

Julian massages his eyes.

"This wouldn't be a house on a hill, would it?"

"A gated neighborhood on a hill outside of Charlotte. She's putting herself and her family at risk. The Charlotte PD won't know her back story. It's a death wish for someone with that many enemies, but once Darcy Gellar makes up her mind, nobody talks her out of it."

Julian shuffles back to his desk, head spinning. After he falls into his chair, he sits in silence, listening as the light fixtures hum above his head. Darcy is moving her family to Charlotte. And Genoa Cove keeps sticking its nose into his business.

"Dammit, Ames," he says toward the detective's closed door. "Stop giving me the Daddy treatment."

If there's one thing he agrees with Ames on, it's Darcy is making a mistake. What is she thinking moving her children? Julian understands her fear. Darcy knows

Michael Rivers will come for her, and when he does, she wants the showdown on her terms. But this is lunacy.

Julian shuffles through the caseload on his desk and wishes he wasn't off work today. Now he'll be a prisoner to his thoughts, too amped up to fall asleep tonight. As he raps his knuckles against the desk, Officer Faust crosses the bullpen area and sticks her head into Ames' office. Julian likes Faust and hopes she isn't the cop who ratted him out for buying Darcy tea. What Julian needs is a vacation.

He checks his contacts and locates the phone numbers for police departments in Miami and Raleigh. Bigger cities, fewer neighbors looking over his shoulder. And a chance to advance quicker than he will in Genoa Cove. If Darcy leaves, what's tying him to the coast? His parents left for Florida two years ago, and though Julian likes his coworkers, he never spends time with them outside the office.

Maybe Darcy has it right. Get the hell out of Genoa Cove and go some place where no one knows your name.

# CHAPTER FIVE

Darcy blows the hair off her forehead and taps her fingers on the laptop case. After a moment of consideration, she retrieves the computer and opens the browser. This time she skips the killer websites and clicks on her saved links.

The color of honey, the Cape Cod appears on the screen. In the picture, a mix of potted flowers and ornamental shrubs border the stone driveway and small front yard. Sunlight beams down from a perfect blue sky and reflects against the solar panels fixed to the roof and angled southward. A six kilowatt generator, hidden behind the house, provides backup power.

Darcy's finger wavers over the *request information* button. The asking price seems fair, but it will drain the last savings from Tyler's life insurance payout and put Darcy in debt for the next thirty years. Not to mention the war she'll have on her hands when she explains to Jennifer and Hunter they're moving. She understands the second she clicks the button the Realtor will hound her until she enters an offer.

You can't put a price on safety.

Darcy clicks the link and lowers the screen. One eye watches the door, expecting Jennifer to bust into the room, demanding to know why Darcy is moving them again. Both doors to her kids' rooms remain closed, the drone of a YouTube video audible when Darcy peeks into the hallway. One quick glance at the security cameras, then she slips on her flip-flops and unlocks the deck door inside the kitchen.

The heat blasts her when she steps outside. Waves ripple off the wooden deck and turn the backyard into a dream sequence. She slides into the Adirondack chair and thinks better of it, opting to grab a beach towel from the hallway closet and lay it across the seat so she doesn't singe her thighs. Opening the umbrella, she eases against the chair and lets her eyes wander across the yard. A meadow dotted with trees borders the backyard. The onshore wind carries a salty ocean scent, and she can almost smell wet sand and sun lotion when she turns her face to the breeze. Her Virginia neighbors had warned her about the North Carolina heat, but Darcy brushed them off, assuming temperatures would remain comfortable along the coast. And last year they had, even when a nasty heatwave hit interior portions of the state. Not so this year. Mother Nature opened a blast furnace and aimed it at Genoa Cove.

Darcy won't wait for Michael Rivers to resurface and butcher her family. But relocating won't keep her children safe. Given enough time, Rivers will find her. She needs to be ready when he comes.

Darcy jumps when the phone rings. Her old FBI partner's name appears on the screen.

"Did I catch you at a bad time?" Agent Hensel asks.

"Just trying not to melt in this heat," Darcy says,

plucking at her shirt when the breeze dies.

"Listen, I need you to remain calm, but we may have had a Rivers sighting last night."

Darcy's back goes rigid. She sits forward with her elbows on her knees, face lowered away from the sun.

"Where?"

"Outside Allentown, Pennsylvania, around midnight. A woman claims she spotted Rivers climbing into an Audi outside a gas station off I-476."

"Nothing we haven't heard before. What makes you think the claim is legit?"

Office conversation in the background tells Darcy Hensel is at his desk.

"She wrote down the plate number. Turns out the Audi was reported stolen two weeks ago, and that has my curiosity piqued."

"You mentioned a gas station. There must be security footage."

"We've got the local PD checking it out now. They'll send us the footage, and we'll run it through facial recognition software."

It's an eight-hour drive from Pennsylvania to Genoa Cove. Rivers might already be here. A shiver rolls down her skin as Darcy steps into the kitchen and throws the security bolt.

"Keep your eyes peeled, but don't overreact," Hensel says, continuing. "I put a call into the Genoa Cove PD and spoke with the chief. They'll ramp up surveillance on your house. Detective Ames will contact you."

Ames is the detective who arrested Hunter when he suspected her son of murder. She finds it difficult to forgive the detective's misstep, though Ames eventually realized his error and defended her family.

"The Full Moon Killer is loose and wants my family dead, but you don't want me to overreact?"

"All we have to go on is one eyewitness account about a stolen sedan. And potentially one other thing."

"Be honest with me, Eric."

"We seem to have misplaced Warden Ellsworth." Darcy met the warden of the Buffalo prison when she interviewed Rivers last year. "I tried calling him two days ago, and his assistant told me Ellsworth hadn't come into work and wasn't answering his phone. As of this morning, Ellsworth is still missing."

"You think Rivers went after the warden?"

"I can't deny the possibility. Ellsworth was the only authority figure standing in his way. No doubt they clashed."

"Seems like a helluva risk to go after the warden when the entire country is looking for you."

"You profiled Rivers, Darcy. Tell me the truth. Do you think he'd risk going after Ellsworth?"

Darcy shuffles her feet and scuffs the toe of her sneaker against the floor.

"Yes."

"Why?"

"He's vindictive. Not only did Rivers send hired killers after me and my family, he murdered Amy Yang because she escaped. That's the ultimate insult to a man like Rivers. Let's assume he tried to buy Ellsworth off like he did the prison guards. The warden spurned him, so Rivers waited until the time was right and went after Ellsworth as a matter of principle."

"I agree."

Darcy checks the windows. The house next door has sat vacant for over a year. The once nicely landscaped yard looks unruly, shrubs growing up the side of the house, branches snaking over the siding as if nature is dragging the home into a shallow grave. Anybody could be inside the house.

"Eric, we're not safe in Genoa Cove."

Hensel coughs. She pictures him choking on his soda and wiping the spill off his desk.

"You can't keep running. Darcy, we talked about this. You're protected where you are."

"A lot of good the police did my family last autumn."

"It's different now, Darcy. Ames is on your side and looking out for you. Everyone in the village knows you're innocent."

"Not everyone. I still have neighbors who believe Hunter helped Chaney murder those girls."

"Only one neighbor, and Harold Gibbons is a crazy old fool."

"A crazy old fool who holds court with half the neighborhood. Eric, I see them pointing at my windows. They're scheming."

"You don't know what they're saying. Maybe they formed a watch committee to monitor your property." When Darcy doesn't reply, Hensel stammers. "Okay, they didn't form a watch committee, but having snoops for neighbors has its advantages. Nobody's sneaking up on you without half the village knowing about it. Lock yourself away in a community where nobody knows your back story, and the police won't be there when you need them."

In the living room, Darcy falls onto the recliner and closes her eyes.

"Neither the police nor FBI are protecting me now. You're in Virginia, Eric."

"But you have Ames and the Genoa Cove PD watching your back."

"Officer Haines is keeping an eye on the house."

"You're spending more time with him, I take it.

"Julian is a lot younger than me. We're just friends. He's had a soft spot for Jennifer since the night Chaney kidnapped her, and he seems to get along with Hunter."

"Be careful, Darcy. Don't get too close."

Hensel remembers Darcy welcoming Bronson Severson into her home. She made a mistake. But Julian is different.

Climbing off the couch when she hears Jennifer approaching, Darcy slips out to the deck again. Being outside feels different now. She's exposed.

"I'll keep my eyes open, Eric."

"There's another reason to keep your eyes peeled."

"This had better be good news."

"Not exactly. Leo Vescio is in the wind."

Darcy's heart skips. She'd first met Vescio when the FBI investigated an organized crime ring in Western New York. Vescio secretly aided the FBI to bring down his competitors, and since then he'd risen from a small operator to the top of the food chain. Last year, Darcy contracted Vescio to attack Rivers in prison. Her plan backfired, and Rivers murdered Vescio's entire crew. The serial killer sliced their throats and punctured their chests with a shank. The failure made Vescio look weak and diminished his army. Upon their releases, the inmates would have rejoined the mob boss.

"Why would Vescio run? He has a good rapport with the FBI."

"He got what he asked for. Once he took over for his predecessors, he drew the crime task force's attention.

Between you and me, the FBI plans to take Vescio down. Someone must have tipped him off."

"When did he go missing?"

"Forty-eight hours ago. Look, Darcy, if there was ever a criminal who'd leave the country at the first sign of trouble, it's Vescio. But you need to remain vigilant. He hasn't forgotten what happened at the prison."

"Say it, Eric. You think Vescio might come after me."

"He's an idiot if he tries. No, he fled the country. That's what I believe."

After the call ends, Darcy rubs her forehead and glances up at the security camera overlooking the deck. Now she has two murderers to watch out for. She hides the phone inside her pocket when the deck door slides open. Darcy exhales when she realizes it's Hunter, not Jennifer. Jennifer would have sniffed a conspiracy and questioned why Darcy took the call outside.

Hunter yawns and uses his fingers to brush the knots out of his blonde hair. His eyelids droop, not surprising since he played video games until sunrise.

"What's up?"

"Just getting some fresh air," Darcy says, stretching out her legs as Hunter crawls into the neighboring chair.

"It's two hundred degrees," he says with a cock of his eyebrow. "The air won't be fresh until fall."

"You were up late."

"Or early. Depends on how you look at it."

"It wouldn't hurt to fill out a job application."

Hunter rolls his eyes.

"I already tried the mini golf place, and the three pizza delivery applications got me nowhere."

"So that's it, you give up after a few tries and hide in your room all summer?"

"Come on, Mom. I'll keep looking."

"You better. How else can you afford to take Bethany out to dinner every Friday?"

Since they returned to Genoa Cove, Hunter and Bethany have been inseparable. And that worries Darcy. How will Hunter react if she forces him to leave again? Selling the merits of a fresh start will be difficult enough without crushing Hunter's relationship with Bethany.

There are also Bethany's feelings to consider. She's not Darcy's child, but a part of Darcy wishes Bethany was. Bethany's brother, Aaron, turned into a monster. Was it nature or nurture that made Aaron? Last fall, Hunter endured Aaron's bullying, and it was Aaron and Sam Tatum who beat Hunter while Bronson Severson watched. Aaron and Sam were already looking at jail time for assault before the news of Aaron and Sam raping Bethany broke. In Darcy's eyes, the parents allowed this to happen. Instead of heeding the warning signs, they looked the other way until the unthinkable happened. Yes, Hunter needs Bethany, but Bethany also needs Hunter, especially with Aaron and Sam out on bail and awaiting trial.

"Speaking of money, I need to borrow ten bucks."

"Ten dollars for what?"

"There's a party tonight."

Darcy levels her eyes with Hunter's.

"Whose party is it?"

"Just some guys I play *Call of Duty* with."

"Not Bethany?"

"You know she doesn't go out like that. Not since..."

"Yeah, I get it."

Darcy sits back in the chair and crosses her arms. It occurs to Darcy Hunter must have heard about Aaron and Sam getting out of jail. The thought of either boy showing up at the party causes Darcy's skin to itch.

"I don't like you going to parties, Hunter. A lot of kids caused you trouble last year, and you don't know who will show up. Besides, if anyone catches you drinking, the coach will cut you from the team."

"We talked about this. I don't want to play football this year."

"I figured with Aaron and Sam gone—"

"It's not about them. Sports aren't for me."

The wind kicks up as a cloud crosses over the sun.

"Well, okay. But I don't want you sitting inside all fall in front of the computer."

"What about the ten dollars?"

Darcy chews her lip.

"Grab a bucket out of the garage. Wash the sand off the Prius, and we'll discuss the ten dollars over iced teas."

"In this heat?"

"You don't want the money?"

Hunter groans.

"I'll get the bucket."

"That's my boy."

The door closes. Darcy sits alone on the deck as the back of the house draws her gaze. Studying the walls, she discerns the fresh paint masking the smiley face Richard Chaney drew on the siding. Remembering forces her to envision scenarios where she must defend the house. She closes her eyes and pictures herself on the living room couch. It won't be easy for Michael Rivers to break through the front door, and she'll have time to react if he tries. The front window is the most vulnerable entry point. Either there of the glass deck door.

If he breaks through the glass, she has two choices: stand and fight, or run for the bedroom and retrieve her gun, the same model Glock-22 she carried with the FBI. The gun gives her the best odds of surviving an encounter with the most feared serial killer of the last fifty years. But running for her bedroom at the end of the hall leaves her children's doors unguarded. And he might attack them first.

Opening her eyes, Darcy squints against the sunlight and peers through the glass. Knives in the kitchen drawer make great close combat weapons in a pinch. Knives served her well at Laurie's house when she fended off another serial killer. But if Rivers comes through the deck door, he'll cut her off from the kitchen.

Darcy's priority: defend Hunter and Jennifer to the death.

The bathroom stands across from Jennifer's room. If she conceals a weapon inside the cabinet, she can reach it faster than she would the gun. But it frightens her to leave a weapon inside a cabinet her son and daughter open daily to grab their toothbrushes.

The wind thickens, chasing Darcy inside.

# CHAPTER SIX

The rain does little to thwart the heatwave. If anything, it thickens the air with humidity. Like breathing in swamp water.

Steam floats above the blacktop like little ghosts when Darcy steps outside. Gray clouds, shredded by the wind, hang low over Genoa Cove, but the storm is well inland. Hunter raises the garage door and places his hands on his hips, searching for an excuse not to wash the already wet Prius. Then he seems to remember the ten dollars and jogs across the sodden lawn toward the garden hose.

Out of oat milk and eggs, Darcy pockets her wallet and crosses the street. Hunter calls to her.

"Hey, why don't I give you a ride?"

Darcy turns back to Hunter.

"The Corner Store is only three blocks. I'd rather walk."

Hunter shrugs.

"Don't say I didn't ask."

The rain chased most of her neighbors inside. Darcy cringes and lowers her head when she spies Mr. Gibbons clearing fallen tree branches off his driveway. Gibbons was

Genoa Cove's most vocal advocate of locking Hunter up and throwing away the key. Maybe if she walks fast, he won't notice—

"Only a fool would go for a walk in a thunderstorm," Gibbons says, tossing a branch to the curb. "Don't want to get struck by lightning."

"And yet you're outside."

"I'm a few steps from the front door if the wind picks up." He shakes his head. "Women today. Give them rights, and they think they're invincible."

"Excuse me?"

He huffs and turns back to his work. The anger coursing through Darcy's body encourages her to argue. Instead, she keeps walking.

"Saw that boy of yours all over that girl who had sex with her brother," Gibbons calls.

Darcy halts in her tracks. Before she realizes what she's doing, she wheels around and marches toward Gibbons. He takes a step backward in his driveway, and Darcy wonders if Gibbons is recalling the time she pulled a gun on him after he followed her into a dark storefront in Smith Town.

"Repeat what you said."

"You heard me."

She wants to scream. Gibbons refuses to accept Hunter had nothing to do with the Darkwater Cove murders.

"That poor girl was raped by her own brother, but I wouldn't expect you to believe the police. After all, you still think my son murdered those girls even though the FBI captured the actual killer. It must be fascinating to live inside that shell of yours."

Emboldened by his growing anger, Gibbons puffs out

his chest and stands face to face with Darcy.

"Let me tell you a story about Genoa Cove, Ms. Gellar. Before you set foot in my village last year, we had one of the lowest crime rates in the country. Since you arrived, multiple teenage girls murdered, and the police keep cruising through our neighborhood like we're some slum with a gang problem."

"How are those murders our fault?"

"Well, let me think." Gibbons makes a show of tapping his forehead while squinting his eyes. "You captured a mass murderer three years ago, but instead of putting a bullet in his head, you sent him to prison like a good little liberal."

Darcy's knees buckle. She assumed Gibbons knew about her FBI career but had no idea he blamed her for not killing Rivers when she had the chance. She was lucky to survive the serial killer's attack, but that doesn't prevent Darcy from blaming herself for letting him live.

"Oh, I've done my homework on you, Agent Gellar. Or should I say former agent? Every horror we've experienced in Genoa Cove is because of you. I don't even blame your son for being who he is. He grew up surrounded by stories of murder, and no doubt they affected his psyche. But he is who he is. If he didn't kill those girls himself, he surely aided Richard Chaney. I understand the FBI found them together in the park."

"You're twisting the truth. They were together because Chaney paid two boys to kidnap my son."

"Your story, not mine. One needn't be a mathematician to see the direct correlation between the sudden rise in rapes and murders in Genoa Cove and your family's arrival. As it's logical neither you nor your daughter raped and murdered those teenagers, it must have been your son."

She's a split-second from striking Gibbons. Laying him out on the steaming macadam. Her fingers curl and uncurl. Getting herself arrested won't do her family any good. She takes a deep breath. Gibbons still wears the same smug grin when she refocuses.

"There's no point arguing with a man who refuses to acknowledge the truth. You'll give yourself a coronary, if you don't do something with all that hate floating around inside you. Have a pleasant day, Mr. Gibbons."

She feels his glare burning into her back as she marches away. Across the street, Mrs. Andrews ventures onto her front stoop to watch the confrontation. Darcy often sees Andrews and a circle of neighbors conferring with Gibbons as they cast glances at Darcy's house. Another reason to move her family. The neighborhood gossipers will never accept the Gellar family.

Darcy walks the three blocks to the Corner Store before her hands stop trembling. The sky looks fitful, fragments of black clouds warring for supremacy with the sun. Perhaps she should have let Hunter drive her to the store.

The little brick-faced shop is smaller than the downstairs of a middle class home. Boxes of cereal, many adorned by cartoon characters on the box, line one shelf. A second shelf serves as a miniature newsstand. The local paper sits front and center, but one can also purchase newspapers from Raleigh and Charlotte. Today's *New York Times* sits in the center. Darcy locates the oat milk inside the refrigerator along the back wall. A chilly cloud puffs out when Darcy slides the door open, and she revels in the cool air.

But she isn't free from the scrutiny she escaped when

she left Gibbons in his driveway. A middle aged mother in designer clothes clutches her adolescent daughter to her hip when she sees Darcy. At the front of the store, the gray haired man behind the counter looks warily in her direction as he bags a loaf of bread for a man in a business suit. They're all passing judgment on her. They might cheer for Darcy to capture Michael Rivers and end the village's nightmare. But inwardly, none of them would shed a tear if the FBI found Darcy and her family slaughtered in their bedrooms, the leering mark of the Full Moon Killer painted on the walls with their blood.

After the store owner bags the groceries, Darcy hands him the money and doesn't wait for change. She's through the door and into the searing heat before he can thank Darcy for her patronage. The anger from her encounter with Gibbons resurfaces in her quickened gait, and she nearly plows over a boy walking his bike down the sidewalk as she turns the corner. Gibbons watches through the living room curtains when she passes.

Darcy places the phone on the kitchen counter and unpacks the groceries. As she closes the refrigerator, Jennifer shoots Darcy a withering stare. Her daughter's inky hair is pulled back in a ponytail, a style which reminds Darcy of herself at Jennifer's age. She's grown a lot in the six months since they returned from Georgia, her hips and chest filling out, drawing the eyes of her male classmates. Despite the bubbly personality, Jennifer explodes when someone angers her. And by the thousand-yard stare she's shooting at Darcy, Jennifer is furious.

"A real estate guide arrived in the mail. Who is Mrs. Kudlow?" As Darcy stammers, Jennifer types a query into her phone and turns it so Darcy can see the screen. It's the Kudlow Realty website. "You're looking for another house."

"Honey," Darcy says, motioning for her daughter to sit beside her at the kitchen table. Jennifer sits across from Darcy instead, arms folded and a scowl twisting her face. "I'm only looking at options."

"That's a lie. I bet you made an offer. So where is it this time, Mommy Dearest? North Dakota? The Antarctic?"

"It's a house in North Carolina, Jennifer."

"But not in Genoa Cove, right? I knew you'd screw everything up again. Just when Hunter and I are making friends. Remember when you said no one in school would accept Hunter after what happened last year? Well, he has friends now and a steady girlfriend. How do you think Hunter will feel when you make him leave Bethany?"

Hunter's door opens and closes. He stands in the corner of the kitchen, itching the mop of hair atop his head as he sends a confused look toward the garage.

"Did you shut off the music?"

"Yeah, Mom killed your tunes," Jennifer says. "She always does stuff without asking our opinions first."

Hunter glances between Darcy and Jennifer.

"Wait, what's going on?"

Darcy shakes her head, but Jennifer doesn't stop.

"She's talking to a Realtor and wants to move again."

"Is that true?"

Darcy opens her hand and motions for Hunter to take the open chair. He doesn't. Her son spins on his heels and marches toward his bedroom.

"Too bad, because I'm not leaving," he says a moment before the door slams. His voice booms from inside the bedroom. "I'm a legal adult now! I'll live where I want to."

Darcy rearranges the salt and pepper shakers.

"Thanks for upsetting your brother and blowing this out of proportion."

Jennifer leans back and raises her palms.

"Who's upsetting Hunter? I'm not the one telling him he made new friends for nothing, and now he has to break up with Bethany."

"I'd never make Hunter and Bethany break up."

"Don't you see that's exactly what you're doing? How can they stay together if you move us across the state?"

"It's not that far."

"So it's like the next town over, close enough for us to visit our friends after school?" Jennifer slaps her palms on the table. "Yeah, I didn't think so."

Before Darcy replies, Jennifer shoves the chair back and stomps out of the kitchen. The slam of the bedroom door shakes the walls.

So that's it. The kids will stay in isolation and avoid Darcy for the rest of the day.

Why don't her kids recognize the danger? They can't stay in Genoa Cove. As her mind wanders, Darcy's gaze drifts to the vacant house next door. She half-expects to see a stolen Audi tucked inside the garage and a face at the window. It's dark inside. Quiet.

Like the moment before a funeral bell tolls.

# CHAPTER SEVEN

Fretting with her skirt as she stands in the driveway, Darcy tugs the hemline, which rides too high above her knees. She's sending the wrong message. What will Julian think of her?

Julian's call came as a surprise. They'd had lunch together earlier, and now he wants to take Darcy to dinner at Harpy's, an upscale seafood restaurant on the Genoa Cove pier. Despite her reservations—she knows Julian considers her too old and only wants to be friends—Darcy agreed to dinner. Anything to avoid Jennifer and Hunter. Neither will speak to her, not since the Charlotte realty magazine arrived. Before she left the house, Hunter was in the shower and getting ready for his party. He'll drop Jennifer and Lindsey off at Kaitlyn's on the way.

Dammit. She forgot to put out the trash. No chance Hunter or Jennifer will do her the favor. She checks the time on her phone. If she hurries, she can pull the can and the recyclables to the curb before Julian picks her up. She opens the Prius and clicks the automatic garage door opener. The door rattles and grinds upward, revealing the garbage can and four yellow recycling containers stacked against the back wall. As she steps inside the cooler garage, a Honda Civic pulls to the curb. It's Lindsey, dressed in a plaid skirt and white top. The sea-blue hair band matches the bracelet Lindsey borrowed from Jennifer. The Civic beeps and drives off.

Noticing Darcy in the garage, Lindsey waves and jogs to catch up to her.

"Let me help, Ms. Gellar."

"Oh, thank you, Lindsey. But you don't need to take out my garbage."

"Nonsense," the girl says, waving Darcy away. "I'll grab the can and come back to help you with the recyclables."

While Lindsey drags the can to the curb, Darcy trails her with two stacked containers in her arms. Then they return to the garage and carry the last two containers down the driveway. Darcy rubs the grit off her hands, wishing for a hand wipe.

"Come inside where it's cool," Darcy says. "Jennifer should be ready in a few minutes."

Escaping the heat, Darcy heads to the kitchen and rinses her hands off. Her brow dotted by sweat, Lindsey follows behind.

"That was very kind," says Darcy as Lindsey sits at the kitchen table.

Lindsey shrugs.

"I take out the trash at my Mom's house. It's no big deal."

Her Mom's house?

"Was that your mother who dropped you off?"

"No, that was my Dad. I stayed at his apartment the last two days, but I'm going back to Mom's after the party." Darcy tries to hide the question on her face, but

Lindsey already noticed. "My parents separated this spring."

"I'm sorry, Lindsey. That must be hard on you."

Lindsey twirls a strand of hair around her finger and gives it a tug. Subtle, but Darcy notices the anxiety driven hair pulling.

"It's not as bad as it was. The last year seemed weird with them fighting all the time. Their separation was inevitable, and I suppose the divorce will come sooner or later. Sucks to be me."

Darcy remembers tension between her parents when she was a teenager. There were times Darcy felt certain her parents would divorce, or at least separate. Her mother was hard to get along with, stern and judgmental. But Darcy's parents stayed together until her father passed.

"Lindsey, if you ever need someone to talk to, or you just want to get away, our house is always open to you."

Darcy's offer wins a smile from Lindsey. Before she can reply, Jennifer hustles into the kitchen in bare feet, two flats tucked under her arm as she struggles with an earring.

"We're gonna be so late," Jennifer says. "What is Hunter's issue?"

Darcy stops Jennifer in her tracks and places her hands on her daughter's shoulders.

"Calm down. You know your brother. Hunter just stepped out of the shower and will spend the next thirty minutes making his hair perfect. The party doesn't start for another hour. Now, what's going on with the earring?"

"The hole closed again. That's why I keep telling you I need to wear earrings more often."

"Stand still."

Darcy grasps the earring between her thumb and forefinger and studies Jennifer's ear. As her daughter said, the hole closed. She must force the post through the small opening. Easing the post into the hole, Darcy grits her teeth. Jennifer's eyes close, and she flinches when the post pops through the back side.

"There. That only took five seconds."

"Is it bleeding?"

Darcy grins over Jennifer's shoulder at Lindsey, who struggles not to burst into laughter.

"No blood. Behave yourself at Kaitlyn's. Remember, if anything happens at the party that makes you uncomfortable—"

"I'll call you to come get me."

"And that goes for you too, Lindsey."

"Yes, Ms. Gellar," Lindsey says, hopping up from the chair.

Lindsey smooths Jennifer's dress as Jennifer balances on one foot, slipping on her flats. The microwave clock catches Darcy's eye. Shoot. Julian is probably waiting in the driveway, wondering what's taking so long.

"I need to run, girls. Have a wonderful time, and please behave at the party."

In the driveway, Darcy bounces on her feet, willing Julian to arrive before Mrs. Andrews and Mr. Gibbons venture outside. While she checks her text messages, Julian's car turns the corner. Two quick beeps, and he pulls into the driveway.

She gives him an awkward wave and crosses around the car, but he's out of his seat and opening the passenger door before she can protest. She slips into the seat, the damn skirt riding up her thighs as though it shrank two sizes after the door closed. Realizing she can't stretch the skirt further without ripping the fabric, she crosses one leg over the other and leans her elbow against the door with her palm pressed to her face.

Julian wears white dress pants and a black textured mock, casual yet dressy, something he could wear beneath a sports jacket or as a t-shirt.

"Ready to go?"

"Sure," she says, sliding her purse between her feet.

A charged, uncomfortable quiet lingers in the car until he fumbles with the radio dial and tunes in a pop station. He glances at her for approval, then fiddles with the dial again.

"No, that channel is fine," Darcy says.

"I wasn't sure what sort of music you liked."

Over the next five blocks, he clears his throat now and then as if he has something to say. She didn't expect the bashful act. Darcy never saw this side of Julian before. She covers the furtive grin with her hand, but he notices.

"What?"

"Oh, nothing," she says. "I'm just trying to decide which one of us is more nervous."

"Wait, you're nervous?"

"Aren't you?"

She frets with the hemline again, and that leads her eyes to her shirt. Is it cut too low? Dammit, she's a middle school girl on her first date again.

"Stop worrying about the dress. You look great, Darcy."

The fire in her cheeks spreads down her body.

"Thank you. I wasn't sure what was appropriate...for Harpy's, I mean."

He nods, a knowing smile on his face.

"Anyhow, there's no reason for either of us to be nervous. We're two friends having dinner."

"Right."

That confirms her suspicion. They're just friends. Her heart sinks.

Fishing nets hang from the walls inside Harpy's. A cacophony of voices travel over the room, the restaurant at peak capacity as a teenage boy in a shirt and tie leads them to their table. Julian pulls Darcy's chair out for her, and after she takes her seat, she senses eyes on her from across the room.

"What was that you told me—most everyone in Genoa Cove likes me?"

"Don't pay them any attention," Julian says. As the waiter hands out menus, Julian shoots pointed looks at the nearby tables. That keeps the wolves at bay for now. "Oysters came fresh from Maine today. Are you up for an appetizer?"

"I feel bad. You already bought me lunch."

"That was tea, and if it's important to you, you can get the check next time."

"You're already planning the next...dinner?"

She bites her tongue for almost saying *date*.

The appetizers arrive. As advertised, the oysters taste fresh and perfectly salty. Julian hits his oysters with a touch of hot sauce, but when she tries, she ends up sneezing from the heat. By the time the waiter removes the appetizer plates, the ice breaks between them, and they ease into the conversation. He keeps mentioning his house and renovations he made. She senses him steering the conversation, but she can't decide where he wants it to go. When she checks her messages for the second time, he tilts his head toward the phone.

"What has you so anxious?"

She sighs and stuffs the phone into her purse.

"It's my kids. They're both out tonight, and I turn

into a mother hen when they're out of my sight."

"Understandable. What are they up to?"

"Hunter went to a party at his friend's house, and Jennifer is spending the night with a girl from school. Well, it's a party, but I'm not supposed to call it a party."

"So you have the house to yourself tonight?"

Darcy clears her throat.

"Until midnight. That's Hunter's curfew."

He passes her a basket of garlic knots and wipes his hands on his napkin.

"But Hunter is going into his senior year. You're not used to him going out?" When she presses her lips together, his eyes light with comprehension. "I'm sorry. With all that you and the kids went through last year, I don't blame you for watching over them. I'd do the same." He leans forward and lowers his voice. "But nobody has seen or heard from Michael Rivers since December."

"Except for me. I hear from him three times per week."

"You assume it's Michael Rivers on the phone. Even if it is, he hasn't come after you. The entire GCPD is waiting if he tries."

"Still bothers me that he finds my phone number no matter how many times I change it. And what about the stolen car in Allentown?"

"It's one woman claiming she saw Michael Rivers. And why would he be in Pennsylvania?"

"Because the FBI wouldn't expect him to be there. Maybe it wasn't him, but I'm not taking chances." Darcy groans. "I'm not sure it's a good thing if you get to know me."

"Why would you say that?"

"Who wants to be around a train wreck?"

"You're not." Julian tears the last garlic knot in two and hands her half. "We all have secrets. I have to admit I wasn't honest with you this afternoon."

"Oh?"

"You asked me why I became a police officer. The story about my father is true. He worked the dangerous side of Newark for almost two decades."

"Did something happen to your father?"

Julian wipes his mouth and sets the napkin on his lap.

"*Someone* happened to my father. What does the name Jerry Reichs mean to you?"

Darcy drops the appetizer.

"Oh, God. The serial killer, Jerry Reichs? He was a child murderer during the nineties."

"That's him. Reichs owned a consignment shop on the edge of the city. Really it was an old house; he converted the downstairs into a shop, but it had a fenced-in yard, an upstairs and basement. The house sat three blocks from the elementary school. By the end of autumn, nine kids had gone missing within a five-mile radius of the school. Reichs would lure the kids into his shop with video games and toys in the front window. Nobody noticed. The police found the remains of nine children buried under the basement's dirt floor. My dad was one of the first cops on the scene when they discovered the first body."

"I can't imagine how that affected your father."

"That was the end of Newark for Dad. In his eyes, living there put his family at risk. So he took an early retirement and moved us to Genoa Cove. Never looked back."

Darcy holds her reply while the waiter sets the entrees in front of them.

"You must have been young then. Did you

understand what was happening?"

"Kids talk," he says with a grimace. "Before I left, I'd learned more than I ever wanted to know about Jerry Reichs and what he did to those kids. I started having dreams about Reichs coming after me. This one time before we moved, I woke up screaming because I saw Reichs in the doorway to my bedroom. Now, I know what you will say. It was just a nightmare. But it was so vivid. I saw every pore on Reichs's face. He just stood there in the doorway, swaying like an invisible wind set him in motion. Then he smiled and walked into the room. That's when my father shook me awake."

"That's terrifying. I'm sorry, Julian."

He cuts into the salmon fillet and pops a chunk in his mouth. He chews, holding up a finger.

"Don't feel sorry for me. Every kid has night terrors. Mine just involved a real monster. But something good came of it. After we came to Genoa Cove, I got on the Internet and learned everything I could about the victims —who the kids were, their grade levels in school, whether they loved the Yankees or the Mets. And I guess I knew from that day that I wanted to be a cop. I didn't want that to happen to any kid again."

"Well, you achieved your dream. It's like you told me. Genoa Cove was the perfect destination for you."

"But not the final destination." He sips from his glass of water. "I guess we're a lot alike, you and I."

"How so?"

"We're planning our getaways." Darcy pauses with the fork outside her mouth. He knows. "Kudlow Realty. You chose well. They're the most reliable company in the area."

"Who told you?"

"People around here talk too much. You said so yourself."

"I apologize, Julian. This isn't how I'd planned to tell you."

Julian pushes his plate aside and levels his eyes with hers.

"You can't do this, Darcy. Don't you see the risk you're taking? I understand your motivation. The GCPD, the FBI, we promised to keep your family safe last year, and we failed. But moving to Charlotte...I wish you'd give this more thought."

Darcy blanches. Is this the reason Julian invited her to dinner?

"I haven't signed the papers. Nothing is finalized."

"But are you sure, Darcy? Is this what you want?"

A tear creeps out of her eye. Darcy swipes it away.

"All I want is to keep my family safe. Living in a gated community affords me advantages I don't have here."

"Such as?"

"There's a security guard at the entrance."

"As if Michael Rivers will drive a Volvo to the gate and sweet talk his way past."

"He won't find us. Not immediately."

She sets her chin on folded hands and ponders how the conversation got to this point.

"Eventually, he will. Stay, Darcy. I can protect you."

Before she can protest, he reaches across the table and places his hand over hers. The warmth of his touch stops her hands from shaking.

"I'll give it more thought, Julian. Let's not talk about it anymore tonight."

After dinner, they walk the pier and watch a family of

four catch blue crabs off the side with nets and string. The sun hangs low behind them, coloring the water golden. Darcy feels night's approach, but for the first time in almost a year, she doesn't let the trepidation bother her. They lean against the pier and look out at the rolling sea, Darcy holding his arm and leaning her head on his shoulder.

As gloaming colors the sky, Julian drives them into the village where they walk a lighted path through the community park. Only a few people remain in the park besides them, and as they stroll between two pink magnolia trees, Julian's hand finds hers. When she glances up at him, he stops. Before she can react, he leans forward and presses his lips to hers. A gentle kiss, one that melts away the last vestige of caution. After their lips part, she allows the contented silence to speak for her.

There's a bounce to her step as they follow the circular path back to the beginning. Neither wanting the night to end, they sit upon a park bench beneath a weeping willow. Street lights along the shopping district push back the darkness. She's tempted to lean over and kiss him again, but she doesn't want to push things. Julian touches her cheek.

"If Michael Rivers died tomorrow, would you consider staying in Genoa Cove?"

Darcy lowers her head.

"That's morbid."

"But you wish for it."

"Yes."

"So would you stay if Rivers disappeared?"

"I don't know. Jennifer made friends and wants to finish high school here, but Hunter leaves for college in a year, and there's nothing to tie me to the region. Especially since I'm persona non grata in Genoa Cove. If I end up on the coast again, it won't be around here. What about you?"

Julian bends down and picks the head off a clover, then tosses it.

"I've turned down offers from bigger departments, but I didn't burn any bridges. I'll have options, but there's no rush to take something new."

"But you're not long for Genoa Cove, either."

"When the right offer comes along, I'll make the move and never look back."

As he talks, Darcy's vision shifts to the street. A black sedan sits at the curb. It wasn't there before, and she can't see past the windows. Julian's voice drifts away until she can't hear him. Her instinct whispers danger, though she can't decide why the sedan unsettles her. He catches Darcy not listening and studies her face. His eyes follow hers toward the street and focus on the black sedan.

"Something wrong?"

Darcy bites her lip.

"That car. It wasn't there when we entered the park."

"It's a busy street, Darcy. The entire block is lined with vehicles."

"But I swear I saw someone inside. He's watching us."

Julian bends forward and strains his eyes.

"Tinted windows. I can't see inside. Are you sure you saw someone?"

Darcy shakes her head.

"It's nothing. This Michael Rivers report has me on edge."

"The FBI said Rivers stole an Audi with Pennsylvania plates, right?"

"Correct."

"Well, that's a Lincoln with North Carolina plates."

A wave of embarrassment comes over Darcy. She waves away a mosquito when it lands on her cheek.

"I don't know what's gotten into me tonight."

"It's been a long day. You want me to drive you home?"

She doesn't. If Julian asked, she'd spend the entire evening with him. But things are moving too fast, and she needs a night to put their relationship into perspective.

"If you don't mind."

Darcy regrets the premature conclusion to their date when he pulls into her driveway and circles the car to open the door. At the front door, he waits until she unlocks the house and silences the alarm, but he doesn't make a move to come inside. After she gives him the all-clear, they kiss again in the driveway. This kiss lingers longer than the one in the park. Though it's a cliche, she swears she sees a light flash on the backs of her eyelids.

Loneliness hangs heavy when Julian's car motors out of the neighborhood. In the kitchen, she pours a glass of water and sips at the counter, the realization that she had her first date in more than a decade buzzing through her mind.

But when the excitement wears off, her eyes lock on the silhouette of the vacant house next door. Sudden paranoia crashes into her. And she's alone again. Exposed. Targeted.

She craves the anti-anxiety medication. Just one extra pill to numb her fears. Darcy withstands the medication's siren song.

That night, sleep proves difficult. And when she sleeps, she dreams of a dirt floor basement in the house next door. Three bodies lie lost and buried beneath the soil.

The bodies of Hunter, Jennifer, and Darcy.

# CHAPTER EIGHT

The beat from the stereo's speakers rattles the window and follows Hunter out the front door. Inside, the party kicks into full gear, the downstairs choked with teenagers spilling booze and yelling over the music. He's happy to be outside, especially with Bethany on his arm. The teenage girl's perfume smells of flowers. It tickles his nose as they stop at the curb and kiss.

"I can't believe you made it to the party," Hunter says.

Her arms wrap around his shoulders as she looks up at him.

"Well, I couldn't sleep knowing you'd be inside with half the school's cheerleaders."

She had one drink. Just one. Keeping the promise he made to his mother, Hunter avoided alcohol, though he smells like a brewery after Squiggs tripped and dumped a cup of beer down the front of his shirt. Hopefully, the cops don't pull him over on the way home. He'll never talk his way out of this one.

Bethany leans against his shoulder as they follow the sidewalk toward the end of the block where Hunter's car sits beneath a dead, leafless tree that won't survive the next gale. The sea breeze whips Bethany's hair across his face, and he catches a whiff of her shampoo. He can't leave her. Never again. So how can he explain his mother's plan to move them to Charlotte? There has to be a way around this. If he can't talk Mom out of moving, perhaps he can stay in Genoa Cove on his own. He's eighteen now, a legal adult and old enough to make his own decisions. But that would mean leaving Jennifer.

She senses his unease and touches his cheek.

"Hey, what's gotten into you?"

"What do you mean?"

"It looks like something is eating you up. Tell me. I can help."

He can't tell her. Doing so will ruin an otherwise perfect night. The last thing Bethany needs is the stress of their relationship ending.

As she prods him to answer, a shape emerges from the dark and blocks the sidewalk. The person stands in the shadows so Hunter can't see who it is, but he can tell it's a male. A teenage boy.

Bethany gives Hunter an uncertain look. He urges her forward, but they walk with a cautious gait as the silhouetted figure lingers ahead of them. Hunter wants to turn around, head back to the party, where he knows it's safe. But Bethany will think he's a coward.

When they grow closer to the figure, the boy steps forward. The streetlight catches the teenager's face. Bethany pulls up.

"Shit, it's my brother. He's not supposed to leave the house."

Aaron Torres does a lot of things he's not supposed to do, Hunter thinks to himself. Aaron closes the distance between them. Maybe he sneaked out of the apartment without his father knowing. It's just as likely the father allowed the boy to leave. Aaron Torres doesn't live by society's rules. Was he born evil, or did somebody teach him?

Hunter moves Bethany behind him when Aaron blocks them from passing. Tears streak the boy's face, and Hunter catches a whiff of whiskey when Aaron edges closer.

"You can't be here," Bethany says around Hunter's shoulder. "If the police find out—"

"Nobody will let me talk to you, Bethany. Not Mom or Dad. You have to understand…it wasn't supposed to happen that way. If it wasn't for Sam…"

"You're blaming Sam? You always put yourself above the law, Aaron, but this is too much."

Bethany tenses. Hunter feels the angry heat rolling off her body. Aaron hitches. More tears spill as Hunter blocks Bethany from getting at Aaron. God knows how she'll react if she gets her hands on her brother.

"I'm sorry, Bethany. Is that what you want to hear? Because I'll say it as many times as I need to until you believe it's true. You're my sister. I love you."

"You raped me, you son-of-a-bitch!"

Her shout echoes through the neighborhood. A porch light flicks on across the street.

"No, it was Sam. You know it was Sam, Bethany. If you tell the police the truth, I won't go to jail."

"That's what this is about? Daddy can't save your ass this time, so you want me to lie for you."

"Bethany, please. You don't understand. Do you know what it's like inside prison? Do you know what they do to people accused of rape?"

"It's not an accusation anymore. You're a rapist. What happens in prison is your own doing."

Something changes in Aaron's eyes. They narrow and burn.

"This is his fault," Aaron says, pointing at Hunter. "Ever since this scumbag moved to Genoa Cove, everything has gone to shit."

"That's enough. You've been drinking, Aaron. If you want me to call a ride for you—"

"No. What I want is for you to break up with this asshole before he wrecks our family."

"Go home, Aaron," Hunter says. "You can't be anywhere near Bethany."

The corner of Aaron's mouth quirks up.

"What if I don't? What the hell are you going to do about it?"

Hunter steps back and bumps into Bethany. Memories of the beatings Aaron and Sam gave Hunter last year return to him. Being rushed to the hospital. The concussions. His neurologist warned him another blow to the head could cause a seizure. Or worse.

"Look at the pussy back away," Aaron says, grinning. "Is this who you want defending you, Bethany? He's a waste. Fuck this prick. If it wasn't for him, none of this would be happening."

Aaron is too far gone. Now he blames Hunter for the rape. Hunter can't reason with Aaron. Nobody can.

As Hunter and Bethany back away, Aaron smashes his fist against the window of a car parked along the curb. A spiderweb of broken glass forms along the window. He slams his fist against the glass a second time and shatters the window. Safety pellets pepper the passenger seat.

One jagged shard hangs off the top of the window, a

bloody stalactite.

Aaron rips the piece of glass out of the window. Bethany screams as Aaron lunges at Hunter.

The shard tears Hunter's shirt, but he spins away before the tip finds his flesh. Shoving Bethany off the sidewalk, he yells for her to get help.

Aaron rushes Hunter as Bethany runs back to the party. This time Hunter is ready. When Aaron slices the glass at Hunter's face and misses, Hunter lets the boy's momentum carry him forward. Hunter strikes Aaron in the jaw.

When Aaron steadies himself, the uncertainty in his eyes belies his promise to beat Hunter unconscious. Aaron jabs the glass at Hunter's stomach. Hunter spins away and catches the boy's arm, landing a hard punch to his attacker's nose. Blood spurts, and Aaron drops the glass and stumbles forward.

Then Hunter leaps atop his prone enemy. Punches rain down, Hunter's fists a blur as he strikes Aaron again and again.

A police siren grows closer as Hunter smashes his fists against Aaron's bloody face.

# CHAPTER NINE

The phone rings on her nightstand and frightens Darcy out of sleep. She sits up and looks at the clock. It's after midnight. Hunter isn't home yet.

Panic jolts her nerves when the phone rings again. She snatches the phone off the nightstand, expecting to see Hunter's name on the screen. But it's a local number she can't identify. She recognizes Detective Ames's voice when she answers, but his words make little sense. There was a fight. A boy was rushed to the hospital. Hunter hurt someone.

She struggles into her clothes, hands trembling as her mind races through the possibilities. Running to the kitchen, she looks for her keys and remembers Hunter has them. Shit.

The next call she places goes to Julian, who answers in a groggy stupor.

"The police have Hunter. Something about a fight at a party."

"Slow down," Julian says. The springs squeak as he crawls off the bed. "Did they arrest Hunter?"

"I don't know, Ames didn't say."

The pause makes Darcy wonder if Julian and Ames aren't seeing eye to eye. Maybe Julian is at odds with his coworkers. That would explain his desire to move.

"Ames would have told you if he'd arrested Hunter, so that's good."

"Hunter has the car, Julian. I can't drive myself to the station."

"Hang tight. I'll be there in fifteen minutes."

He arrives in ten minutes instead. Darcy races to the passenger door and throws herself onto the seat. He's dressed in sweat pants and a t-shirt, and she feels guilty for dragging him out of bed in the middle of the night. They don't talk during the drive to the police station. Julian focuses on the road, cutting down side streets and taking short cuts Darcy didn't know existed.

A skeleton crew of overnight shift workers man the bullpen when Darcy arrives with Julian. Officer Faust, the female officer who accompanied Julian to the house last fall, nods at Julian and calls back to Ames. Darcy spies Hunter in Ames's office. There's an icepack on his hand. A red bruise rises off the side of his face.

He's not alone. Bethany sits beside him.

Julian grabs Darcy's arm to keep her from rushing forward. Ames emerges from his office and turns back to Hunter and Bethany, holding up his hand so they stay put. The detective pops an antacid into his mouth as he crosses the bullpen. He halts when he sees Julian, more evidence the detective might be the source of Julian's frustration.

"What happened to Hunter?"

Ames raises a placating hand.

"Hunter will be all right."

"I don't understand. You said Hunter got into a fight?"

"According to multiple witnesses, Aaron Torres attacked Hunter on Jensen Road."

"Aaron Torres shouldn't leave his apartment. Isn't his father keeping an eye on him?"

As if summoned, the Torres father storms through the door with his wife in tow. Though it's one in the morning, the man wears black, pleated slacks, a white shirt, and a tie. His pepper-gray hair is perfectly combed, and a Bluetooth device sticks out of his ear. Black circles gird the mother's eyes. She wears a bathrobe over pajama pants, her hair mussed.

"I just came from the hospital," Mr. Torres says, glaring at Ames. "My boy has a concussion and needed seven stitches."

"Calm down, Mr. Torres," Ames says.

"Calm down? I want the maniac who did this arrested." The man takes in Julian and Darcy. "Jesus, it's you. You're the reason our village went to hell."

With Faust's assistance, Ames leads the Torres family away. The mother glances back at Darcy. The apologetic look in her eye tells Darcy she's given up.

"So it was her boy who did this?" Torres shouts over his shoulder. "Why am I not surprised? I'll sue the hell out of you, Gellar. I'll sue the village for what happened to my boy."

A door closes down the hall. Ames returns a moment later.

"Sorry you had to see that, Ms. Gellar."

"You'd better not consider arresting my son."

"It looks like self-defense. Bethany Torres claims her brother came at Hunter with a weapon...a piece of glass. We found a vandalized car at the scene and blood on the windowsill. We'll match it to Aaron Torres once we get the

DNA test back." Ames swings his eyes toward Julian. "Don't you have an eight o'clock shift, Officer?"

"I gave Ms. Gellar a ride to the station. I'm staying until she's finished here."

The detective's gaze holds Julian a second longer before he turns back to Darcy.

"Until we get this sorted out, it would be best if Hunter stayed with you at home. I realize he's a legal adult, but it would be in your best interest if Hunter kept a low profile."

"That sounds like house arrest."

"Like I said, Hunter isn't under arrest."

"At this time. You admitted Hunter defended himself."

"That's what it looks like. We haven't concluded our investigation."

"What's to conclude?" Julian asks, folding his arms. "Witnesses saw Aaron Torres attack Hunter Gellar, and it won't be long before you match his DNA to the broken car window. And let's not forget Aaron shouldn't have been there in the first place, especially with his sister present."

"You weren't a responding officer. This isn't your case."

Julian braces for an argument, but Ames tells Darcy he'll speak with her soon and returns to his office.

It's after two when Julian drives Darcy and Hunter back to Jensen Road, where they pick up the Prius. Hunter doesn't like leaving Bethany with her father, but he doesn't have a choice. Julian follows Darcy and Hunter home, and Darcy can't stop herself from picturing her son in a fight. Witnesses claim it took a small army to pull Hunter off Aaron. A concussion, seven stitches. She doesn't harbor the least bit of remorse for Aaron Torres, but Hunter's violent streak sends a chill through her body. When she visited the prison outside Buffalo with Hensel, Michael Rivers predicted Hunter would become a serial killer. If he wasn't a murderer already.

Nonsense. Her boy wouldn't hurt anyone. It was self-defense.

She repeats the mantra in her head until they arrive home.

# CHAPTER TEN

She's slept less than three hours when the sun forces Darcy up from sleep. She glances at the nightstand. Six in the morning.

Groaning, she drops her legs off the bed and lowers her head. A novel's worth of messages from Jennifer await Darcy on her phone. Someone told Jennifer about the fight, and for the last two hours she's messaged Darcy for answers. Which means her daughter hasn't slept.

Darcy calls Jennifer, who fires panicked questions through the phone.

"I've been messaging you and Hunter all night. Why won't anyone respond?"

"Your brother is asleep, Jennifer," Darcy says, starting the coffee maker.

A hurt sound comes out of Jennifer's chest, and Darcy realizes there's something deeper going on than the attack on Hunter.

"Hon, are you all right?"

Jennifer sniffles and clears the sob from her throat.

"Lindsey killed herself last night."

The shock knocks Darcy against the counter. No, not

Lindsey. At no point did the girl strike Darcy as suicidal, though she recalls her parents' impending divorce. Was Lindsey's outgoing, helpful personality a mask to conceal her pain?

"My God. How could this happen? I'm so sorry, Jennifer."

"I found out in a group text. A fucking group text. The whole school is talking about it."

Darcy slumps into a chair and waits out the dizzy spell threatening to topple her. She always takes it hard when a child dies, but this is one of Jennifer's friends, a girl her daughter's age. A teenager Darcy had quickly come to like.

"Was Lindsey…depressed?"

"No, she was so happy all the time. None of this makes sense."

"Honey, sometimes people overcompensate when they're in pain and hide what they're going through."

Like Jennifer? Darcy worries her daughter works too hard to bury her own traumas. But she wouldn't kill herself like Lindsey. Would she?

"That's not it, Mom. Trust me. You weren't there. We'd know if something was going on with Lindsey. She was just here nine hours ago. Why would she kill herself?"

Darcy's heart catches. She switches the phone to her other ear and stands.

"So Lindsey seemed herself at Kaitlyn's."

"Yes. She kept talking about going to Europe at the end of summer vacation and how much she was looking forward to it."

Darcy wants to ask how Lindsey killed herself, but she can't frame the question in her head without it sounding cruel and heartless. Though it pains her to jump to conclusions, Darcy worries about drugs. Maybe Lindsey took something and turned suicidal. She'll ask Julian. He must have talked to someone in the department about the suicide by now. Instead, she lets Jennifer talk and cry herself out.

"Why is all this happening to us? First Lindsey commits suicide, then Aaron starts a fight with Hunter. Is Hunter okay?"

"Don't worry about your brother. He just has a few bruises."

"What caused the fight?"

Darcy recounts what Ames told her about the attack.

"That asshole. Why is Aaron on the street at all?"

"He shouldn't be."

"They should put him away forever. Coming after Bethany and attacking Hunter...Aaron doesn't care about anyone but himself."

"He'll have assault on top of the rape charges now."

"The police charged him with assault?"

Darcy stops. No, Ames didn't explicitly state they'd charged Aaron with assault.

"I'm certain they will."

"In Genoa Cove? Don't count on it. The father knows the mayor and the chief of police. He'll get Aaron out of the assault charge. Wait and see."

Yes, Genoa Cove has its hierarchy, and the Gellar family isn't part of it. Darcy's worry the police will turn on Hunter lingers after the call ends. Darcy blows the hair out of her eyes. Kaitlyn's mother wants Jennifer to get a few hours sleep before she brings her home, which gives Darcy the morning to finish chores around the house and put last night's events into perspective.

Venturing outside, she confirms nobody spray-painted her car overnight, recalling Aaron's vandalism last fall. Her eyes stop on Mr. Gibbons's house down the road. Before long, the entire neighborhood will hear about the fight. Gibbons and Mrs. Andrews will twist the story until Hunter becomes the aggressor. Darcy needs to get Hunter and Jennifer out of Genoa Cove.

After she finishes the laundry, Darcy parts the living room curtains and sees Mr. Gibbons, arms folded over his chest, holding court with Mrs. Andrews and two other neighbors. He gestures at Darcy's house, his arms flailing with misplaced anger she'll never understand.

Hunter emerges from his room, an icepack pressed against his cheek. Wearing only his shorts, his blonde hair sticking out in every direction, he brushes against the wall on his way to the kitchen where he searches the refrigerator for breakfast.

"How's the eye?" Darcy asks.

Hunter cracks three eggs and drops them into the frying pan.

"Hurts when I blink too fast."

She wants to wrap him in her arms and never let go. He gives her a wary, sidelong look as he pushes the eggs around with the spatula.

"Did Detective Ames say anything to you about the police pressing charges against Aaron?"

Hunter shrugs and scratches his head.

"Not specifically, but I guess it doesn't matter. He's going to jail for what he did to Bethany."

If the police don't press charges, the village will think Hunter was at fault.

"How is Bethany handling this?"

Hunter pops a slice of bread into the toaster.

"She already gave up on Aaron."

"The father sure took Aaron's side last night."

"Well, that's why Bethany's mother kicked him out."

"I thought the father got an apartment because Aaron couldn't live in the same house as Bethany."

"No, she kicked him out of the house. Bethany thinks they'll get a divorce."

Darcy sits down at the kitchen table. At least Bethany's mother holds her son accountable. The father continues to justify his son's actions. Darcy can't blame the mother for wanting a divorce. But Bethany doesn't need the stress of her parents separation hanging over her head. Darcy has to hand it to her son. He's dealing with the attack and Lindsey's suicide as well as can be expected.

"How well did you know Lindsey Doler?"

Hunter digs through the cupboard for the salt and pepper and snickers.

"You make it sound like she died or something."

Oh, no. Darcy tries to cover the horror on her face. Too late.

Dropping the spatula, Hunter turns off the burner and stares at his mother, unblinking.

"I'm sorry, Hunter. I thought you heard."

Hunter can't focus. He swings his attention from Darcy to the window, then back to the stove and his half-cooked breakfast.

"Lindsey Doler died?"

Swallowing the knot in her throat, Darcy tells Hunter about the suicide.

"Your sister says Lindsey didn't display signs of depression. Did any of the other kids at school think Lindsey needed help?"

Hunter drops his eyes to the floor.

"No way. I mean, she was a little young to hang with

my friends, but she was cool. Everyone liked her. I can't believe she killed herself. Do you know how she…?"

"No, and don't go asking your sister for specifics," Darcy says with caution in her voice. "Jennifer took the news hard. Lindsey came to Kaitlyn's house last night."

"And Lindsey didn't act like something was wrong?"

"No, she seemed in good spirits." Darcy nods her head at the stove. "I'll finish making your breakfast."

Hunter does a double-take and remembers he turned off the burner.

"I've got it," he says.

"You're upset."

"Well, yeah. That's about the worst thing you can hear about another kid."

While Hunter turns his attention back to cooking, Darcy chides herself for upsetting her son. He would have found out today, she reasons. After last night, the last thing Hunter needed was for his mother to deliver another shock of terrible news. They make small talk while Hunter cooks his breakfast, his mood brightening.

Hunter's phone blasts a heavy metal song when a call comes in. From his side of the conversation, Darcy knows it's Jennifer on the phone. He shifts into big brother mode, comforting Jennifer and gently asking her about Lindsey. Hunter possesses an uncanny ability to set Jennifer at ease. Soon, the conversation shifts. Hunter tells her about the fight as if it was just another evening in his life, laughing with his sister as he plates the eggs. After he pours a glass of orange juice, he hands Darcy the phone.

"Here. Jennifer wants to talk to you."

Hunter sets the plate on the table and digs into his noon breakfast.

"How are you doing with all of this, Jennifer?"

"Is it okay if Kaitlyn and I go to the nature preserve? Her mom said she'll bring me home after dinner."

Darcy sighs. One second Jennifer can't sleep because she's worried about her brother and upset Lindsey committed suicide, the next she'd rather spend the day with her best friend than come home. Perhaps it's a blessing. Jennifer needs to be with her friend today.

"Is hiking wise? You stayed up all night."

"I slept three hours. I'm good now."

"You should reconsider. I don't want you getting sick."

"Mom, it's totally fine. I'll sleep tonight."

"What about the heat advisory in effect? Wouldn't you rather go swimming or hit the mall?"

"It's not that hot out. We were just on her deck talking, and it's not bad."

When last Darcy checked, it was ninety degrees outside.

"Well, if this is what you want. Drink plenty of water and don't push too hard. And don't come crying to me if you wake up with a sore throat tomorrow."

Darcy pictures Jennifer's eye roll before the call ends. A measure of relief falls over Darcy when Julian's cruiser pulls into the driveway. Though she's seen him in uniform, she's burned an image into her head of how Julian looked last night. He tips his cap when he catches her spying through the window.

"You're supposed to be working," Darcy says, greeting him in the doorway. "Slow day?"

"It's too hot for the criminals. How's Hunter?"

Darcy searches over her shoulder for her son, but he already ate, washed his dishes, and vanished into his bedroom.

"He's handling it well. I didn't realize Aaron's parents are getting divorced."

"That's news to me too. Then again, I don't keep up with village gossip the way some of my coworkers do."

She wonders if he's talking about Ames.

"Speaking of which, what happened to Lindsey Doler?"

Julian shifts his gaze to the doormat. He places his hands on his hips and shakes his head.

"So you figured out the reason I stopped by."

"You want to speak to Jennifer about Lindsey's death."

Memories of last year resurface, and Darcy recalls the police railroading Hunter. Julian catches Darcy's concern.

"I figured Jennifer might want to talk about it." Julian removes his cap and wipes his face on his forearm. "Teens don't talk when they're under stress. It's like they're afraid their classmates will think they're weird or weak. When a teen takes her life, all her friends share the pain."

"You can speak with Jennifer anytime. But she's still at Kaitlyn's house."

"She hasn't come home yet?"

"It's for the best. The girls are spending the day together. They can reassure each other in ways a parent can't."

"You're probably right."

"Julian, I need to ask. How did Lindsey..."

"Kill herself?"

"It's hard enough to say."

"She hung herself. The father found Lindsey in the garage."

Darcy falls against the jamb. In her mind, she pictures a teenager with her entire life ahead of her, a noose looped around her neck because her parents couldn't make their marriage work.

"Women don't hang themselves, Julian. It's usually a guy thing."

"And it's rarer among teenagers. The statistics don't favor Lindsey hanging herself, but it happened."

The quiet between them draws out, and Julian shifts from foot to foot.

"I should get back to work."

Darcy sneaks a look over Julian's shoulder.

"Yes, before one of my nosy neighbors gives the chief a call."

"Technically, I'm on an official visit. Jennifer spent the evening with a girl who committed suicide. I'm just asking how Lindsey acted last night."

"Listen, Hunter and I are grilling a steak for dinner, and Jennifer should be home by then. You're welcome to join us."

"I'd love to, but Reynolds called out sick on the swing shift. I'm covering for him until eight."

Darcy scratches her face to conceal her disappointment.

"All right. If anything changes, let me know. We'd love to have you. Over for dinner, I mean."

Damn, that sounded awkward. Julian grins and promises to let her know.

# CHAPTER ELEVEN

Jennifer shuts the door to Mrs. Beckley's sports car. Standing beside Kaitlyn, she waves as the car pulls away. The Genoa Cove nature preserve begins on the north edge of the village, a stone's throw from the bustle of downtown, and merges with protected forestland.

"Tell me about the trail again," Jennifer says, shielding her eyes with her hand as she looks up the hill.

"It's a dirt trail," Kaitlyn says, "which is why I brought these."

Kaitlyn lifts her leg and shows off a new pair of hiking sneakers.

"Hilly?"

"Yeah, but don't worry. It's all shaded forestland. You'll love it. Wait until you check out the wildflowers. They're amazing."

A girl's voice calls up from the sidewalk. When Jennifer spins, she sees Lindsey Doler waving at her. Heart thumping, she blinks and looks again. Kaitlyn calls back to the girl. It's Cheryl from the gymnastics team, one of Kaitlyn's friends. Jennifer looks away so Kaitlyn doesn't see the tears crawling down her cheeks. A part of her wanted to believe it really was Lindsey, that the suicide was nothing but a crass Genoa Cove rumor. Her father hadn't discovered Lindsey hanging in the garage, and she's still alive in Genoa Cove, searching for Jennifer to tell her everything will be all right.

Jennifer sniffs and wipes her face on her t-shirt. Sweat trickles down her back and rests on the base of her spine. Her mother's warning about the heat nagging in the back of her mind, Jennifer fidgets with the hem of her shorts.

"Hey, what's up with you? You okay?"

Kaitlyn's voice disappears beneath the village traffic. Jennifer watches Cheryl cross the street and vanish behind a hedgerow fronting a large two-story home. Her heartstrings tug. Though she realizes she concocted a fantasy, Cheryl leaving ends any hope Lindsey is still alive. Her friend killed herself. And Jennifer should have seen the signs. She missed Lindsey's cries for help. Jennifer failed her.

"Jennifer."

Kaitlyn touches her shoulder. Jennifer clears her throat and bends to tie her sneaker, hoping the relentless sun dried her cheeks.

"I'm okay. The heat's getting to me."

"But we just stepped out of the car."

Jennifer contorts her face into a forced smile and turns.

"How far does the trail lead up the hill?"

"The walk isn't long."

"That's a good thing."

"Mother Hen has you fretting over the big bad heat, doesn't she? Well, don't worry. I've got just the thing to cool us off."

Kaitlyn opens her backpack and removes a towel. Six

beer bottles clink together as Jennifer forces a smile. Kaitlyn acted bubbly all morning to cover her grief, and now she wants to get drunk.

"Where did you get those?"

"My Mom hides six packs in the garage. She thinks I don't know where they are."

"Won't she notice a pack missing?"

Kaitlyn waves the concern away.

"Not at all. Hey, are you gonna loosen up, or will you be a killjoy all day?"

"I just don't want you to get in trouble."

With a sly smile, Kaitlyn zips the bag shut and slings it over her shoulder. The nature preserve is empty except for the two girls, the heat too much to bear for the rest of the village. Initially, Jennifer can't stop herself from grinning. Kaitlyn was right. This place is beautiful. A garden of wildflowers native to the east shore parallels the entrance to the trail.

"It's spectacular," Jennifer says. "Can you imagine having a vase of these in your bedroom?"

"So I'll pick you a few. What's your favorite color?"

A black iron gate prevents visitors from stepping inside. Kaitlyn slings one leg over the short barrier and boosts herself up. Jennifer whirls around and searches for a park employee.

"You'll get us kicked out."

"There you go, freaking out over nothing again. It's just a flower."

"But they put the gate up for a reason."

"They can sue me."

Before Kaitlyn chooses a flower to steal, the sharp glint of reflected sunlight causes her to stop and glance at the parking lot. A black sedan idles in an open parking space beside the path. Something about the car constricts Jennifer's lungs. Her eyes fix on the sedan as Kaitlyn peeks through the trees.

"I know who that is," Kaitlyn says, resting her hands on the gate. "Looks like Bryce Carters borrowed his dad's car."

"That's not Bryce Carters," Jennifer says, her voice little more than a whisper.

She jumps when Kaitlyn grabs her arm.

"Come on. Let's hike into the woods and get silly drunk. For Lindsey!"

Kaitlyn leaps over the gate and drags Jennifer up the trail. Over her shoulder, Jennifer spies the sedan through the trees until she can't see it anymore. Now and again, the wind pulls the engine's growl up the hill. They're over the crest when a car door slams in the parking lot.

"He's coming," Jennifer says, her anxiety growing.

"Maybe he wants to kiss you."

Jennifer blushes.

"I'm not into Bryce."

"Obviously, he's into you. Though it's mega creepy he followed us here." Kaitlyn turns back and cups her hands around her mouth. Before Jennifer can stop her, Kaitlyn shouts down the hill. "Go home, loser! She's not interested...but maybe I am."

Kaitlyn doubles over laughing. The trees dance and sway as the wind picks up.

"That wasn't smart."

"Oh, stop. We're just having a little fun with Bryce."

Kaitlyn twirls and marches into a clearing, where the temperature soars fifteen degrees warmer than it was under the trees. Jennifer runs to catch up, looking behind as she closes the distance on her friend. Overrun by grass and invasive weeds, the dirt trail snakes through the trees and vanishes down a hill. It's a quick walk from the clearing to the next tree line. This section of forest runs deeper than the last, extending as far as Jennifer can see. And it's dark. Shadows fall down from old trees and spill across the forest floor.

"Not much longer," Kaitlyn says, recognizing the anxiousness on Jennifer's face. "The trail empties to a pond after a mile. Almost nobody ever goes there."

Kaitlyn pats the bag, indicating they'll drink the beers at the pond.

For a long time, they walk in silence. Animals scurry under the brush when they approach. Leaves from last autumn form a thick mat, silencing their steps. Which means Jennifer won't hear someone coming up behind them.

"Why did she do it?"

Jennifer stumbles. She didn't expect Kaitlyn to broach Lindsey's suicide.

"I don't get it. She seemed so happy last night."

Kaitlyn nods, her misty eyes fixed straight ahead.

"She hugged me before she left. It wasn't a goodbye hug, either. She wanted to get together tonight."

Chewing her lip, Jennifer tries to reason why her friend took her life.

"You knew about the trip to Europe, right?"

Kaitlyn wipes her eyes on her shirt sleeve.

"Knew about it? She called me last April when her father bought the tickets. Lindsey couldn't wait to go. There's no way she'd kill herself."

Except teenagers don't postpone suicides because they're looking forward to a trip to Spain and Italy. Jennifer keeps her doubts to herself, allowing Kaitlyn to vent her frustration.

Soon the girls go silent. Jennifer puts the idling sedan out of her mind. Why make herself crazy over nothing? She's allowing her paranoia to get the best of her, memories of Eric Stetson and the two abductions staining how she sees the world. Bryce Carters borrowed his dad's sedan and spotted Kaitlyn and Jennifer in the parking lot. Nothing more to it. Walking alongside Kaitlyn, Jennifer relaxes and takes in the forest. She never knew this nature preserve existed. Following the trail through the woods, it's difficult for her to believe the busy village lies beneath the ridge, the ocean just over the horizon.

But when the pathway descends a slope riddled by fallen branches and mud from recent thunderstorms, Jennifer feels eyes watching through the trees. She reaches out and grabs Kaitlyn.

"What's wrong?"

Jennifer places a finger against her lips. Scans the forest. In the darkness, her imagination conjures nightmare faces from her past. Richard Chaney. Eric Stetson.

"Let's go," Kaitlyn says. "We don't have all day, and I want to sober up before my mom comes back."

Her mother isn't coming for three hours. Removing the phone from her pocket, Jennifer checks for a signal and can't find one.

"Wait, what happens if one of us gets hurt and needs help?"

"Don't get hurt," Kaitlyn says, arching an eyebrow.

"Seriously, Kaitlyn. No signal, that's not good."

Kaitlyn releases an exasperated groan and starts down the decline, turning sideways to maintain her balance. Jennifer glances back, her heart thundering when a shadow swims through the darkness a hundred feet behind them. Now she rushes ahead of Kaitlyn, urging her friend to hurry.

"What's the rush? I thought you were worried about getting hurt."

Jennifer sees the pond through the trees, the water glistening as she catches a scent of the boggy terrain. They're halfway down the decline when a branch breaks behind them. The snap echoes off the trees. Kaitlyn draws up, worry in her eyes. A small teenage boy stepping on a branch wouldn't have caused a noise that loud.

"I told you it wasn't Bryce," Jennifer says.

She might as well be alone in the forest. Kaitlyn can't help Jennifer, doesn't appreciate the danger. For girls like Kaitlyn—girls who spend their days mired in text conversations—what happened to Jennifer last year was just a television show. A scary movie that ends when the credits run and the monster removes the mask. Is someone stalking Jennifer again? Mom acted weird the last two days. Something has her spooked.

Kaitlyn checks her phone. She can't find a signal, either. All around the girls, the trees crowd together as though conspiring, branches rubbing against each other when the wind picks up, joints groaning under the weight of years. It's dark as night inside the forest.

"Should we hide? Jennifer?"

Listening, Jennifer filters out the birdsong and animal sounds. She tells herself she doesn't hear the crunch of boots on branches and dried pine needles behind them. Her instinct screams *run*. Only a girl who has faced the devil twice can sense the evil trailing their steps. As she swings her vision along the hillside, a sapling bends to the side when someone forces it out of the way.

When Kaitlyn opens her mouth in question, Jennifer

covers the girl's mouth and warns Kaitlyn with her eyes. They stand behind a thick grouping of elms and hickories, their location invisible to anyone descending the ridge.

"Who do you think it is?" Kaitlyn asks, whispering.

"How would I know? You're the one who said it was Bryce. Just stay quiet."

Kaitlyn drops to one knee and presses her body against a tree trunk. Jennifer studies the ground for anything that might serve as a weapon. Nothing but fallen branches, no rocks visible beneath the bed of leaves. A snapped log lies beneath the tree, too large for either girl to lift.

Then footsteps draw near. Jennifer doesn't dare peek around the tree. Kaitlyn digs through the leaves and comes away with a sharp-tipped branch. That will do in a pinch, Jennifer thinks, nodding her approval. Kaitlyn clutches the branch against her chest, her breaths shooting in and out.

The footfalls are almost on top of them when Jennifer shakes Kaitlyn and drags her around the tree. A moment later, a shadowed figure stomps past. He would have seen them had Jennifer not pulled Kaitlyn back.

As they hide in the darkness, the man stops and searches the forest. Looking for Jennifer and Kaitlyn. The man swings his head toward the tree. Jennifer flattens herself against the bark before he sees. It's too dark to see their pursuer's face. The strong, lumbering body tells her it's a man.

The man resumes his search down the hill. Jennifer releases a held breath and edges around the trunk. But instead of descending the hill to the pond, the man stops and studies his surroundings. He knows they're close. In a moment, the man will reverse course and search the hillside again, and this time he'll find them crouched beside the tree.

When he turns around and stares right at them, Jennifer covers Kaitlyn's mouth. A tear crawls out of her friend's eye and wets Jennifer's fingers. She just needs to keep Kaitlyn quiet a little longer. Until the man turns his gaze on the rest of the forest.

But he doesn't. He senses their presence. Knows he passed them.

When the stalker angles across the hillside with his back to them, Jennifer nods at the broken log at her feet. Kaitlyn questions Jennifer with her eyes, and Jennifer pantomimes a kick. Kaitlyn's face lights with understanding. One little nudge is all it will take to get the log rolling down the hill. In the dark, it won't be easy to discern the cause of the noise. If they're lucky, he'll think one girl ran for the pond.

"When I kick the log, run for the trail. Don't wait for me, just go. I'll be right behind you."

"Are you sure this will work?"

"It has to. But Kaitlyn, you need to leave the backpack."

A protest forms on her face, then she nods.

"All right. Ready to go?"

"Do it."

Jennifer shoves the heel of her sneaker against the log and starts it rolling. At first, she fears the tall grass will snag the log and impede its progress. Momentum takes control, and the log hops over a hummock and crashes down the hillside. Kaitlyn shoots into the dark and runs for the trail, Jennifer staying behind to ensure the diversion worked. Except she can't see the man. He disappeared.

When he crashes through the brush, falling for the distraction, Jennifer turns and runs. She doesn't stop until they reach the parking lot.

Kaitlyn leans over with her hands on her knees. Spittle drips off her lips, a puddle of sick between her sneakers as she wipes at her eyes with a tissue. Jennifer paces out of breath and places a call to her mother. Civilization beams under the afternoon sun, vehicles whipping past on the thoroughfare. Jennifer has never been so happy to see the village of Genoa Cove.

"Are you sure you don't want me to call my mother?" Kaitlyn asks, sniffling.

"My mom is on the way. Just stay near the sidewalk, okay?"

Kaitlyn nods. As they pace the sidewalk, the girls earn strange looks from people driving past. One woman in a Volvo slows to a crawl along the curb and mouths, "Is everything okay?"

Jennifer raises her thumb, and the woman drives off.

Where is Mom? She should have been here by now. Glancing back at the parking lot, Jennifer shakes her head. The black sedan is gone. The stalker couldn't have outrun them to the parking lot and driven off. As she ponders where the man hid the sedan, Mom beeps and pulls the Prius beside them.

"What happened?" Mom says, climbing out of the car.

"Please drive us home," Jennifer says in between breaths. "I'll tell you on the way."

# CHAPTER TWELVE

Darcy chews a nail at the kitchen table. A black Lincoln. That's the vehicle she saw at the park.

"Did you read the license plate?"

"The car was too far away," Jennifer says. She fishes a water bottle out of the refrigerator and chugs half.

"Careful, hon. You'll get yourself sick if you drink too fast."

Jennifer holds up a finger and swallows the remainder, the plastic making a crackling noise as she sucks the air out. She sighs and places the bottle on the counter.

"I don't get why you needed to go to the nature preserve in the first place," Darcy says, running a hand through her hair.

"Mom, is there something you haven't told us?"

Darcy pulls her hand from her mouth, but her fingers drum the chair with nervous tension.

"What do you mean?"

"You've been acting weird the last two days. We know something is wrong."

Darcy massages her temples. Jennifer needs to know

Michael Rivers might be in Genoa Cove, but until now she had no reason to believe Rivers was already here.

"Get your brother. I have something I want both of you to hear."

Jennifer returns with Hunter, who rakes the hair away from his eyes and plops into a kitchen chair, arms folded.

"Okay, what's going on now?" Hunter asks.

"Last night, I went to dinner with Julian…Officer Haines." Jennifer and Hunter share a look. "After dinner, we visited the park in the village center. While we sat on a bench, I noticed a car with tinted windows parked beside the curb. I swore whoever was inside was staring at us. It was a black Lincoln."

"Like the one at the nature preserve," Jennifer says.

"Yes. I've learned not to believe in coincidences."

"But nobody has seen Michael Rivers since he escaped from prison, right?"

Darcy shakes her head. She doesn't want to scare the kids, but they need to know.

"Two nights ago, a woman spotted Michael Rivers outside Allentown, Pennsylvania. Now, she might be lying, and Allentown is a lengthy drive from Genoa Cove, but that's the first time a credible witness came forth with information about Rivers since the escape."

"So it's him," Jennifer says, tugging at a lock of hair.

"The woman said Rivers drove an Audi with Pennsylvania plates. The vehicle we both saw was a black Lincoln, and I'm certain the car had a North Carolina license plate."

"He could have changed cars," Hunter says, resting his chin on his fist.

Yes, that's what Darcy is afraid of.

"That's a possibility. The truth is we don't know where Michael Rivers is or if he'll come after us. To this point he's sent hired hands."

"He only hired people because he was in jail," says Jennifer, wandering to the window. "Now he's out."

"There's another possibility. Aaron Torres has a lot of friends. He wants revenge, especially after the fight with Hunter. Maybe it's a kid harassing us."

Jennifer places her hands on her hips.

"Nobody would dare. Besides, who is stupid enough to associate himself with Aaron and Sam?"

Darcy turns the chair toward her son.

"Hunter, think back to last night when you left the party with Bethany. Did you notice a black Lincoln nearby?"

Hunter ponders the question for a moment, then he shakes his head.

"I doubt it, but it was dark out, and cars lined both sides of the street."

"Could you ask Bethany if she saw anything?"

Hunter chews his lip.

"I'll ask, but now isn't the best time. Her mom isn't handling this latest incident with Aaron well."

"Okay, but both of you, please keep an eye out for a black Lincoln. Whoever it is, he's following our family. Watch your backs at all times." Darcy meets their stares. "And no parties or sleepovers until we figure this out. Are we good?"

"Yes," they both say in unison.

When Jennifer and Hunter retreat to their rooms, Darcy phones Julian and fills him on the day's events.

"I remember you worrying over that car," Julian says. The motor in the background tells Darcy he's driving and has her on speaker phone. "And you're certain it had North Carolina plates?"

"Definitely."

"Okay. I'll radio back to the station and have someone run a check on black Lincolns registered in Genoa Cove. Check if anyone of interest pops up."

By *of interest* Julian means someone with a criminal record. A nice plan except Michael Rivers wouldn't register a vehicle. Unless the stalker is someone from town, Julian's search won't bear fruit.

"Hey, am I on speaker phone?"

"Yep."

"Is anyone in the car with you?"

Julian laughs.

"No. You may speak freely, Ms. Gellar."

Darcy grits her teeth, not wanting to sound like a love-struck teenager.

"I had a lot of fun last night."

"Yeah? Well, good, because so did I."

The smile in his voice booms through the phone.

"It would mean a lot to me if you stopped by after work. I remember you said you'd be late, but we'll be here all night."

Her pulse races when he pauses. Is she pushing their relationship beyond his comfort level?

"I'll be there. Give me a chance to run those checks and get you an answer."

"Great. See you then."

Happiness fades after the call ends. A cold thought occurs to Darcy. What if Lindsey Doler didn't take her life? A black sedan followed Darcy and Julian into the village. The same night, a girl who spent the evening with Jennifer was found hanging from a noose in the garage.

And the next day, the same sedan pulled into the nature preserve a moment after Kaitlyn's mother dropped the girls off, and someone chased the girls through the woods.

Not taking any chances, Darcy retrieves the Glock from her bedroom and slides it into the holster. She slips inside the bathroom and tugs the bottom of her t-shirt down. The mirror shows the bulge on her hip. Good enough.

Walking outside, Darcy scans the neighborhood. Everyone remains in their houses, cowering from the heat. But as she checks the windows, she spots matted grass in front of the house next door. Footprints. Couldn't be from the mailman. He wouldn't deliver to a vacant house.

After she ensures no one is around to see, Darcy crosses into the neighboring yard and stops when the grass grows past her knees. She worries about ticks, snakes, anything that might latch onto her leg if she plunges through. Stepping around the overgrowth, Darcy follows the path with her eyes. Someone cut across the lawn and tracked around the house. Kids? Doubtful. The neighborhood consists of wealthy couples without kids, single professionals, and the elderly. Only the Masons have two toddler girls, and they're not old enough to ride bikes without training wheels.

Darcy avoids the property, walking along the bordering meadow as if the neighboring yard spreads disease. The tracks follow around the back of the house and become a confused jumble. As if someone walked back and forth, searching for a way inside.

A cold sensation creeping down her neck, Darcy returns to her house and locks the door. From the kitchen, she spies the vacant house. The tracks end at the back door.

The house leaves a sick feeling in Darcy's stomach.

Sipping water, she narrows her eyes at the house, studying the gloom beyond the windows. This is crazy. The tracks probably belong to the real estate agent.

But as she pulls her eyes away from the house, a shadow creeps across the walls. A black bulk moving slowly down the street. It doesn't take her long to recognize the black Lincoln. Running into the living room, Darcy parts the curtains and watches the car turn the corner. The glare of the sun washes out the windshield, forcing Darcy to pull her eyes away. The sedan can't be traveling faster than five mph.

After the car slides past the curb, it halts at the foot of Darcy's driveway. Blocking her in. A cold sweat drips down Darcy's neck as her fingertips brush the Glock.

Michael Rivers? Or another hired killer?

Or Sam Tatum. Aaron Torres pulled a similar stunt last year. She can only guess what Aaron would have done had she not chased him away with a gun. With Aaron headed back to jail after the fight with Hunter, Sam will want revenge.

Whoever is inside the sedan, he won't attack Darcy in broad daylight with her neighbors watching.

Darcy throws a look over her shoulder. The bedroom doors remain closed. Good. That means the kids are safe.

Darcy whips the front door open and bounds down the driveway, the gun in her hand. The sedan revs and jerks as if the driver, stunned by the woman rushing toward the car, hit the brake instead of the gas. She's a step away from the Lincoln when the tires squeal. The car shoots out of the neighborhood in a cloud of black smoke.

But not before she reads the license plate.

# CHAPTER THIRTEEN

"No, I didn't see the driver," Darcy tells Detective Ames over the phone. "The sun was too bright against the windshield."

The sun drifts lower in the sky, bloody reds kissing the tree tops as Darcy stands in the driveway. Hunter and Jennifer huddle behind her, watching from the doorway. Dammit, she wishes Julian was here.

"Okay, Ms. Gellar. I sent a cruiser to your location. You remember Officer Faust?"

"Yes."

"Expect her in five minutes. In the meantime, I'm running the plates. You're certain you memorized the number?"

"Positive."

"Okay. For what it's worth, I don't expect Sam Tatum drove past your house. He's under parental supervision. One misstep and he goes into lockup until the hearing."

"That didn't stop Aaron Torres, Detective Ames. I don't think Sam considers the implications of his actions. How could he after he raped Aaron's sister?"

Ames clears his throat. Darcy pictures the detective at his desk, the same worn suit jacket hanging in the corner of the room, his shirt threadbare around the neck, sleeves rolled to his forearms.

"Anyhow, let's not jump to conclusions. The driver could have been lost and searching for an address."

"Then why did he speed off?"

"I've seen you angry, Ms. Gellar. If I saw you sprinting at me with a gun while I idled outside your house, I'd slam my foot on the gas too."

He's trying to settle her nerves with humor, but she hears the concern in his voice, senses the detective's anxiety that last year's horror show is about to get a sequel. The FBI already warned him about the Rivers sighting in Pennsylvania, so he must worry the Full Moon Killer will come after Darcy in Genoa Cove.

Officer Faust arrives two minutes later and parks her cruiser behind the Prius. She's stocky, a full head shorter than Darcy. Black hair curls up beneath her cap as she meets Darcy in the driveway.

After inviting Officer Faust inside, Darcy recounts seeing the Lincoln while in the park with Julian. The officer cocks an eyebrow, but the concern etched into Faust's face suggests she's taking the incident seriously.

"And you've never seen this vehicle in your neighborhood before?"

"No, I don't recall seeing any of my neighbors driving a black Lincoln."

Faust holds up a finger when a voice comes over the radio.

"Excuse me," the officer says, stepping into the foyer.

Darcy huddles on the couch beside Jennifer and Hunter. Gone are the sullen dispositions and vitriol toward Darcy. The kids are scared. They should be. She doesn't want to rip their lives apart by uprooting them again, but her priority is keeping them safe.

"That was Detective Ames," Faust says. "The plates belong to a vehicle reported stolen two nights ago outside of Rocky Mount."

"So he's here."

"Who?"

"Michael Rivers. Have the locals search for an abandoned Audi with Pennsylvania plates near Rocky Mount. He switched vehicles to throw the police off his trail."

"Don't jump to conclusions. Thieves steal cars all the time. All we know is the Lincoln came from Rocky Mount."

Faust speaks into the radio. A moment later, a motor guns outside the house. At the sound of a car door closing, Faust moves to the front door. She glares back at Darcy when Julian appears on the stoop. It's clear Faust doesn't approve of her partner dating Darcy.

"You have company, Ms. Gellar."

"All hell breaks out the second I get off shift," Julian says when Faust lets him inside.

He wears a red t-shirt that clings to his muscular frame, the ridges of his chest evident beneath the cloth, sun-bronzed biceps stretching the fabric. Officer Faust briefs Julian before leaving with a vague promise that the department will send a cruiser past the house overnight. After she departs, Hunter and Jennifer mope into the kitchen. In times of crisis, they cling to one another.

"So I guess you didn't grill," Julian says, trying to thaw the chill in the room with a sarcastic grin.

"Something came up."

"Just kidding. I've got us covered." Julian waves his phone at Darcy. "How do margherita pizzas sound?"

"You ordered us dinner?"

"They're thin crust so I got three."

"Thank you, but we'll never eat that much."

Julian rubs his belly.

"You've never watched a cop put away an entire pizza pie after a twelve-hour shift. Back to this car you saw. Tell me what happened."

Darcy motions Julian to take a seat on the couch, and Darcy sits beside him. He wears Nike sneakers and white ankle socks. She still isn't used to seeing him out of uniform. Darcy recites the events of the last hour. Julian's hands fidget in his lap as if he isn't sure what to do with them. He settles the internal argument by clasping them together.

"You're certain it's Michael Rivers," he says.

"It has to be."

"Finding the Audi in Rocky Mount will lend credence to the theory. In the meantime, I suggest you pack an overnight bag and take the kids to a hotel. You'll be safer there. The GCPD will keep a vehicle in the parking lot and make sure nobody causes you trouble."

Darcy glances around the room. The house will look more ominous after the sun sets.

"Honestly, I kinda like the sound of that."

"Good. Let's call around and see who has vacancies. There's a convention in the village. That might make getting a reservation more difficult than usual, but we should be able to find you a room."

"What about you?"

He clears his throat.

"I figured I'd make sure you made it to the hotel

safely, then head home."

"You work tomorrow morning?"

"Nope, got three days off before I start swing shifts." Julian's eyes move to the kitchen. The kids' murmurs float back to them, and Jennifer sniffles. "Someone sounds upset. We should check on your kids…or maybe you should. I don't want to overstep."

"Come with me."

When Darcy and Julian enter the kitchen, Jennifer meets Hunter's eye, silencing the conversation. They sit with their hands in their laps and study their reflections on the tabletop. Jennifer chews her lip and glances away from Julian. She wants to like the young officer, but having Bronson Severson under their roof shattered her trust. It will take time before she accepts Julian.

Darcy wants to ask what they were talking about. Instead of prying, she says, "Julian ordered pizzas for dinner."

Hunter gives Julian a half-hearted nod, and Jennifer mutters something that sounds like thanks.

"Anyway," Darcy continues, coughing into her hand. "How would you like to stay in a hotel tonight?"

"Do we have the money for that?" Jennifer asks, swiveling in her chair to face them.

Darcy folds her arms in front of the refrigerator.

"There's a resort hotel with a pool on the south end of the beach. Free breakfast. How's that?"

Jennifer shrugs and picks a piece of fuzz off her shorts.

"Okay, I guess. I mean, it's not safe here anymore, right?"

Darcy exchanges a glance with Julian, who steps forward and kneels in front of Jennifer.

"You have every cop in the village looking out for you." Jennifer purses her lips as if swallowing an argument. "Last year was horrible, but it's not happening again. If we need to, we'll put twenty-four-hour surveillance on the house."

"And we'll be prisoners," Jennifer says, chewing her thumbnail. "What if you were our age? How would you deal with never leaving the house?"

Julian looks to Darcy for help.

"The pizza won't arrive for a half-hour," Darcy says, brushing the hair off Jennifer's face. "That gives you time to think about what you want to pack. How about we start with a night or two in the hotel and take it from there? By then the police will have figured out who drove past our house."

"What about the party tomorrow night?" Hunter asks. "You said I could go."

Darcy sighs.

"Circumstances change. I can't let you go out until the police catch whoever is stalking us."

"This will never end."

"Hey, I need both of you on board. No sulking and complaining. It sucks to hear this, but there will always be another party, another get together. You're disappointed, I get it. But focus on what's important."

Hunter nods, unconvinced.

Tilting her head toward the living room, Darcy leads Julian out of the kitchen and gives Hunter and Jennifer space.

"The hotel," Julian says. "Was it a bad idea? They don't seem thrilled."

"It's a fine idea. They've both been through hell the last year. Now they're worried it's starting all over again.

Or that it will never end."

"What about you? Is that what you think?"

Darcy shuffles to the window. Peeking between the drapes, she glances up at the sky. Blue dusk spills down from the heavens, the first stars glimmering above the streetlights. Her fear of the dark awakening, Darcy fingers tremble at her sides.

"It's starting again. And this time it won't be another Richard Chaney or Eric Stetson who comes after us. Michael Rivers is here, Julian. He's in Genoa Cove."

Julian touches her arm. Darcy spins to face him.

"Ames will bring the FBI to Genoa Cove. You're not fighting Rivers alone. Not this time."

"You don't get it, Julian. Even inside the hotel, we won't be safe. Locked doors don't stop him. He contracted murderers to kill us from inside a federal penitentiary."

The pizza arrives as shadows spread across the yard. Julian pays the delivery girl and tells her to keep the change, refusing Darcy's offer to cover the tip. Closing the door with three boxes balanced on one arm, Julian points at Darcy.

"Save your money. This order is on me."

Darcy sets the pizzas on the coffee table. Jennifer brightens when her mother opens the first box. Hunter hangs his head in the corner and nibbles at a slice. His earbuds hang around his neck. Darcy feels thankful Hunter hasn't shut them out with his music, but she worries he's going into a shell again. While the others eat, Darcy dials the Cove Inn and books a fourth floor room for two nights. She wants guests below and above their room, an extra layer of safety should the Full Moon Killer track her down.

An hour later, three packed bags lie inside the front

door. With Darcy and the kids inside, Julian stands in the driveway and waits until the cruiser arrives. It's Faust again, and she's accompanied by a boyish officer Darcy hasn't met before. Julian mentioned a recent recruit named Wolpert. This must be him.

If Faust is stocky, Wolpert looks like a small tank. He's a hair taller than Faust. The thick trunk and legs mark him as a running back or linebacker. The cap mats down his light brown hair. Darcy can't hear them speaking. Now and then, Julian looks back at the window, causing Darcy to pull the curtains closed and step back. A few seconds later, Julian enters the house with the two officers.

"Darcy Gellar, this is Officer Wolpert," says Julian, standing aside for the officers.

Wolpert tips his cap at Darcy and the kids.

"Here's how we'll do this," Wolpert says as he takes them in with his eyes. "Ms. Gellar, you and the kids will ride with Julian to the hotel. Officer Faust and I will take the lead, and we have a second cruiser stationed outside a gas station a mile down the road. That's to ensure no one tries to follow you. Once you're settled inside the hotel, Officer Faust and I will watch the hotel until the graveyard shift takes over. In the meantime, we'll have an officer swing by the house to pick up your car so you're not stranded. May I have your keys?"

Darcy retrieves the keys from the kitchen counter.

"Very good," Wolpert says. He tries to exude confidence, but Darcy catches him glancing out the window as if expecting the darkening sky to rush inside. "One rule. Tell no one where you're staying. Not even family. Let us do our job, and we'll get you to the hotel without anyone knowing. Provided you keep a low profile, there's no reason to believe anyone will find out you're at the hotel."

Darcy climbs into the passenger seat while Jennifer and Hunter scoot into the back. Julian reaches behind him and removes his gym bag from the seat so they have room. Then Faust pulls her cruiser into the street and heads toward the coastal route. Julian waits ten seconds. When no other vehicles pull off the curb to follow, Julian backs up and trails the cruiser, maintaining a city block's distance between them and Faust's cruiser.

Gibbons holds court in Mrs. Andrew's driveway with several neighbors. No doubt the police car arriving at Darcy's house attracted the looky-loos like moths to a flame. Oh, the juicy tales they must be telling. Their eyes swing to Julian's car as it passes. In a world without rules, Darcy would roll down the window and shoot them a vulgar gesture. Instead, she bites her lip and looks away, sensing the heat behind their glares.

They arrive at the Cove Inn without incident. Julian speaks with Faust in the lobby while Darcy checks them in. A college-age girl with straight honey-brown hair and green eyes hands Darcy the room key.

Julian accompanies them to the room. He won't allow them to enter until he walks through. After he finishes, he stuffs his hands into his pockets and shifts from foot to foot.

"Sit and relax," Darcy says. "You're welcome here."

While Hunter tries in vain to fit the leftover pizza into the tiny refrigerator, Julian moves to the window and parts the translucent curtain. He inspects the parking lot before closing the blackout drapes.

"I should head out," Julian says, tapping his hand against his leg.

"You're sure you don't want to stay awhile?"

Julian glances at Darcy's bed, then at the neighboring queen where Jennifer and Hunter set their bags. Jennifer sits on the edge of the bed, one leg crossed over the other as she reads her phone.

"I'd better not. I'll head down to the cruiser and see how soon we can get your car over here."

"It's not that important. Hey," Darcy says, lowering her voice. "The more I think about Lindsey Doler's suicide, the less sense it makes. Who were the investigating officers?"

Julian waits until Hunter passes and sits beside Jennifer on the bed.

"Medlock and Isaacs responded last night. We talked in passing at the station, but they didn't say anything that indicated a wrongful death."

"Something about her suicide seems a little too coincidental."

"Why would the Full Moon Killer go after Lindsey Doler?"

"You tell me. Why did Richard Chaney murder those teenagers last year? What if Rivers went after Jennifer last night, followed her to the party, and—"

"And what? Saw Lindsey and decided to kill her instead?"

"Maybe she fits his type."

"Which is?"

"Young, pretty teenage girls."

"I suppose it's worth looking into. I'll check with Medlock and Isaacs and take a look at the photos."

"We're missing something important. I don't trust this suicide, Julian. Will you let me know as soon as you know more?"

"I will. Text or call if you need anything. Otherwise, I'll catch up to you in the morning. Please get some sleep. Genoa Cove's finest have eyes on the entrance to the hotel. You're safe here."

A pang of disappointment hits Darcy when the door closes. She didn't expect they'd take the next step in their relationship and sleep side by side with the kids in the next bed, but she wishes he'd stayed longer. She can't blame him for feeling uncomfortable.

While Jennifer and Hunter stay up late talking, Darcy wanders to the elevator and rides down to the lobby where she purchases three protein bars from the shop in the corner. Through the automatic doors to the parking lot, she spots the police cruiser nestled between two hotel vans. The officers are silhouettes. Faust raises a cup of coffee to her lips.

Tired parents carting two toddlers and a stroller struggle toward the elevator. Darcy offers to help them with their bags, but the woman gives her a wary glance and says they can handle it themselves. When the elevator closes and ushers the family upstairs, Darcy unwraps one of the protein bars and bites off the top. A swarm of guests rush through the lobby. They're probably here for the convention. Darcy can't stop herself from scrutinizing everyone as a potential threat.

A sizeable man with a beard stands in the far corner with a phone pressed to his ear. He's staring at Darcy. Then a woman in business attire clicks by on high heels, pulling a suitcase behind her. When she passes, the man is gone.

Darcy slips through the crowd and searches for the bearded man. She can't find him. But now there's a slender man wearing a designer leather jacket looking at Darcy from across the lobby. Paranoia suffocates. She remains vigilant, interrogates every guest as a potential threat to her and her family. Darcy searches the faces, concentrating on people standing on their own. The most likely eyes of the Full Moon Killer. She's never felt so alone in a crowded room.

When Darcy rides the elevator back to the fourth floor, she finds Hunter and Jennifer asleep. Quietly, she places the two protein bars on their bed stand and slides the covers back on her bed. Before she turns in for the night, she checks the parking lot. The police cruiser hides between the two hotel vans. She sees the bumper peeking out. More guests drag their bags through the parking lot, and Darcy decides it's safe to sleep.

But as she settles under the covers, the sensation that something is terribly wrong slicks her flesh with a cold sweat.

# CHAPTER FOURTEEN

I could get used to living in a neighborhood like this, Julian thinks as he flips the keys around in his hand. Julian studies the little house Darcy Gellar calls home, curious over the neighbor staring at him from a driveway halfway down the block. That must be Mr. Gibbons.

Intending to unlock the Prius and bring the car back to the hotel, Julian glances down at the key chain. Darcy's house key hangs off the chain. Spinning around, he inspects the neighborhood. It's after eleven now. Gibbons abandons his neighborhood watch post, and nobody else is out at this time of night.

The breeze wrapping around the house fails to relieve the suffocating humidity. A beetle crawls over his toe, and Julian loses his sandal as he kicks the black insect into the grass. Something feels wrong.

Darcy wouldn't mind if he checked out the house and ensured nobody tried to break in. He had his doubts about the Michael Rivers theory. A fugitive would go into hiding, and he certainly wouldn't pursue Darcy and her family with the police present. But someone drove past Darcy's house today in a stolen vehicle and left two black tire skids.

Julian slips the key into the lock and jiggles it until the mechanism clicks. The door slides open, and he steps into the dark entryway. Which is strange. He swore Darcy left a light on in the living room. So much for considering Darcy paranoid. Julian's fingers brush against the holstered pistol on his hip.

He flicks on the entryway light and squints against the sudden glare. In the living room, he leans over and turns on the table lamp, the one he's certain Darcy kept on. No, the bulb hadn't burned out. The lamp was simply off.

Scratching his head, Julian assesses the downstairs. Searches for anything out of place. Inside the kitchen, he turns on the next set of lights. Darkness presses against the windows. As he crosses the floor, movement catches his eye. Instinctively, he twists behind the refrigerator and pulls the pistol from his holster. Something beyond the deck, too fast to make out what it was. Breaths crawl in and out of his chest. Despite the air-conditioned interior, his hair turns sweaty. Removing the police radio, he pauses. Maybe he should remain quiet until he's certain nobody is standing outside the deck doors. Impossible to tell with the kitchen lights reflecting off the glass. He doesn't like that an intruder can see inside, but Julian can't see out.

He leaps from the refrigerator to the wall and kills the lights. At first, stars cloud his vision. When his eyes adjust to the sudden darkness, he glares through the deck doors. Three Adirondack chairs surround a table with an umbrella jutting out from the center. Starlight turns the deck gray. He was sure a shape shot through the yard. Could have been a deer. Yet there hadn't been a sound. Had he seen his own reflection in the glass?

Julian places the radio in his back pocket and steps toward the doors. Unlocks the door and pulls. It won't budge. He forgot the bar locking the door at the base, the added measure of security Darcy added last year during the Darkwater Cove murders. He slides the bar back and steps onto the deck. Cricket songs ring out in the otherwise silent night. He can't see beyond the meadow grass bordering the yard. Not taking any chances, he keeps the gun in his hand and steps off the deck. One glance along the back of the house reminds him of the security cameras. If someone was in the yard, the camera should have caught him.

But it's the house next door that draws Julian's attention. The vacant house.

Last month, the realty company sent a lawn care crew to mow the grass, but nobody has touched the property since. The grass grows knee high around the house, the shrubberies untrimmed and clawing at the siding. A young tree standing off the vacant home's deck looks disturbingly like a person hiding in the shadows. Julian chides himself for letting the empty house set his nerves on edge. He's a little old to believe in haunted houses and monsters hiding in the dark.

But when he steps toward the unruly yard, a thump comes from inside the house. He throws himself against the side of Darcy's house, the camera fixed to the roof above his head. Listening, he reaches down for the radio and presses the button. His throat goes dry when he swallows. Before he speaks, the thumping sound comes again. And this time he's sure it came from inside.

The female dispatcher answers his radio call. Julian pauses before speaking, the sensation that someone is watching him drawing the hairs up on his arms. When the dispatcher asks Julian for his position, he requests backup. There might be a trespasser next door. It's common on television shows and in movies for the hero to bust into the house alone, guns blazing. But that's not how officers react in the real world. He has no reason to believe this is a matter of life and death. The noises could be anything—the wind knocking a branch against the house, vermin crawling around inside.

Or Michael Rivers looking for Darcy.

Slipping the radio into his pocket, Julian kneels at the corner of Darcy's house. It's pitch black inside the neighboring home, too dark to discern movement. He watches and waits, losing his nerve. If the officers show up and find no sign of anyone inside the house, he'll be the butt of their jokes for the next month. If he's lucky. Cops are relentless.

No additional thumps come from next door, and he doubts his judgment when an approaching siren brings his head up. The cruiser pulls to the curb.

Julian steps out from behind the house.

# CHAPTER FIFTEEN

Unfortunately for Julian, the two responding officers happen to be veterans with a knack for riding younger officers. Their eyes light with the possibility Julian panicked over nothing.

"It might have been a demon," Medlock says, puffing out his gray handlebar mustache.

"Or Sasquatch," Isaacs adds.

Isaacs, just six months from his retirement date, raps Medlock on the shoulder. They share a laugh.

"Very funny," Julian says with his back leaned against the cruiser, hands in his pockets. "You two geniuses get word back from Rocky Mount on that stolen Audi?"

Officer Isaacs, a burly man with a full beard and mustache, shakes his head.

"Haven't found a misplaced Audi in Rocky Mount. Could be the FBI is way off on this."

Julian's gaze drifts between Darcy's house and the vacant property. Intuition tells him the situation is more dangerous than the evidence suggests, but if Michael Rivers stole the Lincoln, the Audi should have turned up by now. Then again, all they had to go on was an eyewitness account in Allentown and grainy video footage of a man who never turned toward the security cameras. As if he knew their positions.

"Tell me again what you heard," Medlock says, the joviality gone from his face.

"Two loud thumps inside the house. Like somebody was walking around in the dark and bumped against the wall or knocked something over."

"And you thought somebody came through Ms. Gellar's backyard?"

"Yeah, but it was dark out. Maybe it wasn't a person. It could have been anything."

Isaacs tilts his chin at Darcy's house.

"She's got the place locked down like Fort Knox, security cameras covering every edge of the home's exterior. If someone cut through the yard, he'd be on camera, right?"

Julian scratches his chin.

"Darcy monitors the footage on her laptop, and I don't recall her taking it to the hotel. It should be here."

"You know how to log on to her computer?"

"I've got the password in my phone."

Isaacs raises his eyebrows at Medlock. The veteran officers follow Julian to Darcy's door. He fits the key into the lock and opens the house, the living room lights shining as he left them. While Medlock and Isaacs wait in the foyer, Julian searches the kitchen for the computer. Not there. It must be in the bedroom. He senses their stares on his back as he follows the hallway to Darcy's bedroom door. Edging the door open, he scans the room and spots the laptop bag in the corner beside a half-packed overnight bag. Must be Darcy forgot a bag while rushing to leave.

Julian carries the overnight bag and laptop case to the kitchen. Opening the laptop, he waits for the computer to awaken from sleep mode, then he checks his phone and enters the password, knowing how this must appear to Isaacs and Medlock. If he has Darcy's passwords, they must be in a relationship. He stifles a groan. For several months, he danced around the possibility of asking Darcy on a date. Taking her to Harpy's felt akin to walking a tightrope over a pit of snapping flames. Though they've become close friends, an invisible wall exists between Julian and Darcy. She struggles with addiction and fear of the dark, and Julian senses she'll never be over Tyler's death.

He locates the icon for the security system and loads the app. The screens display the property in real time. It takes him a moment to remember how to load archived footage. Scanning the time stamps, he reverses one hour and plays the recording.

"Any idea when you saw the guy?" Medlock asks, hands on hips.

"Must have spotted him five minutes before I called dispatch."

That gives Julian a time window to work with. He speeds up the replay until he sees himself walking onto the deck. He went too far. Backing up, he sets the speed to normal and stands back to watch with Isaacs and Medlock looking over his shoulder.

There.

A shape blurs past the edge of the screen. The camera doesn't catch the figure, but the broad shouldered shadow sliding across the grass marks it as a man.

"I'll be damned," Medlock says, drumming his fingers on the counter top. "Roll it back."

Julian reverses the footage to the point before the shadow blackens the yard. This time he replays the footage in slow motion.

"He knows where the cameras are," Julian says, pointing at the screen. "Two steps to the left, and we'd have his mug on camera. This guy knew the radius of the camera view and stayed just outside the perimeter."

"Cat burglar," Isaacs says without conviction.

"I don't know. Look here." Julian starts the replay again and nods at the shadow. "You'd think the guy would make a run for the meadow, at least get behind the trees. Instead, he beelines toward the vacant house next door."

"And you never saw him again?"

"Exactly."

"I suppose we should check the house." Isaacs grimaces. "Hey, could be the guy tried to break in, and that's the noise you heard. He took off after he couldn't find a way inside."

"Then he should have left a print on the window or on one of the doors," says Julian, glaring at the two officers. "We need to walk through that house."

Isaacs shares a glance with Medlock.

"I was afraid you'd say that."

Another GCPD cruiser pulls to the curb. By now, the commotion has attracted a slew of neighbors. They convene in the middle of the road, speaking in hushed tones which the wind carries to the officers. Julian catches Darcy's name and a derisive slur before Officer Faust climbs out of the cruiser and makes her way across the lawn.

"Heard you had a possible break-in at the Gellar residence," Faust says, quieting the squelch booming out of her radio.

"Boy Wonder here thinks someone broke into the haunted house next door," Medlock says, cocking his head toward Julian. "And now he wants to go in, guns blazing."

"I just want to check things out," Julian says, shoving his hands into his pockets.

Faust stares at the vacant house. The doors remain closed and the windows intact.

"Did you find signs of forced entry?"

"Gellar's cameras caught someone move across her yard toward the vacant house."

Hands on her hips, Faust studies the adjoining yards.

"If these two chickens are too afraid to go inside," Faust says, winking at Isaacs and Medlock. "I'll back you up."

Isaacs spits.

"Who's chicken? Tell you what, hot shot, why don't you skim through Boy Wonder's footage and tell me what you see on the camera. Medlock and I will make sure Julian doesn't get scared in the dark."

Faust turns to Julian. There's concern in her eyes.

"Did you catch a face on camera?"

"Negative. At least, not that I could see. If you want to take a second look at the footage and keep an eye on the Gellar residence, we'll check out the neighbor's house."

Julian can count on one finger the number of times he's entered a residence with the perpetrator still inside, and that was when a single father drove home drunk and ran over his neighbor's mailbox before passing out in the upstairs hallway. With Medlock and Isaacs close behind, he follows the sidewalk to the porch stoop. Skittering in the grass hints at vermin overrunning the knee-high overgrowth.

His nerves on edge, Julian swears the entryway tilts

toward him. As if inviting him inside. His spine feels encased in ice. Medlock nods at Isaacs, who takes off around the back of the house in case an intruder tries to slip out unseen. The officer grits his teeth when he wades into the dewy grass and weeds. Something darts away from his feet and draws a fading line through the overgrowth.

When Medlock stands in place at the back door, Julian slips on a pair of gloves and grabs the door knob. It's unlocked. He glances at Medlock, who exhales through his nose and sends Julian a *why-me?* look.

The door slides open. Julian expects stale, stuffy air to assail him in the entryway. It doesn't. Someone's been inside the house, and he doubts it was the realty agent. The foyer opens to the living room. White bedsheets cover a couch and two chairs left by the previous owner. In the dark they seem like graveyard monsters. A kitchen lies off to the left. Water leaks from the faucet with steady plunks. While Julian enters the kitchen, Medlock splits off to the right and follows a dark hallway toward three open doors. Though Julian expects to find Isaacs at the back door off the kitchen, his heart skips when the officer's face appears at the window. Isaacs jiggles the handle. The door pops open.

"Unlocked," the officer says, running his eyes over the dark kitchen.

The floor is bare, no table or chairs. A thin layer of dust covers the counter. Julian twists the faucet and stops the leak. Examining the basin, he spots the shadow of a water line two inches off the bottom. The drip wouldn't have caused the line. The faucet was used in the last day.

A groaning floorboard turns Julian's head around. It's Medlock entering one of the rooms off the hallway. In the hollow interior of the home, sounds crawl through the walls and seem to come from everywhere.

"See anything in the backyard?"

Isaacs glances over his shoulder at the window overlooking the yard.

"Trampled grass heading toward Gellar's yard."

"That could have been me," Julian says.

Isaacs nods, then tilts his head toward the hallway.

Crossing through the living room, Julian flicks the wall switch for posterity. No power. Medlock's flashlight blinds him as the officer turns out of a room at the end of the hall. For a brief moment, Julian's heart races with the possibility it's the intruder aiming the light into their faces. Then Medlock lowers the beam to the floor.

"The bathroom and bedrooms are clear," Medlock sighs. "I checked the windows. They're all latched from the inside."

Julian sets his gun inside his holster and folds his arms.

"No reason to climb through a window with the doors unlocked."

"You think the Realtor forgot to lock up?" Isaacs asks with false hope in his voice.

Julian doesn't.

Though Medlock cleared the rooms, Julian peeks inside the bathroom, then crosses the hall to the two bedrooms. Both bedrooms are empty. An oval throw rug covers half the floor inside the master bedroom. Pale starlight washes over the windows. He's about to turn away when an imperfection in the paint catches his attention. Medlock and Isaacs glare at him in question.

Flicking on his flashlight, Julian directs the beam toward the corner window. The black mark on the wall looks like an insect as Julian crosses the floor. As he gets closer, the imperfection takes shape. It's a carving.

Still wearing his gloves, Julian kneels beside the window and moves his eyes closer to the wall. His stomach turns. He's seen this symbol before—painted on the back of Darcy's house, and branded into the flesh of young women in crime scene photos. The leering smiley face is the mark of Michael Rivers, the Full Moon Killer.

"Shit," Medlock mutters.

"Take a picture," Julian says, leaning out of the shot while Medlock frames the photograph.

While Medlock aims his flashlight over the symbol, Julian runs a gloved thumb over the carving. It's etched with a sharp object, almost certainly a knife. He can feel the ridges through the rubber glove. The window offers an unobstructed view of Darcy's house. From here he can see into her kitchen. If Darcy stood at the sink washing dishes, he could watch her for as long as he chose without her knowing. Julian's eyes flick along the house and into the living room. A shadow passes over the window. Please let that be Officer Faust.

"Get the crime scene techs out here," Medlock tells Isaacs as he kneels beside Julian at the window.

Unease creases the officer's eyes. Julian pulls the radio off his hip.

"Faust, you find anything on the security footage?"

When Faust doesn't reply, Julian shoots his gaze back to Darcy's house. Now a shadow moves through the kitchen.

"Shit," Medlock says, wiping a hand across his mouth.

Julian jams his thumb down on the call button.

"Faust, do you copy?"

"Copy." Tension rolls off Julian's shoulders at the sound of Faust's voice. "I checked out the house. Everything appears to be in place. No evidence anyone broke inside."

"What about the footage?"

"It's like you said. Someone moves through the backyard at the edge of the cameras. It's too dark to make out a face. How's it going inside the neighbor's house?"

Julian rises to his feet and massages a knot out of his shoulder.

"Either Michael Rivers came through the house, or someone has a sick sense of humor."

A pause.

"The Full Moon Killer was next door?"

"I'll explain in a second. We're coming out."

"Techs should be here in half an hour," Isaacs says in the doorway.

Making a note to have the crime techs lock the doors after they dust for prints and gather evidence, Julian leads the two officers inside Darcy's house. One last examination of the camera footage reveals nothing new. Without another object in the picture to use as a reference, there's no way to determine the prowler's size. The speed with which it moves marks the unknown subject as athletic, agile. The possibility Michael Rivers watched Darcy and her children from the next yard sends a chill through Julian.

He glares out at the darkness past the deck, sensing they aren't alone. The night is full of footsteps that never come.

After Officer Faust responds to another call, Julian locks Darcy's house and follows Medlock and Isaacs back to their cruiser.

"Are you headed back to the inn?" Isaacs asks,

leaning against the passenger door.

Wonderful, Julian thinks. Does everyone in the department know about his relationship with Darcy? Secrets don't keep in villages like Genoa Cove.

"Did the medical examiner get back to you regarding the Doler suicide?" Julian asks.

Medlock scuffs at a rock with his shoe.

"We're not dead set on calling it a suicide."

"What changed?"

"Two sets of ligature marks on the neck. It's subtle, but one looked more vertical than the other."

"And what does that tell you?"

Medlock pantomimes a taut rope in his hands.

"Let's say someone came up behind Doler like so and strangled her with the rope nearly horizontal across her windpipe. Then he props her up and hangs her from the ceiling to make it appear like a suicide. The knot will pull the noose higher on Doler's neck."

"This could have been a murder."

Isaacs waves his hands.

"Slow down. It's a preliminary report. We shouldn't get ahead of ourselves."

"By all accounts, Doler wasn't a suicide candidate. Everyone keeps harping on the parents divorcing, but according to Doler's friends, she handled the break up well."

"Kids hide shit, Julian. Suppose she puts on a smile for her friends, but inside the divorce is tearing her up."

Julian glances at the vacant house, its windows like black eyes watching him.

"But if we're wrong about the suicide…"

"I know. It's last year all over again."

Medlock stares at Isaacs. It's going to be a long night.

# CHAPTER SIXTEEN

Darcy sits at a table along the periphery of the breakfast buffet. Hunter and Jennifer stand in line, Jennifer grabbing second helpings of oatmeal and fruit while Hunter waits for the waffle maker to beep. Breakfast in hand, Jennifer follows Hunter to the table.

"I don't know where you hide it all," Darcy says, winking at the double stack of waffles on Hunter's plate.

Jennifer sits down with a huff and pulls out her phone. When Darcy doesn't ask her what the problem is, Jennifer groans again.

"Okay, Jennifer. You got my attention. What's going on?"

"Kaitlyn is having everyone over tonight, and it looks like I'm the only one not going."

"You mean she's throwing another party."

"I didn't say that," Jennifer says, stabbing a piece of honeydew with her fork. "It's just friends hanging out."

"If she goes to Kaitlyn's, I'm going to my party," Hunter says, sawing a chunk off his waffle as he looks at Darcy through the tops of his eyes.

Darcy sets her hands on the table.

"Nobody's going to any parties tonight. We discussed this. It's too dangerous."

Jennifer's face reddens. Then she points the fork at Julian passing through the lobby. Hunter looks up as the off-duty officer weaves between the tables.

"Can I talk to you for a minute?" Julian asks, casting a look at the back of the room.

Darcy offers him a chair, but when he levels his eyes with hers, she knows this information isn't for the kids' ears. Hunter and Jennifer grunt when Darcy tells them she'll be right back. After they find a spot at the back of the room, Julian touches her shoulder.

"Someone broke into your neighbor's house last evening."

"The empty house?"

"Yeah. I went back to pick up your car and decided to do a walk-through at your place. I hope you don't mind."

"No, not at all. Was the house okay?"

"Darcy, you left the table lamp on before you left, right?"

Darcy thinks for a moment.

"I'm sure I did. When I was a kid, my parents always left one light on whenever we left the house. A theft deterrent. Old habits die hard. Why do you ask?"

"It was off when I unlocked the door."

Her skin crawls at the possibility of someone inside her house.

"You're certain the light hadn't blown."

"The light works fine. Either we're both mistaken, and you turned the light off before leaving, or someone came inside." Darcy's knees wobble, and Julian directs her to a chair. "I checked the place out. No damage, nothing missing, and there sure as hell wasn't anyone inside the house."

"What about the house next door?"

Julian looks across the room at Hunter and Jennifer. The kids are too busy eating to wonder about their conversation. He recounts seeing a figure run through the yard. The floor buckles as Julian continues, explaining how the security camera caught the man's shadow. Last year's terror is about to repeat itself.

Feeling her balance waver, Darcy pinches the bridge of her nose. Julian sits across from her and reaches over the table, setting his hand on her arm.

"We covered every inch of the house next door. Whoever was inside, they were long gone, but—"

"It's Michael Rivers, Julian. And he didn't leave a print. Michael's too careful."

"We're still investigating. The crime techs dusted for prints, and we expect Rocky Mount PD to give us an answer on the missing Audi by the end of the day. At least you're safe here."

Darcy laughs without mirth and gestures to the lobby and elevator.

"You really think the hotel staff would notice if Michael Rivers strolled through the lobby? This isn't a movie, and he isn't going to show up looking like Hannibal Lecter. He'll dress to fit in. With the hotel packed to capacity, he'll just be another guy heading to his room. For all we know he booked a suite."

Julian exhales and raps his knuckles on the table.

"Let me talk to the hotel manager. We might be able to place an undercover officer on your floor."

Julian stands up from the table.

"Where are you headed now?"

"Back to the neighbor's house. Then I'll put a call into

Rocky Mount PD."

"Isn't this your day off?"

"It is."

***

Hunter drops his phone on the bed and falls on the mattress. Staring at the ceiling, he clasps his hands behind his head as Jennifer sits on the edge of the bed, her thumbs flying across her phone as she composes a message. Mom is downstairs with Julian.

"How long before she makes us leave?"

Jennifer's thumbs freeze at his question. She makes a flustered sound in her throat and continues her text.

"She was on the phone with that Realtor the other day. Didn't you notice how quickly she changed the subject when we called her out?"

Annoyed, Jennifer shoves the phone into her pocket and lies beside her brother.

"It's so unfair. She never asks us what we want. Like that time she dragged us to Georgia. How did us being there make things better?"

Hunter shrugs.

"She was worried about Laurie."

"Well, it's not Laurie who ended up kidnapped."

Wincing, Hunter recalls his panic when Eric Stetson abducted his sister. He's embarrassed to admit there was a time when he worried he'd never see Jennifer again. Hunter slipped into a grim shell, steeling himself against the likelihood the kidnapper killed his sister. On one long night, he lay awake at four in the morning with tears rolling down his cheeks. Each time he drifted into sleep, he heard Jennifer talking to him, so close she could have been in the next bed. She told him not to worry, that she was with Dad now and everything would work out.

He won't lose Jennifer again.

"I figured out where she's moving us."

Jennifer blinks and rolls over to face him.

"How?"

"I checked the browser history and found the house she wants."

"Tell me she isn't still looking for a place in Charlotte."

When he doesn't reply, she turns over and slams her fist on the mattress.

"Shit. So where? It has to be someplace nicer than Genoa Cove. Why couldn't she move us to Sunset Beach or Durham? I could get used to living near the universities."

"It's a snobby Charlotte suburb."

"What?" Her scream reverberates off the walls and rings inside his ears. "I don't want to live in Charlotte. How is a city safer than where we are?"

Hunter rolls to his side and props his head up on his hand.

"Because it's secure. It's a gated community."

"What the hell, Hunter? Has she lost her mind? She doesn't have the money to afford a neighborhood like that."

"This Michael Rivers guy…she means to kill him. And with the way the cops botched the last investigation, I get why she doesn't want to depend on them."

"Don't take her side."

"I'm not. I'm just saying…"

"Spit it out."

Taking a composing breath, Hunter sneaks a peek at

the door when someone moves past.

"I'm starting to understand the way she thinks. No way Mom wants to keep running. She wants to strike first —kill Rivers before he comes after us. And that scares the hell out of me. What if she goes after him without the police to back her up?"

Jennifer swallows.

"Mom wouldn't do something that stupid. Anyway, I figured you'd throw a shit-fit over leaving Bethany. I don't get why you're taking this in stride."

"We've both come close to dying during the last year. I want it to end. Don't you?"

The idea of leaving Bethany cuts deep. Hunter doesn't know how he'll explain it to her. Maybe it's better if she doesn't know. But he's old enough that he can come back to her. He doesn't need his mother's permission anymore.

A door slamming in the next room breaks his train of thought. While Jennifer texts her friends, Hunter wanders to the tiny refrigerator and grabs a soda off the shelf. Taking a sip, he walks to the window and looks down on the parking lot. The Genoa Cove police car sits in the same spot. The glare on the windshield is too intense to make out the officers inside. He turns away from the window as a figure moves between two evergreen trees beside the lot. At first, he assumes the man standing in the shadows is a maintenance worker. But a maintenance worker wouldn't stare at their window for that long.

And there's a car parked at the curb on the other side of the street. A black sedan.

Hunter steps back from the window and draws the curtains, feeling as if someone placed an icy hand on his neck.

"Hunter?"

Jennifer sits up, concern twisting her face.

Hunter swallows.

"Get Mom."

# CHAPTER SEVENTEEN

Officers swarm along the thoroughfare as Darcy stands with the kids at the window. Julian watches over Darcy's shoulder, pacing beside the door as he speaks into his radio.

"Ames is on the way," Julian says by way of breaking the ice, but Darcy can't stop trembling. "The FBI should arrive in two hours."

Hensel is en route. He messaged Darcy while Julian spoke with his chief.

Julian steers Hunter away from the window and walks him to the door. Darcy overhears Julian prompting Hunter to describe the man.

The likelihood Michael Rivers trespassed onto the hotel's property and stood a stone's throw from a police cruiser stuns her. He's brazen, and it only took him a matter of hours to track her to the hotel. For all she knows Rivers could have been here the entire time.

"There's a traffic cam right there," Julian says, directing Darcy's gaze toward the crosswalk at the end of the block. "There's an excellent chance we caught him on camera when he drove through."

Darcy nods, but getting a picture of Rivers won't do her any good. They already established he's in Genoa Cove. The media will plaster his face in the newspaper and on the evening news, and by tonight every person in town will claim they saw the Full Moon Killer hiding in the shadows. Across the street, Officer Wolpert interviews a mechanic outside a vehicle repair shop. The man shakes his head at Wolpert's questions until the officer thanks him for his time and moves on.

Darcy's phone rings.

"It's Hensel," she says to Julian. "I need to take this."

Julian gives her a concerned stare as she walks away. She locks herself inside the bathroom for privacy, groaning when the mirror displays the black circles under her eyes.

"The state police set up check points around Genoa Cove," Hensel says, the SUV motor loud in the background. "If Rivers is in the village, he's not getting out."

"Rivers came to the hotel. Somehow he knew where we were, and he didn't think twice about the police presence."

"He'll think twice when they take him down, Darcy. Right now, I want you and the kids to stay put. You're surrounded by law enforcement. He can't get to you."

Running the sink, Darcy splashes water on her face and dabs it away with a towel.

"Every time the police, sheriff's department, and FBI tell me we're safe, one of my kids goes missing."

"He won't fight his way past dozens of armed officers. Don't move until I get there. It won't be much longer." Hensel presses the phone against his chest when Agent Fisher speaks to him. Tall and lean, Fisher accompanied Hensel to Georgia when Jennifer went missing. "Darcy, I need to go. Hang in there a little longer. We're almost to the hotel."

In a dreamlike state, Darcy shuffles out of the bathroom. They all turn to look at her—Julian, Jennifer, Hunter.

Julian eyes Darcy.

"Everything okay?"

"Yes, everything will work out. The state police closed off the village."

She stands between her children and stares through the window. A swarm of police officers and county sheriff's deputies move about the grounds like worker ants. If Rivers left a trace of evidence, they'll find it.

By the time Hensel and Fisher arrive at the hotel, Hunter is half-asleep on the bed, Jennifer slouched in the corner with her head against the wall. Julian stands at the far end of the room with his phone pressed to his ear, nodding as he speaks with Detective Ames. Darcy taps a nonsense beat on her thigh while she sits at the window. Much of the law enforcement contingent cleared out in the last hour, but two cruisers park near the entrance and keep watch on everyone coming and going.

Five minutes after Hensel and Fisher pass through the sliding glass door to the lobby, a knock brings Darcy out of her chair. Though Julian knows the FBI is coming, he holds up a hand and prevents Darcy from opening the door. He stands to the side of the door and leans over, pressing his eye against the peephole. Satisfied, he opens the door.

Hensel looks like he rode for twenty-four hours in the SUV, his face drawn and pallid. Fisher reaches across Hensel and shakes hands with Julian as Hensel makes introductions. But someone is missing from Hensel's team.

Agent Reinhold, the profiler who worked the Eric Stetson case in Georgia.

"Agent Reinhold isn't with you?" Darcy asks, searching over Hensel's shoulder for a third body.

"She left the FBI and started teaching."

"You're kidding. When did this happen?"

"Two months ago. She teaches profiling at College Park now."

Maryland has a top-notch Criminology program, but Darcy never pegged Reinhold for a professor.

"So who's profiling for you now?"

Hensel itches the back of his neck.

"Nobody. At the moment."

He glares at Darcy, holding her eyes until she sweeps them into the room. Julian briefs them.

"Detective Ames is interviewing the girl who accompanied Jennifer to the park," Julian says, crossing his ankle over his knee. "He should be here within the hour."

"Perfect. I'd like to hear his thoughts on—"

They all stop when Darcy's phone rings. Except for her cousin, Laurie, everyone who would call Darcy is inside the hotel room. Sensing it might be the Full Moon Killer, Hensel catches Darcy's eye before she answers.

"Let it go to voice-mail. If it's Rivers, he'll call back." Julian glances at Hensel. "What do you think?"

"I want all calls to Darcy's phone traced," Hensel says.

Fisher gets the FBI on the line after Darcy's phone goes silent. A glance at the screen shows the caller used an unknown number. Jennifer and Hunter raise their heads, and Julian moves to Jennifer to keep the girl calm. Darcy leaps when the phone rings again. Same number.

Hensel holds up his hand until Fisher raises his

thumb.

"Okay, Darcy."

Darcy doesn't speak. She places the phone to her ear and listens. If this is like previous calls since the prison escape, Rivers won't talk to her.

"I hear you breathing, Darcy."

Her stomach lurches.

"I can see you through the window. Agents Hensel and Fisher are there with your children, as well as that young cop you have eyes for."

Darcy mouths, "He's watching us through the window," and Hensel searches the parking lot. He backs away from Darcy and radios the cruisers.

"No need to send the police after me, Darcy. Nobody finds me until I want them to."

"What do you want, Michael?"

"I want you and your beloved dead. You know this by now."

"The last time didn't go so well for you. You shouldn't have lured me into that house. You got what you asked for."

"Like Warden Ellsworth?"

"Are you telling me you have information about Warden Ellsworth's disappearance, Michael?"

Rivers must know Darcy is trying to keep him talking. Hensel grips his hair and marches to Fisher. The look on Agent Fisher's face tells Darcy the FBI hasn't located Rivers yet.

"There's a quarry off route 301 outside Rocky Mount. You'll find a present at the bottom of the quarry, Darcy. I left it especially for you."

"A quarry off route 301 outside Rocky Mount," Darcy repeats so Hensel hears. "Explain what you mean by *present?"*

"It's a vision of your future, and that of your children, Hunter and Jennifer."

"I'm warning you, Michael. This is between you and me. Stay away from my kids."

"Go to Rocky Mount, Darcy. You'll understand."

The line dies. Darcy stares at the phone, her hand trembling.

"Tell me you got him," Hensel says to Fisher.

Using his tablet, Agent Fisher zooms in on a map of Genoa Cove and says, "I've got him narrowed down to a two-mile radius inside Genoa Cove."

Hensel sets the tablet on the desk and points at the map.

"Here's the hotel. Rivers watched us during the call, which means he must be in this sector."

Hensel and Fisher examine a narrow stretch of rural terrain outside the hotel. The land climbs away from the ocean.

"With a powerful set of binoculars, he could have watched from here," Fisher says, zooming in on a hillock a half-mile from their location.

"Call the cell company and get a closer estimate. Officer Haines, I want the locals to set up a one-mile perimeter around this hill." Julian nods and radios headquarters. "We need road blocks. Stop anyone driving out of the perimeter. And get Ames on the phone. He'll want to review the medical examiner's report. The two distinct ligature marks tell me Lindsey Doler didn't commit suicide. Someone murdered her."

Darcy stands at the window and runs her eyes over the horizon. She can see the hill, but from here it's an indistinct green space of trees and meadow. One road arrows over the hill and disappears on the other side of the ridge. No black sedan.

Edging away from the window, Darcy ducks when the bullet pierces the glass.

# CHAPTER EIGHTEEN

Inside an unused conference room on the hotel's lowest floor, Darcy sits with her arms wrapped around her children's shoulders. Jennifer trembles beneath a blanket, her eyes red and wary. A group of deputies and GCPD officers sneak peeks at the Gellar family from across the room. Even Hunter leans against his mother's shoulder with his hands buried inside his sweatshirt pockets.

A mauve rug patterned by concentric figures stretches the length of the rectangular room. Black tablecloths drape over three round tables separated by regular intervals. A long table stands at the front of the room, where Agent Fisher lays out his tablet and studies the terrain around Rocky Mount with Hensel. Carpet cleaner tickles Darcy's nose and makes her eyes water.

Hensel approaches Darcy and her family, sighing and shaking his head.

"You didn't find Rivers," Darcy says, already knowing the answer.

"He couldn't have slipped through the checkpoints. My guess is he's still inside the perimeter. We'll smoke him out."

"You won't, Eric."

"About this trip to Rocky Mount. The locals are on the scene, but their chief wants the FBI on site when they investigate the quarry."

"You're leaving?"

"Yes. Agent Fisher will stay in Genoa Cove to coordinate the search. I want you to come with me to Rocky Mount."

Darcy drops the blanket off her knees and glances at Hunter and Jennifer.

"I'm not leaving my kids. Whatever present Rivers left for me, I'm not interested."

Hensel glances at Julian, who guards the double doors beside Officer Faust.

"What if you left Hunter and Jennifer with Officer Haines? It would only be a few hours."

"We're right here, you know?" Jennifer glares bullets into Hensel. "You don't need to act as if we can't hear you."

"Okay, Jennifer," Hensel says, dropping to one knee in front of Darcy's daughter. The teenage girl leans back in her chair. "I'll ask you directly. Both you and your brother. Are you willing to stay with Officer Haines for the rest of the afternoon while your Mom and I drive to Rocky Mount?"

"Doesn't sound like my mother wants to go," Hunter says, watching Hensel from the corner of his eye.

"No, she doesn't," Hensel says before swinging his eyes to Darcy. "But your mother wants what you want. To end this forever. We don't know why Michael Rivers feels it's important for your mother to accompany me to Rocky Mount, but this might be our best chance to catch him."

Jennifer shakes her head.

"It's a trap."

"Is that what you're worried about?"

"Think about it. If this guy wants you and Mom out of the way, this is the perfect opportunity with both of you exposed."

Jennifer's clear thinking knocks Hensel back on his heels. He lowers his head and rubs the back of his neck.

"Words of wisdom, Jennifer. You're a Gellar, there's no questioning that. But we won't be alone. The local police and sheriff's department will be on the scene, and that's not counting the crime scene investigators. You want us to catch Michael Rivers, right Jennifer?"

Darcy bites her tongue. Though he makes sense, Hensel is manipulating her daughter. Jennifer takes a quick glance at Julian, who stares straight ahead on the right side of the double doors. Darcy's daughter exhales through her nose.

"You really think you can catch him?"

"I do. No guarantee this trip will lead us to Michael Rivers, but we have to follow every lead."

Jennifer tilts her head toward Hunter. Hunter whispers something Darcy can't make out.

"We'll stay with Officer Haines," Jennifer says, pulling the blanket tight around her shoulders. "But we'll never forgive you if anything happens to Mom."

The ride to Rocky Mount takes Hensel and Darcy over hills that seem to climb to the clouds. Ahead, rain draws a gauze curtain over the highway as the wind whips the trees into a frenzy. Then the heavens let loose, the talons of an angry god tearing through the underbelly of a descending sky. Hensel runs the wipers on high, but a torrent of rain batters the windshield as hail pings off the roof. Nearing the quarry, Hensel slams on the brakes when a tree limb crashes into the road.

"Careful of the ditch," Darcy says when Hensel swerves onto the shoulder. Beside the road, flooding waters carve a new river through the ditch.

While thunder booms behind them, the rain lets up on the outskirts of Rocky Mount. Before Hensel rounds the bend paralleling the quarry, Darcy spots the swirling reds and blues of the emergency lights reflecting off the puddled roadway.

Afraid the SUV might lose traction in the mud if he descends the hill, Hensel parks at the quarry entrance. A male police chief with a black horseshoe mustache climbs the dirt path and greets them on the shoulder.

"Agent Hensel? Chief Broden."

Broden offers his hand.

"Thank you for inviting us. This is Darcy Gellar." Broden's handshake is strong, his palm callused. "She profiled for the FBI's Behavior Analysis Unit and studied the Full Moon Killer. I brought her in to consult on the case."

Darcy arches an eyebrow at Hensel, who continues without missing a beat.

"Catch me up on where things stand," says Hensel, following Chief Broden down the quarry road.

"You arrived at the right time. Our sounding equipment indicates a large object at the bottom of the quarry, likely a vehicle. Damn water is cloudy and full of rusted equipment that people dump when nobody's watching. It didn't feel right sending divers into the water until I was sure what we were looking for."

"Can't blame you."

"This is a hot spot for underage drinking. Teens come here to party because the quarry is hidden from the road, and as long as they don't shine flashlights like a bunch of idiots, nobody knows they're here. All the rusted junk floating around in that muck, and these stupid kids take off their clothes and skinny dip. You believe that?"

Darcy grimaces. It's easy to imagine a teenager slicing their flesh open on a jagged piece of metal below the surface. Bacteria overruns the water. Would Jennifer or Hunter do something this stupid and risky?

"Nothing surprises me when it comes to teenagers, Officer."

"We're using an old-fashioned plan of attack." Broden motions to the canoe floating atop the water. A red haired woman with a star on her hat watches from the shore. She must be the county sheriff, Darcy assumes. Two male deputies flank the sheriff and shoot distrustful looks at Darcy and Hensel. Two police officers man the canoe, one aiming a spotlight at the water while the other paddles. Every few yards, the officer holding the oar prods the water, searching for the object the sounding equipment located. "If it's a car, we'll drag it ashore and turn the investigation over to you."

Broden leads Hensel and Darcy to the water's edge. They're fifty yards deep inside the excavated bowl. A green, milky stain floats on the water, residual rain drops drawing circles on the surface. Trees sprout from the dirt walls rising up around them. The clink of wood against metal brings Darcy's head up.

"You found it, Richardson?"

Officer Richardson nods back at Chief Broden as the second officer redirects the spotlight.

Sensing someone behind her, Darcy turns her head and finds the red haired sheriff glaring at her.

"You Agent Gellar?" Darcy nods. "I'm Sheriff Berks.

I read your FBI report on Michael Rivers. Excellent work. What makes you believe he came through my county?"

Darcy brushes the chill off her arms.

"Bad luck, Sheriff. You just happened to stand between Rivers and his ultimate destination."

"Which is?"

"Genoa Cove, North Carolina." When the sheriff's eyes question her, Darcy explains. "That's where I live now."

"You must have really pissed him off, Agent. What did you do?"

"I caught him."

Commotion at the shoreline breaks up their conversation. The sheriff tips her cap at Darcy and joins Chief Broden near the water's edge.

"It's a car," Richards calls out. "Too murky to determine the make and model."

"All right, boys. Let's drag this baby out of the water."

A female diver wades into the water and angles toward the spotlight's beam. She attaches chains, and ten minutes later, a beige Audi with Pennsylvania plates surfaces. Water surges through the busted side windows. When the flood abates, the officers shine flashlights into the vehicle.

Richardson, wearing a boyish face that marks him as a rookie, shakes his head at Broden.

"I don't see anything inside. Just mud and weeds."

To accentuate his point, Richardson pulls the passenger door open, releasing more water.

"Don't touch the vehicle, Officer," Hensel warns. "The vehicle is evidence."

Hensel steps forward with Darcy at his side. Peering

through the windows as she rounds the Audi, Darcy looks for anything Rivers might consider a sick present. There's nothing to see, just a sodden interior, the inside coated with mud and smelling of mold and decay. But a death scent wafts from the back of the car. Darcy coughs into her hand, bracing herself. She doesn't want to get sick in front of the deputies and officers.

"What do you think?" Hensel asks, watching Darcy over the roof.

"Pop the trunk."

Donning gloves, Hensel reaches down and pulls the lever. The trunk opens, a gore-dripping maw. Mud splashes against the bumper and colors the gravel driveway black. The smell that rolls out of the trunk causes two officers to turn away and bend over. Darcy stands at the corner of the bumper, resisting the urge to look inside. Hensel inches forward with a flashlight aimed at the trunk's interior.

"Jesus," he says, covering his mouth.

Darcy tells herself she doesn't need to look. This is what the Full Moon Killer wants. But she already sees the human head from the corner of her eye. Disgust roils around in her stomach before she rounds the bumper.

Staring up at her is the severed head of Warden Ellsworth.

# CHAPTER NINETEEN

Darcy catches a sob in her throat. Stars sparkle across the night sky, uncaring. After they discovered Ellsworth's grisly murder, their investigation took longer than anticipated. Texts to Hunter and Jennifer go unanswered, but Julian assures Darcy they're fine and parked in front of his television. It's after ten. Two hours of driving time stand between Darcy and her children as the black FBI SUV motors down the interstate.

Hensel opens his mouth and stops. There's nothing he can say.

The killer's *present* feels like a violation. As if he raped Darcy and stole her dignity. She fidgets with her hands in her lap, terrified that if she was home, she would have abused the anti-anxiety medication and fallen off the wagon, betraying the trust of her loved ones. Even now the call is strong. The bottle sits on the counter inside the hotel bathroom. Later, she'll slog inside the room to collect her belongings. It will take all her will not to pry off the cap and swallow the remaining pills.

When they return to Genoa Cove, Hensel will drive her to Julian's, where she'll spend the night with her kids until the police find a safer place for them to stay tomorrow. As if such a place exists.

"If I'd known what Rivers intended…"

Hensel trails off with his mouth hanging open. He sneaks a look at Darcy, who leans into the corner formed between the seat and door.

"It's not your fault. You couldn't have known."

"I should have seen this coming. At least I should have expected Rivers to…oh, hell."

He rubs his face and shakes his head like a dog splashing out of a river.

"You want me to drive so you can rest?"

"That's not necessary," he says. "I'm wide awake now. Don't expect I'll sleep a wink after the quarry."

In the sky, the screaming face of the moon seems to follow the SUV down the interstate. Hensel catches Darcy observing the sky.

"The moon isn't full yet," Hensel says. "Rivers is getting active earlier than usual."

"He's breaking patterns. It's almost as if he's toying with the profile. The strangulation of a teenage girl, but no marking burned into her neck. He tried to shoot me with a long-range rifle, while he's always murdered with a knife. And now he's killing enemies ahead of schedule."

"Doler's murder, if it was a murder, might have been one of opportunity. He struck fast and got out of there before someone noticed. No time to leave his mark, regardless of how much the ritual means to him. Either way, he's escalating."

"Because it's personal this time. Four years ago, he killed out of desire. Now he wants his enemies dead, and with Ellsworth eliminated I'm the last one standing."

Hensel lowers the visor to block out the moon glow.

"Last winter I gave you an opportunity to return to the BAU. Have you given it any more thought? With Reinhold leaving the FBI, the door is wide open."

"That's a commitment I can't make, Eric."

"Perhaps when we capture Rivers and this nightmare is finally over."

"Capture Rivers? I caught him once and look where it got me. He's as dangerous from behind bars as he is loose. No, this won't end until I put a bullet in his head."

Hensel drags the back of his hand across his lips.

"Then I'll help you end the nightmare. Whatever it takes." Darcy glances over at Hensel. His eyes meet hers. "Like I said. The door is open when you're ready to come back. I'm proud of how you handled the medication addiction, and your color is a thousand times better than it was over the winter. You're too strong for him, Darcy."

"And yet most nights I wake up in a cold sweat, holding back a scream. The nightmares never stop. Sometimes it doesn't seem like I've progressed at all."

"Don't underestimate your accomplishments, Darcy. You're an amazing woman."

Hensel fiddles with the radio dial as Darcy closes her eyes. The humming tires draw her toward slumber, but there's a barrier standing between her and sleep. The invisible wall shocks her when she pictures the eyeless head of Ellsworth gaping up at the sky. It seems to look at her. Accusatory.

The SUV pulls into the Cove Inn after midnight. A pair of state troopers lead Hensel and Darcy through the lobby and into the elevator. Darcy unlocks the door with her key card, and Hensel follows the larger trooper into the room. A minute later, he gives the all-clear. Hensel waits inside the door while Darcy grabs her medication and a change of clothes.

Inside the bathroom, her hand pauses on top of the pill bottle. A part of her wants to empty the bottle's contents into the toilet and flush away the temptation. Another part, the self-destructive side, concocts reasons to take an extra pill. Or three. The trauma of the quarry. The bullet aimed at her head. Turning her head away, she plucks the medicine off the counter and stuffs into the bottom of her bag.

Hensel drives across Genoa Cove to Julian's house with the headlights of the state trooper's SUV shining in the mirrors. As they had at the hotel, the troopers lead Darcy and the FBI agent to the door where Julian stands waiting. The officer rubs his eyes and smiles at Darcy. With a yawn, she swings the bag to her other shoulder.

"Everything good here?" Hensel asks, bouncing on his toes in an effort to stay awake.

"I got it, Agent Hensel," Julian says.

Hensel promises to contact Darcy in the morning. The two vehicles drive into the night, and Darcy leans on the jamb with Julian holding the door for her.

"The kids aren't still up, are they?"

"Hunter is watching a movie in the den. Jennifer fell asleep an hour ago."

Good. Her daughter barely slept at Kaitlyn's. Darcy drops her bag inside the door and flops onto the couch.

"Anything new on the search for Rivers?"

"Nothing," Darcy says, peeking around the corner into the den. "Except another victim. I suppose the GCPD heard about Warden Ellsworth."

"Yes, we did."

Julian sits beside Darcy on the couch. He makes a move to touch her arm, then pulls back, uncertain. She breaks the ice by resting her head against his shoulder.

"It was terrible. That poor man. I feel guilty to admit this, but the warden always struck me as snobbish and above law enforcement. He ran a tight ship, and in my heart, I always knew he did his best to contain Rivers and keep him from reaching out to the outside world. Ellsworth made life difficult for Rivers, and that's what got him murdered."

A tear rolls down Darcy's cheek. So much pain and sorrow. How many more need to die?

The light goes off in the den. Hunter cranes his neck around the corner and rakes a knot out of his hair.

"I thought I heard you come in," her son says, leaning in the entryway.

"Come here, buddy," Darcy says, motioning Hunter over to the couch.

"What's up?" he asks, feigning indifference.

But when she draws him into a hug, he nestles his head against hers. And for a frozen moment, he's a child again. The wide-eyed, blonde boy with a million questions who only wanted to spend his day with Mommy.

"I needed this," she says. "How's your sister?"

He pulls away and shrugs.

"Lindsey's suicide is bothering her, and she's scared about what happened at the hotel."

"How about you, Hunter? Are you scared?"

"I guess."

"It's okay to be. But we're closer to catching the Full Moon Killer than we've ever been before. I promise we'll figure this out."

Hunter appears doubtful as he kisses Darcy on the cheek before heading to bed. He's sharing a room with Jennifer at the end of the hall next to Julian's bedroom.

Which makes Darcy wonder where she's going to sleep.

The bedroom door closes, and in the ensuing silence, Darcy's doubts and fears grow loud. Her relationship with Julian is moving faster than she believed possible, making her question her motivations. This isn't the time to forge an emotional bond. And she still harbors doubts. The explanation he gave for volunteering at Bronson Severson's gym settled her stomach, but now she recalls Julian's apprehension to charge Aaron Torres and his friends after the security cameras showed them vandalizing Darcy's car.

"Something is on your mind," Julian says, sitting on the edge of the couch.

Darcy's fingers curl over the edge of the couch cushion.

"Last fall you came to my house after Aaron Torres vandalized my Prius."

"I remember."

"I showed you the security footage, and it took you a long time to admit Aaron and Sam were the boys on camera."

Julian bites his lip.

"I needed to be cautious. The night footage looked grainy, and I wanted to be certain before I charged four teenage boys with vandalism."

"You're not telling me the entire truth." Julian's eyes flick to her, then back to his hands. She senses his anger. "Is this because the Torres family has a lot of influence in Genoa Cove?"

"Not exactly."

"Then tell me."

Julian sets his chin on his fists, considering his words. She wants to trust him.

"I played tailback on my high school football team. Wasn't big enough to play in college, but I always stayed close to the game. After I joined the force, I approached the middle school football coach about volunteering. He put me in charge of running backs and receivers, and when I proved I knew what I was doing, he made me offensive coordinator."

"That's how you met Aaron Torres."

Julian steeples his fingers against the bridge of his nose and nods.

"I knew all four of those kids. Aaron was the star tailback, Sam Tatum the offensive tackle. When you're part of a team, the stars blind you. You never believe the best athletes, the kids helping you win every week, are problems off the field. I saw the signs. You couldn't tell Aaron he did something wrong without getting an ear full. I chalked it up to the kid being a perfectionist and having rich parents who spoiled him. But we went undefeated the two seasons I volunteered, and Aaron and Sam were our best players. I lost track of them after they moved up to junior varsity, and then I couldn't juggle coaching and being a police officer, so I stepped away from the team. My last memory of Aaron Torres was this boy with unbelievable speed and agility for a thirteen-year-old racing down the sideline for a game-winning touchdown. That was our last game. I guess I didn't want to accept he was an awful kid."

Julian pauses and taps his hands on his knees.

"But then I saw Aaron's face when he glanced up at your camera, and I knew I'd been wrong about him. Once I was certain Aaron and Sam orchestrated the attack, I went after them. It was too little, too late. I let you down."

Darcy studies the drapes when Julian lifts his head.

"You didn't let me down, Julian. As much as it pains me to picture myself defending Aaron or Sam, everyone deserves the benefit of the doubt. My son knows about false accusation. You needed hard evidence."

"I'm sorry you're still going through the same bullshit you put up with last year. It's beyond ridiculous anyone in Genoa Cove blames Hunter for the murders. Or you, for that matter."

Darcy's eyelids grow heavy. She rubs the sleep from the corners of her eyes and stretches. Julian is an honorable man, but not infallible. Now when she needs him most, he's opened his home to her. He'll protect her family with his life.

"Thank you for believing in us, Julian. It means a lot."

"You're welcome to stay here as long as you like, but I'll understand if you prefer the hotel."

A jolt of worry shoots through Darcy.

"Shit, we're still booked. I better cancel before the bill runs any higher."

"Darcy, if you need money to get you through the short-term—"

Darcy holds up a hand.

"No, I'm not a charity case. Money is tight, but I have enough saved for the kids' educations."

"So cancel the room and stay with me. It's just me here. I have the space."

"I can't do that, Julian. As much as I appreciate you letting us stay past tonight, I'm imposing."

"Not in my mind."

"No, I am. Besides, we still have our house."

"Which you're not returning to without an armed escort," Julian says. "Take my bed. I've got the couch. If you need to return to the house to grab your belongings, I'll drive you. Stay where you're protected."

"At least let me take the couch. You've done enough, and I'm not kicking you out of your bed."

He ponders the situation and scratches the scruff on his cheeks.

"Tell you what. How about we share the bedroom? You take the bed, and I'll blow up the air mattress."

Darcy wishes they could sleep side by side in his bed. They're adults capable of acting appropriately. Not wanting to seem forward, she offers to sleep on the air mattress instead, but he insists she sleep on the bed.

"Fine," Darcy says. "It doesn't matter where I sleep. The minute I hit the pillow, I'll be out like a light."

"You must be exhausted." Reading her face, he squints his eyes. "But if you want to talk about what happened in Rocky Mount first, I'm all ears."

Darcy's mind wanders back to the officers locating the car beneath the murk, then the water pouring from the car while they dragged the Audi ashore. And the smell when they opened the trunk. She'll remember that scent forever.

"I'll talk about it tomorrow. Right now I'm too tired to think straight."

She leans against Julian as he walks her down the hallway. Then she sits down on the bed, feels the gentle bounce in the mattress. The last thing she recalls is Julian inflating the air mattress with an electric pump before she falls asleep in her clothes.

# CHAPTER TWENTY

Darcy awakens after ten, the sun high in the North Carolina sky. Julian brings her a mug of coffee when she arises. He sits on the edge of the bed, dressed in shorts and a t-shirt, casual except for the pistol on his hip.

"Sorry. I never sleep that late," she says, glancing worriedly at the window.

"You had a helluva day yesterday, and you didn't sleep well last night."

Darcy tilts her head.

"I didn't talk in my sleep last night, did I?"

"You shouted a few times, but I couldn't make out the words."

"Dammit. I didn't mean to keep you awake."

"You didn't. I got my required eight hours, and here's my energy for the day," he says, lifting his coffee mug.

She pads to the kitchen where he places breakfast on the table for everyone. Both kids are still in their pajamas, Jennifer leaning over the table as if she's about to drop face-first onto a stack of pancakes.

"It's appreciated, Julian. I'll cook breakfast for you next time."

The pancakes melt in her mouth and fill the rumbling hole in her stomach. While Hunter and Jennifer clear the table and wash the dishes, Darcy joins Julian on the patio. It's little more than two chairs on a rectangle of paving stones, but it's cool and altogether wonderful beneath the shade of a maple tree.

Yet Darcy can't relax. Nowhere is safe. Michael Rivers has a rifle and doesn't care if he murders Darcy from a distance. Unusual. Most serial killers desire the intimacy of using a knife to take a life. Or strangling a victim. Rivers's hatred for Darcy knows no bounds.

"I got off the phone with Detective Ames before you woke," Julian says. "They're treating the Lindsey Doler case as a homicide now. The medical examiner agrees the killer strangled Doler and strung her up to make it look like a suicide. Ames went back to the scene and found a man's shoe print in a flower bed bordering the garage."

"I don't know if I should tell the kids. It might ease their consciences to know it wasn't a suicide. Jennifer is taking it especially hard and blames herself for not noticing the signs. Then again, they might be better off if we avoid talking about Lindsey."

"Keep the info to yourself until this afternoon. If the story leaks before the press conference, the chief will know where the rumor started. That won't look good for either of us."

"Understood."

"With all that's happened over the last two days, I neglected to mention the CSI team found hair fibers beside the window in the vacant house. We sent the fibers off for testing. I should have an answer soon if they're a match for Rivers."

"No need. We both know it was him."

Julian gulps the last of his coffee and sets the mug down.

"All right. In the meantime, I say we drive over to the hotel and gather your belongings before the manager charges you for another night. He's already called the station twice, complaining his crew needs to clean the room for the next guests. He was *thrilled* over the window repair."

Darcy brushes her hair over her shoulder.

"You'd think he'd be a little more understanding given the circumstances."

"Given the police turned the room into a crime scene, I'd say we wore out our welcome."

"Okay. I want to stop by the house later to pick up a few things. Namely, a change of clothes."

"That works. I'm stopping by the station after dinner. We can go after I get back."

Jennifer and Hunter accompany Darcy and Julian to the hotel. During the trip, Darcy can't take her eyes off the mirrors as she searches for a black Lincoln. It troubles her that Rivers could have ditched the Lincoln and stolen another vehicle by now, a tactic he used in Rocky Mount to throw the locals off. Paranoia nudges her to evaluate every vehicle trailing Julian's car. Thinking like a cop, if Darcy pursued someone, she'd hang several car lengths behind to avoid drawing attention. But no vehicles catch her eye before they reach the hotel.

When they pass through the lobby, a bespectacled manager looks down his nose at them. While they wait for the elevator, the manager steps from behind his desk. A female guest complaining about parking stops the manager and averts an argument. The elevator still hasn't arrived. While Hunter texts his girlfriend, Julian takes a call from the GCPD. Darcy glances around.

"Where's Jennifer?"

"I'll call you back," Julian says, ending the call. He scans the busy lobby. "She was standing right next to me."

Darcy's skin tingles. The elevator door opens. A heavyset man hauling an over-sized suitcase glowers at Darcy, who blocks the entryway.

"Ma'am," he says through gritted teeth.

The man barrels past Darcy, clipping her with his shoulder. She's too busy searching for Jennifer to care. Then she spots Jennifer pouring a cup of tea on the far side of the lobby.

"I'll go," Julian says.

Darcy presses her hand against his chest.

"No, I'll get her."

Weaving through the crowd, Darcy focuses on her daughter ripping the top off a sweetener packet.

"You can't walk away without telling someone," Darcy says, fixing Jennifer with a glare.

"Can't I get five seconds alone? You never let me breathe."

"This isn't about your independence. What if something happened?"

Jennifer hisses and hurls the full cup of tea into the trash container. Encountering her daughter in this state is like grabbing a dish out of the oven without a mitt.

"Why won't everyone leave me alone?"

"Jennifer, please," Darcy says, touching her daughter's arm.

Jennifer pulls out of her mother's grip.

"That's all you do is worry someone will take me. Well, what if somebody does? I don't care, I really don't."

When Jennifer tries to storm past, Darcy shifts to

block her.

"Yes, you do."

"No, I really fucking don't. Why would I want to live through another year like the last one? Everyone I care about..."

Her voice breaks. As Darcy pulls her into a hug, Jennifer's shoulders quiver with pent-up tears. For a long time, Jennifer's arms hang past her hips as tension flees her body. Then she rests her head against Darcy's shoulder and wraps her arms around her mother. The same night terrors Jennifer experienced as a child flutters through her body. This has to end. Darcy needs to take the Full Moon Killer's life before he ruins theirs. She owes her children a lifetime free of nightmares. When Jennifer's hitches cease, Darcy places her hands against Jennifer's cheeks and guides her daughter's gaze to hers.

"You haven't given yourself a chance to grieve for Lindsey. That's my fault too. I put you in this situation, and I wasn't here for you yesterday."

"No," Jennifer says, sniffling. "You're trying to stop a terrible person from hurting someone else. Nobody blames you."

Darcy rests her chin on Jennifer's head, wanting to believe her daughter. Every move she's made seems like the wrong one. Jennifer's trauma is damning evidence Darcy has failed as a parent.

"Let's clean you up," says Darcy, grabbing a napkin off the table. She dabs it against Jennifer's cheeks and soaks up the tears. "You ready to grab your stuff and get the hell out of this bougie hotel?"

Choking on an unexpected chuckle, Jennifer touches her chest and coughs.

"Where do you learn these words?"

"Would it be better if I said it's pretentious?"

"It is rather pretentious."

Her arm around Jennifer's shoulder, Darcy walks her daughter back to the elevator. Reading the question on Julian's face, Darcy says, "We're okay now."

The elevator dings and opens. Hunter smirks at his sister.

"Where's my coffee?"

"Get your own, lazy bro."

After Darcy slips the key card into the reader, Julian steps into the room with his gun drawn. Room service trays litter the floor outside several doors. A small woman wearing a maid's outfit and her hair tied in a bun drives a vacuum over the carpet.

"It's clear," Julian says, popping his head through the opening.

With a pair of drawn out sighs, Jennifer and Hunter gather their clothes and stuff them into the suitcase. By the time Darcy adds her belongings to the pile, she needs to sit on the suitcase while Hunter zips it shut.

"Sure you didn't forget anything?" Julian asks Darcy as he bends to glance under the bed.

"If we left anything behind, it's for the best. Who needs this much stuff?"

In the lobby, Julian stands beside Darcy, his badge displayed prominently on the desk. His presence keeps the sullen manager at bay as a young redheaded man with a face full of boyish freckles closes Darcy's account.

"And we'll be putting the balance on your Mastercard, Ms. Gellar?"

"That's perfect," Darcy says, looking over her shoulder when she senses eyes on her.

A quick look around the lobby reveals no danger, but

that doesn't stop Darcy from assessing every face, every stranger in the crowd as a threat to her family. As she wheels her suitcase past the automatic doors, she feels a sense of abandonment. The FBI can't protect her, her neighbors want her dead, and the hotel couldn't wait to kick her out.

Julian cracks the windows to ventilate the steaming car interior while the cooling system catches up. Backing out of the parking space, he finds Hunter and Jennifer in the mirror.

"Tonight, we're driving back to the house to grab whatever you need for the next week. Clothes, music, whatever you forgot to bring to the hotel. Make a list, because we can't keep going back, all right?" Jennifer glances at Hunter. They nod in agreement. "An officer from the Genoa Cove Police Department will follow us to the house and keep watch until we leave. As long as we have a plan to get in and out fast, we'll be safe."

Hunter and Jennifer pop their earbuds in. Darcy wonders if it would be better for an officer to stay with Hunter and Jennifer at Julian's house while she and Julian make the trip alone. She could grab their belongings quicker without the kids to slow her down. Except she doesn't trust the GCPD, and the idea of leaving her kids in the care of an officer she barely knows sets her nerves on edge.

As the day grows long, a pall falls over Darcy. A discomfort she can't place a finger on. While making dinner with Julian, she peers out the window, expecting the Full Moon Killer to glide out of the shadows. Like a shroud, a black cloud blots out the sun after Julian races back to the office. Ninety minutes pass, and the seconds drag like hours as Darcy paces the house. Through the closed bedroom door, she hears Jennifer and Hunter talking. Something about Lindsey. By now, the word is out. Lindsey didn't kill herself. Someone strangled the teenage girl and hung her inside the garage to stage a suicide.

The potential scenarios float like ghosts through the back of Darcy's mind—Rivers following Jennifer to Kaitlyn's party before he noticed Lindsey. Then he stalked the pretty girl to her house. Watched. Waited. And somehow lured her outside. But how? What would inspire a teenage girl to leave her house in the middle of the night and walk inside a dark garage? The puzzle occupies Darcy's thoughts while she awaits Julian's return. Parting the blinds, she spies the GCPD cruiser sent to guard the house. An officer sits behind the wheel. Noticing Darcy at the window, he raises his thermos and nods in her direction. She waves back and checks the clock.

What's taking Julian so long?

# CHAPTER TWENTY-ONE

Clouds stitch a premature twilight over Darkwater Cove. Darcy balances on the edge of panic when the headlight beams cross the windshield and announce Julian's arrival.

"Sorry I took so long," he says, hugging Darcy in the entryway. "Your FBI friends were at the office, providing a profile of the Full Moon Killer."

Interesting. The FBI didn't bring a profiler with them to Genoa Cove.

"Who delivered the profile?"

"Agent Hensel."

Darcy nods. Though he doesn't have a background in profiling, Hensel is intelligent and capable of bringing the police up to speed, and since he worked beside Darcy when she constructed her in-depth profile of Rivers, he already knows what makes the killer tick.

Checking the hall to ensure the kids are still inside their room, Darcy leads Julian into the living room.

"Where does Hensel think Rivers is? Do they have a plan to track him down?"

"The working theory is Rivers is outside Genoa

Cove, holing up inside a residence," Julian says, wiping the sweat off his forehead. "The police are looking for vacant houses—unsold homes, people on vacation. Anywhere Rivers could break inside and not draw attention to himself."

Darcy works her jaw back and forth.

"Except there's a BOLO out on the stolen vehicle. It's too risky to park the Lincoln in a driveway. Someone would notice."

"Which is why the FBI and police agree he's not inside Genoa Cove. I'm thinking country homes."

"Or a no-tell hotel."

Julian lifts his chin in thought.

"That's not a bad theory. Most people pay by the hour, but the clerk won't question someone who hands over a wad of cash and says he wants the room all week. And we know Rivers has unlimited funds."

"I don't figure there's a motel like that in Genoa Cove."

"No, but there's one in Smith Town."

"But then he'd need to conceal the Lincoln. Not easy in a village the size of Smith Town. He can't stash the car in the parking lot and expect nobody will notice."

"No, that wouldn't work. I agree with Agent Hensel. He's outside the village."

Darcy gathers her bag and tosses the strap over her shoulder.

"Rivers materialized when my daughter and her friend walked through the nature preserve. Once you get outside Genoa Cove, the woods stretch several miles along the coast." Julian bobs his head as Darcy talks. "It explains how he disappeared after chasing the girls through the nature preserve."

"He couldn't survive in the wilderness. Not with this heat and all the rain we've had. But a vacant cabin would work."

"Right, like a hunting cabin. Richard Chaney held Jennifer inside an equipment shelter." The bedroom door opening stifles Darcy's next thought. "You guys ready to go?"

Hunter and Jennifer shuffle into the living room, casting nervous looks between them. Hunter's hands are buried in the front pockets of his jeans.

"I left some stuff in my bedroom I need to grab," he says.

"Like I said before," Julian says, holding their eyes. "We go in quick and get out, so have a plan and know what you need to grab before we arrive. Officer Wolpert will follow us and keep an eye on the house while we're inside."

When Julian backs into the street and turns toward the coast, the lights of the GCPD cruiser flash in the mirrors. Darcy keeps one eye on Wolpert's vehicle as Julian drives, the other eye watching for the black Lincoln. The drive to the coast takes longer than Darcy remembers, though they miss most of the red lights. She's a target now. As is her family. The Full Moon Killer could be anywhere.

Darcy doesn't search for her neighbors when Julian parks in the driveway, the worry over a serial killer hiding in the shadows occupying her thoughts. A moment of anxiousness hits when she can't find the house keys in her pocket. Then she recalls stashing the keys inside her bag, and her pulse returns to normal. Julian stops her from exiting the car.

"Stay in the car until I speak with Officer Wolpert."

Jennifer and Hunter turn to their phones while

Darcy's eyes follow Julian to Wolpert's cruiser at the bottom of the driveway. They speak for a minute, Julian pointing toward the vacant property next door. The two men walk to Julian's car and wait for Darcy and the kids to step out. Officer Wolpert hooks his thumbs on his belt.

"Give me five minutes to circle the house and check the backyard, then I'll go inside and make sure it's clear," says Wolpert.

After Wolpert finishes, he stands aside as Darcy unlocks the door. A whoosh of stale, frosty air meets her at the doorway, and she realizes she left the central air running. She punches in the alarm code and waits for the green light to flash, then she backs away from the entrance.

"I'll come inside with you," Julian tells the officer. He turns back to Darcy. "Give us a second to make sure it's safe."

"We'll wait."

When they check the rooms and declare the house clear, Darcy leads her kids inside and sets down her bag.

"Okay, remember the plan," she says.

Jennifer rolls her eyes.

"We know, Mom. We'll hurry."

Julian paces the hallway while Darcy rummages through her bedroom. Outside, Officer Wolpert radios back to headquarters beside his cruiser, the policeman's eyes hot with attentiveness as he scans the expanding shadows.

Darcy stuffs a week's worth of clothes into her suitcase, then sifts through the medicine cabinet in the bathroom with shaking hands. Toothpaste. They're almost out. Julian will share his, but she's imposing as it is. Then Darcy returns to the bedroom and scans the dresser and closet, sensing she forgot something. Down the hall, drawers roll open and slam shut. Thank goodness the kids are following directions and not taking their sweet time.

Back in the hallway she adjusts the temperature to seventy-eight degrees so the cooling system doesn't run too hard while they're away. Then she hustles to the kitchen and throws open the refrigerator, searching for perishables that won't survive the week. As she closes the refrigerator, a flash of movement grabs her eye. The security monitors. Blinking, she rubs her eyes and leans over the counter. The cameras depict empty views of the yard. But there was something...

"Hey."

Darcy jumps and spins around, her hand moving toward the holstered gun on her hip. She releases her breath when Julian crosses the kitchen.

"You scared me."

Julian tilts his head toward the monitor.

"Did you see something?"

"I saw a shadow. Maybe. Shit. I'm not sure what I saw."

Julian doesn't waste time. He snags the radio off his hip and tells Officer Wolpert someone might be in the backyard. Over the small speaker, Darcy overhears Wolpert calling back to headquarters for backup. Jesus. If this turns out to be a false alarm, she'll look like an idiot and draw the ire of the GCPD.

"There's one way to be sure," Julian says, activating the touch screen on the security monitoring system.

Darcy spots his intention and leans over the kitchen counter as he watches the recorded footage in reverse. Back one minute. Then another minute backward until Darcy is certain she's made a grave mistake. Her mind is playing tricks on her again, fear making her irrational. While Julian examines the footage, Darcy catches a sob from Jennifer's bedroom.

"Something is wrong with Jennifer. I'll be back in a second."

Julian gives an almost imperceptible nod, his vision focused on the monitor. Shoving the bedroom door open, Darcy finds Jennifer hunched over her desk with something resting on her open palm. Jennifer drops the object as though it grew legs and skittered across her hand. It isn't until Darcy reaches her daughter's side that she recognizes the bracelet. It's the same sea-blue friendship bracelet she'd allowed Lindsey to borrow. She wants to believe Lindsey gave the bracelet back to Jennifer before the murder, because the implication of the bracelet arriving in Jennifer's bedroom on its own causes Darcy's head to somersault.

"This can't be here," Jennifer says, pointing to the bracelet.

Hunter arrives and follows his sister's gaze. His eyes swerve to Darcy for an explanation. She can't give one. Her mouth is desert dry, and a shard of ice stands where her spine used to.

"Jennifer, I know you're upset. But think for a moment. Did Lindsey give the bracelet back to you at the party? Maybe you'd been drinking and forgot."

Eyes red and rimmed, Jennifer turns on Darcy.

"Stop saying that. I didn't drink at the party, and I would have remembered if my best friend gave my bracelet back to me a few hours before she died." Jennifer snatches the bracelet off the desk and holds it in front of her mother's face. "This wasn't here when we left. *He* put it in my bedroom."

Darcy spins to find Julian in the doorway.

"Nothing yet," Julian says, concern etched on his face. "I'm still scanning through the footage. What's all the yelling about?"

Jennifer slaps the bracelet into Darcy's hand and folds her arms, a tear clinging to the corner of her eye.

"Jennifer found this on her desk." When Julian gives her a confused look, Darcy takes a deep breath. "She gave the bracelet to Lindsey Doler. Lindsey still had it on her the night she died."

"Okay," Julian says, running a hand through his hair. "First things first. Set the bracelet on the desk. Jennifer, did you touch the charm or any of the beads when you picked it up?"

"I don't think so," Jennifer says, looking uncertain. "I thought I picked it up by the cord."

"You did well. I doubt we'll pull a partial print off the bracelet, but it's worth a try. Darcy, grab me a plastic bag from the kitchen. A sandwich bag will do. Hunter and Jennifer, grab your belongings. Everyone sticks together until Officer Wolpert gives the all clear."

In the kitchen, Darcy rummages through the pantry and spills a box of oatmeal in the process.

"Wolpert, Rivers may have been inside the house," Julian says into his radio.

A lengthy pause sends dread through Darcy's body before the officer responds.

"Copy, Julian. Backup is on the way."

The night grows darker outside the window. At the edge of the gloom, the vacant house next door casts a phantom glow. Darcy locates a box of zip-lock bags when Julian stops the footage. As Darcy moves to his side, Julian hits forward, then reverse. Yes, something moved through the backyard. A blur disrupts the footage. Darcy places a hand over her heart.

"What is that?"

"I can't tell," Julian says, screwing up his face in concentration.

He narrows his eyes. Hits play.

A large, black form shoots through the footage. Darcy's breath catches in her chest. What was it? In real time, it's just an indistinct blur.

Julian pauses the footage and reverses again, and the shadow shoots back the way it came. As he steps forward frame by frame, he raises the radio to his lips again.

"Wolpert, someone moved through the security cameras. Be careful."

As Julian sifts through the footage one frame at a time, the shape takes form. Two legs and arms. Not an animal, but a man cloaked in black.

"Dammit," Julian removes the gun from his holster. "Wolpert, the cameras caught a man in the backyard. He's dressed in black."

The officer confirms receipt of Julian's warning.

"Get the kids and bring them inside the kitchen," Julian says. As Darcy turns, he grabs her elbow and runs his eyes over the glass deck door. They're exposed. "Bad idea. Bring them into the hallway away from the doors and windows. Take a deep breath before you tell them. The last thing you want to do is cause a panic."

Darcy nods, but as she rushes through the living room, every nerve twitches in her body like wires sparking, her mind racing faster than her heart. At Hunter's door, Darcy stops herself and grabs hold of the jamb. Black dots fill her vision. Not now. Not another panic attack. The house is well lit, she reminds herself. Surrounded by multiple walls, they're safe in the hallway.

Hunter stuffs his backpack with a sweatshirt he can't possibly need when Darcy pushes the door open. He opens his mouth in question before he reads the danger on her face. Then he drops his belongings and runs past Darcy toward his sister's room.

"We're okay, Hunter. Officer Wolpert and Julian are armed, and the GCPD is on their way. And I have my gun as well."

Hunter doesn't look back. Regaining her sea legs, she hurries after him. One glance between Hunter and Darcy is all it takes to force Jennifer to stop what she's doing. She edges wide-eyed into the hallway, her arms wrapped around her brother.

"He's here, isn't he?" Jennifer swivels her head toward Darcy's bedroom, beyond which lies the backyard. "The Full Moon Killer."

"We don't know that," Darcy says. "There's no need to panic. We're safe provided we stay together in the hallway."

A dark thought occurs to Darcy. An intruder with a knife could slit the screen to her bedroom window and jimmy the lock open from the outside. Who's to say Michael Rivers isn't inside the house, standing on the other side of Darcy's bedroom door?

She removes the Glock from the holster. Listens. Quiet spills under the door and into the hallway.

A man's shape fills the hallway from the opposite direction. Darcy jumps when Jennifer screams, but it's Julian. He presses a finger against his lips. His radio squawks with the lowered voice of Officer Wolpert, who spotted a man in the neighboring yard behind the vacant house.

Julian purses his lips in indecision.

"Help him," Darcy tells Julian. "It's okay. We're safe inside the house."

He glances down at the gun in her hand.

"Lock the door behind me," he says. "And don't open it for anyone except me or Officer Wolpert. The GCPD should arrive in two minutes."

Jennifer shoots Darcy a confused look when Julian closes the door. Is this the right move? She's taking a risk by sending Julian into the dark. But this might be their best opportunity to catch Michael Rivers. To *kill* Michael Rivers, she thinks. The nightmare needs to end now.

The alarm squeals, a red light flashing beside the entry pad. Quickly, she enters the code to quiet the noise and presses her back to the door. What set off the alarm?

"All right," Darcy says, the breaths flying in and out of her chest. "Back into the hallway, away from the doors and windows."

She receives no argument from Hunter and Jennifer. Placing a hand on each of their shoulders, she eases them down until they kneel beside each other. Hunter's glare fills with heat. He's competent with a gun, as is Jennifer. Agent Hensel taught them to shoot at Laurie's house in Georgia, and since returning to Genoa Cove, both accompanied Darcy to the shooting range. But she isn't comfortable allowing Hunter to defend the family. Defending the family is Darcy's responsibility.

The closed bedroom door pulls Darcy's eyes to the end of the hallway. Officer Wolpert claimed he saw a man in the next yard, but Rivers could have circled back to her property before Julian left the house. Which means he could be anywhere right now. Even inside the house with them.

Darcy runs her thumb along the weapon. Chews her

lower lip. She shifts her body between her children and the bedroom door, the gun raised.

Then another noise comes from inside the house. The sleek whisper of the deck door sliding on its tracks. Impossible. She set the bolt.

At the same time, the house alarm blares again. The kitchen fills with light. Throwing Hunter and Jennifer behind her, Darcy races toward the foyer and pauses at the wall. Someone is inside the house. Where is Julian?

As she presses her back to the wall, gun clutched in both hands, her heart a pick hammer inside her throat, a black shadow grows across the living room rug. The floorboard groans under heavy weight.

Darcy spins around the corner. The man is cloaked in silhouette with the beaming kitchen lights behind him. Spotting Darcy holding the gun, the intruder throws up his hands just as another body slams into him from behind. Julian.

The two men become a tangle of limbs on the floor. They roll over and over, struggling for the top position. Darcy sweeps the gun toward the intruder, but she can't find a clear shot without putting Julian at risk. With a groan, the stranger tugs Julian off of him and rolls him to the floor, both hands circling Julian's neck as he straddles his hips. It's almost as if the intruder forgot Darcy and the Glock.

As Officer Wolpert rumbles across the deck and bursts inside the kitchen, Darcy presses the gun against the man's head.

"Freeze!"

The man releases his grip around Julian's throat and raises his hands. He gives an ironic tilt to his head as Wolpert enters the living room. Julian sucks air into his lungs and rolls onto his side.

Wait. Darcy knows this man.

"Leo Vescio," she whispers.

The mob boss leans his head back and laughs. Officer Wolpert reads Vescio his rights as he yanks the man's arms behind his back. A moment later, Wolpert cuffs Vescio and drags him to his feet.

Darcy silences the alarm and flicks the wall switch. With the living room full of light, she can better see Vescio, dressed in black pants and coat, a winter hat that must have been excruciatingly hot in the summer night pulled over his ears. She plucks the hat off his head and tosses it aside. Despite Vescio's rumpled hair, he maintains an air of dignity and style, as though he isn't on his knees in Darcy's living room with his hands cuffed behind his back. He looks as if he's seated inside his favorite restaurant, swirling wine in a glass.

"What are you doing here, Vescio?"

He cocks his head up at Darcy and smiles, displaying all his pearly whites.

"Visiting an old friend."

"I thought you were someone else. You're lucky I didn't pull the trigger."

"Who were you expecting? Michael Rivers?"

A cruiser with flashing lights pulls to the curb outside with the black FBI SUV behind. Detective Ames hops out of the cruiser with Officer Faust as Hensel leads Agent Fisher up the walkway. Julian holds his hand up, a signal they have the situation under control.

When Detective Ames enters Darcy's house, he rubs his head and studies the man kneeling before him.

"That isn't the Full Moon Killer," Ames says.

Hensel leans his shoulder against the wall and folds

his arms.

"No, it isn't. That's Leo Vescio."

"Should I know that name?"

"He's a small-time operator in the Western New York organized crime scene."

"You aren't keeping up with the news, Agent Hensel," Vescio says, craning his neck. "I haven't been small time in years."

"Not since we took down your enemies, no. You know, the ones you answered to for twenty years."

Vescio's face twists.

"Take him to the station," Ames says after confirming Wolpert read the mob boss his rights. After Faust and Wolpert haul Vescio to his feet and lead him out to the cruiser, Ames swings toward Darcy. "You and your family all right, Ms. Gellar?"

"We're alive. That's all that matters."

"Any idea what this Vescio person was doing inside your house?"

"Looking to save face," Darcy says, remembering the men he lost inside the Buffalo prison after she contracted Vescio to take out Michael Rivers.

Ames glances between Darcy and the two FBI agents for an explanation. When he gets none, he sighs and shrugs his shoulders.

"Organized crime crossing state lines is FBI jurisdiction. You plan to take the lead on this investigation, Agent Hensel?"

"If you don't mind.," Hensel says, holstering his weapon. He wants to keep Ames in the loop and nurture the improved relationship between the FBI and GCPD. "I'd like you in the room when I question Vescio. This is your village, Detective."

Ames rolls his gaze over the interior of Darcy's house.

"This place is locked down tighter than a state penitentiary. How the hell did he get in?"

A breeze crawling through the living room ruffles Darcy's hair. She remembers the sliding glass door to the deck. Funny, she never heard glass break or the bolt popping. Cupping her elbows, Darcy follows the breeze into the kitchen and finds a hole in the glass above the bolt.

"He used a glass cutter," Hensel says. "Shit. That officer didn't find a glass cutter on Vescio, did he?"

Ames understands Hensel's meaning and speaks into his radio to warn Faust. Though they hold Vescio in cuffs, the glass cutter is probably buried inside his boot. Darcy shivers. It only took a glass cutter, a trademark tool for any criminal worth his salt, to break inside.

After Ames departs, Darcy moves to follow. Hensel blocks her in the doorway. Julian and Fisher stand beside the kids, watching the interaction between Hensel and Darcy play out. Only Hensel knows Darcy hired Vescio to eliminate Rivers in prison.

"I want to speak to Vescio," Darcy says.

"No chance."

"It's my house he broke into. This is personal."

Fisher cocks an eyebrow, and Darcy realizes she's revealing too much. Hensel glances over his shoulder and watches the cruiser pull off the curb.

"You say it's personal," Fisher says, glaring at Darcy. "And before you theorized Vescio needed to save face. I want an explanation."

Hensel meets Darcy's eyes. Her former partner's glare reminds Darcy he once warned her the stunt would come back to haunt them. She's sure he's about to tell

Fisher the truth, but Hensel thinks fast on his feet.

"Darcy was instrumental in disrupting Leo Vescio's criminal activities when the task force went after his foes."

"Didn't Vescio grow stronger when you brought his enemies down?"

"Eventually, yes. That much was inevitable. But Vescio lost a lot of ground during our investigation after Darcy cut off his money supply. It should have bankrupted Vescio's operation, but he found a way to survive."

Fisher nods, not accepting the entire story. Hensel turns to Darcy and lifts his chin.

"You may watch the interrogation from the observation room, but you're not sitting in on the interview. Let's go."

—

# CHAPTER TWENTY-TWO

A flurry of activity greets Darcy inside the Genoa Cove Police Department. Short-handed, the police department struggles to keep up with the Michael Rivers case. The new case throws a second wrench into the works —a notorious New York mob boss captured in Genoa Cove. And again Darcy Gellar sits at the epicenter. Ames passes her in the hallway, doing a poor job at hiding his scowl before he enters the interrogation room.

"As always, I'm persona non grata," Darcy sighs as she slips into an uncomfortable plastic chair in the observation room.

"Don't take it personally," says Julian, silencing his radio. "Ames is overworked."

The closet-sized observation room is even smaller than the one inside the sheriff's office near Scarlet River, Georgia. One florescent fixture provides light. Julian leans over and turns off the wall switch. Keeping the observation room dark is the best way to ensure Vescio can't see them, though the mob boss must expect she'll be there.

Officers Faust and Wolpert lead the cuffed Vescio into the interrogation room and sit him down across from

Hensel and Ames. Down the hall, Fisher interviews Hunter and Jennifer in the break room. Vescio wears a bemused grin. Smug. He knows they don't have much on him. The police charged Vescio with breaking and entering. At best, the mob boss will serve a year in prison. Odds are they'll release him after several months, though Darcy hopes the justice system will tack on additional time because he carried a deadly weapon.

Or did he? Vescio didn't have a knife or gun, only the glass cutter. As expected, Vescio hid the glass cutter inside his boot, stuffed inside a soft, padded case which made it difficult to detect when Wolpert searched the suspect.

Inside the interrogation room, Hensel sets down his pen and leans back in his chair.

"You're a long way from home, Leo. What brings you to Genoa Cove?"

Vescio shrugs.

"The sun never shines between Rochester and Buffalo. I needed the vacation."

Ames glances at Hensel from the corner of his eye. Hensel grins and locks his fingers behind his head.

"Seems a man of your means would rent a condo by the beach. Instead, you broke into a private residence. What's your interest in Darcy Gellar?"

The amusement leaves Vescio's face. His mouth twists, the vein in his neck pulsing. But he doesn't answer.

"Come on, Leo. This wasn't a social call. Breaking and entering is a serious offense. You'll do time."

"The only person who should do time is that slut on the other side of the glass."

Vescio stares at the two-way mirror. That he shouldn't be able to see Darcy doesn't stop her skin from crawling. It's as if he knows where she sits. She shifts in her chair, worrying something is wrong with the two-way mirror.

"Harsh words."

"She deserves worse," Vescio spits.

Hensel nods at Ames, who hands him the plastic bag holding the bracelet. He places it on the table in front of Vescio.

"Recognize this, Leo?"

Vescio's lips twist with amusement.

"Is this a joke?"

"Answer the question."

"It's a cheap trinket someone bought at one of those tourist traps on the pier. The ones that charge twenty dollars for a bag of seashells."

Hensel taps his finger beside the bracelet.

"How did you come upon the bracelet?"

"I have no idea what you're talking about. I've never seen the bracelet before."

"Come now, Leo. You broke inside the Gellar's residence."

"You're going down the wrong path, Agent Hensel. The bracelet means nothing to me. Remove it from my sight, please."

Hensel holds Vescio's eyes as he slides the bag over to Ames.

"Let's begin with why you broke into the Gellar's house. Tell me, Leo. Did you intend to harm Darcy Gellar and her children?"

"I would never hurt a child. My daughter is only a few years older than Ms. Gellar's. Why would I want to hurt the girl? Neither she nor the boy mean anything to me."

Inside the observation room, Darcy leans over to

Julian and whispers.

"I believe him. Vescio loves his daughter, and I can't picture him hurting a child. No way he'd play with Jennifer's head like that. Michael Rivers was inside my house, Julian. He slipped past the security cameras and disabled the alarm."

"That's impossible."

"Is it? This man murdered several girls from a prison cell and took out five of Vescio's thugs with a shank."

In the interrogation room, Hensel folds his arm and tilts his head.

"What about Darcy Gellar, Leo? Why attack the woman who took down your most powerful opponents?"

Vescio leans forward, the cuffs holding his wrists behind his back as his chest bumps the table. "Darcy Gellar impersonated a federal agent."

Hensel's calm demeanor falters for a moment, but he wins it back before Ames notices.

"Don't pretend you don't know, Agent Hensel," Vescio says, leering.

Rubbing his chin, Ames turns his attention toward Hensel. Hensel's legs drum beneath the table.

"If you're referring to the incident at the prison involving Michael Rivers and several of your associates, you're off base."

"Liar."

"It's true Darcy Gellar is no longer a full-time investigator with the FBI's Behavior Analysis Unit, but we bring her in for consulting. It so happens Ms. Gellar worked unofficially for me in Scarlet River, Georgia, after a killer abducted three teenage girls."

"Including the slut's daughter."

Hensel slides forward in his chair and rests his chin

on his knuckles.

"When Darcy Gellar contacted you, she did so because you knew five inmates inside the prison. The FBI understood Michael Rivers orchestrated the Georgia abductions, and we needed whatever information we could gain to locate those girls. Desperate times call for desperate measures."

Vescio shakes his head.

"That's not what happened, Agent Hensel. Darcy Gellar wanted Michael Rivers murdered."

Now Ames stares at the two-way mirror.

"You're mistaken," Hensel says, battling to keep his voice calm.

"Bullshit. You know what Darcy Gellar asked of me."

"Leo, I was in the room when Ms. Gellar spoke to you. She wanted information on Rivers. We all did. You read too much into her request."

"Oh, this is rich. I always believed the FBI was more crooked than the mob. Gellar wanted me to stick a knife in Rivers's chest."

Hensel tilts his head.

"Are you admitting you ordered your associates to attack and murder another inmate?"

Vescio opens his mouth and clamps it shut.

"No more talking. I want my lawyer."

"You'll get your lawyer, if that's how you wish to handle things. But it strikes me as more than a coincidence that Michael Rivers arrived in Genoa Cove around the same time Leo Vescio did. Makes me wonder if you're working together."

Vescio lowers his head. His shoulders pulse with silent laughter.

"That son-of-a-bitch murdered five of my men."

"Just like you want to murder Darcy Gellar."

Vescio scoffs.

"I didn't intend to hurt Gellar, just put a scare into her. Let her understand what would happen if she crossed me again."

"So if Ms. Gellar crossed you again, then you would have murdered her."

"Don't put words in my mouth, Agent Hensel. Michael Rivers hurts children. You think I'd help a creep like the Full Moon Killer?"

Hensel flips open his notebook and clicks his pen.

"Maybe not, but you broke inside Darcy Gellar's residence. Seems to me you came to Genoa Cove with two scores to settle. You say he's a creep. So hit him where it counts. Breaking and entering doesn't carry a life sentence. This will go easier for you if you help us catch Rivers."

Ames stares at Vescio. Darcy releases a held breath. Somehow Hensel swerved the conversation away from Darcy's illegal proposal. But now she feels Julian's eyes on her face.

"Come on, Leo," Hensel says when Vescio lifts his head. "You hate child predators like Michael Rivers. Your anger toward Darcy Gellar is misplaced. The man you want revenge on is the Full Moon Killer. Michael Rivers killed five of your men, made you look weak. We understand your motivation. He takes out a piece of your army, you take him out. Now you're strong again. Your enemies fear crossing Leo Vescio. It just so happens we're working for the same team this time. I want what you want —Michael Rivers behind bars."

"That's not what I want," Vescio says, shifting himself in his seat so he no longer looks the authorities in their eyes.

"Right. You want him six feet under. Nobody inside this room will shed a tear if the Full Moon Killer disappears from the world."

"Am I to believe you intend to hunt down Michael Rivers and shoot him like a dog? Don't lie to me, Agent Hensel. You'll catch him and put him back into the system. He'll remain a common enemy, and a powerful one behind bars."

"Think this through, Leo. Help me catch him, and I'll go to bat for you."

Vescio's body trembles. During the times Darcy encountered Leo Vescio, she never saw him lose his cool. He looks like a pot boiling over as Hensel pushes all the right buttons. When Darcy accepts Vescio has nothing more to say, he faces Ames and Hensel, watching the two lawmen from the tops of his eyes.

"He's not inside Genoa Cove."

"We figured that much. You'll need to give us more than that."

"If I knew where Michael Rivers was, this hunt would be over by now. You'd be dragging the river for his remains. But I have reason to believe he's somewhere north of Smith Town."

"There's nothing north of Smith Town," Detective Ames says, sitting forward. "Just wilderness for ten miles."

Vescio's eyes smile.

"A marvellous place to hunt, if I may say so."

Darcy glances at Julian. Their theory about Rivers hiding out in the forest, possibly holed up inside a vacant hunting cabin, suddenly seems plausible.

"How did you come by this information?" Hensel asks.

"I have eyes everywhere, Agent Hensel."

"Are you suggesting your influence extends into the Carolinas?"

Vescio laughs and shakes his head.

"I'm a simple businessman. And like any intelligent businessman, I diversify."

That's all they get out of Vescio—a vague hint that Michael Rivers is somewhere in the wilderness north of Smith Town. When it becomes obvious the mob boss has nothing else to say, Faust and Wolpert lead the cuffed man to the holding cells.

Darcy rubs her face. Exhaustion from a week of troubled sleep makes her body feel as though a layer of decaying rubber lies beneath the surface. She checks the time and is shocked to see it's almost midnight.

"Let's get you and the kids home," Julian says, helping her out of the chair.

Darcy fights the urge to get behind the wheel and search the countryside for Rivers. She won't get a full night of sleep until the Full Moon Killer dies. But sleepiness tilts the scales toward reason, and she accepts Julian's arm.

But when Detective Ames meets them at the door, Darcy realizes their long night has just begun.

# CHAPTER TWENTY-THREE

Feeling like a prisoner, Darcy faces Detective Ames over his cluttered desk, the door closed to outsiders. Julian sits in the bullpen, waiting for Ames to finish so he can take Darcy home. Anxiety trickles through her bones now that Hunter and Jennifer left the building. Officer Wolpert took the kids back to Julian's house and volunteered to stay with them until Darcy returned. There's no telling how long the detective's interrogation will drag, and by the tight-lipped grimace he sends her, she worries it will be dawn before she escapes the Genoa Cove Police Department.

The inside of Ames's office is as Darcy remembers it —a hodgepodge of folders spilling papers, a garbage can stuffed with potato chip wrappers and fast food containers. Stress must be an efficient calorie burner, for Ames hasn't gained a pound this year. A layer of dust clouds the lip of the desk and irritates Darcy's sinuses. No windows inside the office. Only the drab interior of a tiny room that screams for natural light. The desk lamp dumps light on the papers and ignites Ames's face from below, drawing strange shadows around his eyes. He looks like a skeleton.

Darcy opens her mouth to apologize, certain Ames is furious over her deal with Leo Vescio to attack Michael Rivers in prison. Before she can speak, he slams two open hands on the desk, forcing her to jump in her seat.

"You're lucky I don't call the FBI and lock you up for conspiring to murder. You might have Officer Haines and Agent Hensel fooled, but not me. I'm confident there are plenty of higher-ups inside the FBI who'd love to know about the stunt you pulled in Georgia." Ames lifts the phone receiver off his desk. "Better yet, why don't I call the interim warden up in Buffalo. He'll be interested in your conspiracy. You put his staff at risk, and five inmates died on his predecessor's watch. One could argue you're responsible for Warden Ellsworth's death. Michael Rivers killed Ellsworth in response to the prison attack."

The old desk chair squeaks as Ames swivels. He swipes his arm across the desk and cusses when he inadvertently tips his soda can over.

"You need to understand I acted out of need," Darcy says. "You don't have children of your own, but put yourself in my shoes. If a murderer abducted your daughter, wouldn't you go to any length to find out where he'd taken her?"

"Conspiring with a noted mob boss? No. I'd find another option."

"My actions didn't just save my daughter. They spared another girl he kidnapped and held for ten years."

"And cost five lives. Six, if you count Warden Ellsworth." Ames picks up a pen and waves it at Darcy. "And you're ruining the career of an officer with untapped potential. Officer Haines will make detective in the next year and could be running the department soon after. Now he's forced to cover for you."

"My actions are my own. They don't reflect on Officer Haines."

"Guilt by association, Ms. Gellar. People judge Officer Haines by the company he keeps. You should have let the FBI and County Sheriff handle the Georgia kidnappings. Instead, you ran off on your own, risked compromising the investigation, and could have gotten Agent Hensel fired."

"My decisions weren't always the best ones, but two girls are alive today, including my daughter."

"But two other teenagers died, as did Sheriff Tipton."

"That's not fair."

Ames closes a fist over his hair and fights the urge to yank.

"Trouble follows you, Darcy Gellar. As long as you're a Genoa Cove resident, your troubles become mine."

Darcy bites her palm as Tipton taps the pen against his palm.

"What do you want from me, Detective? A full confession? I'll give it, if it means you'll let me go back to my children. I'm happy to face the justice system."

Ames opens his mouth and closes it. He jams a pen into a container on the corner of his desk.

"Putting you in jail won't solve Genoa Cove's problems."

And arresting Darcy will put Julian at risk, Darcy theorizes. As Ames stated, guilt by association could bring Julian down. How will it look if Julian had a romantic relationship with a felon? Darcy scrutinizes the detective. His eyes light with protectiveness whenever he mentions Julian. Ames sees himself as a father figure to the younger officer.

"If it helps matters, I swear Julian...Officer Haines... had no knowledge of my relationship with Leo Vescio until it came to light during the interrogation."

Ames lifts a bottled water to his lips and drains the container, causing the plastic to crinkle and pop after he sets it down. Wiping his mouth with the back of his sleeve, Ames stares back at Darcy.

"Noted. Officer Haines doesn't deserve to lose his career because of your actions. But you need to recognize you don't make choices in a vacuum. People get hurt."

"So you aren't turning me over to the FBI?"

Ames tosses the empty water bottle into the trash. He sets his elbows on his desk and squints.

"No. And it's not because I believe you're innocent. Turning you in would cause a chain reaction. People would lose their careers, perhaps their freedoms. My priority is keeping Genoa Cove safe, and right now I need Agent Hensel and Officer Haines in the field, tracking down the murderer you..."

"Say it, Detective. The murderer I brought to your village." Darcy fills with heat. Her hands clasp the chair arms. "Thank you so much for blaming the victims. You're no better than the rest of Genoa Cove."

Darcy shoves her chair back. Ames's mouth hangs open, his shoulder curled forward. That the detective knows he made a mistake doesn't lend Darcy solace. Moving to Charlotte feels inevitable, and she counts the seconds until she puts Genoa Cove behind her forever.

Slamming the detective's door on the way out, Darcy draws surprised stares from the officers working the late night shift. The glass rattles. Inside the office, a rolling chair squeaks on old casters, but the detective doesn't emerge.

Concern stilting his gait, Julian leads Darcy toward his desk and offers her his chair.

"I'm not staying a minute longer," Darcy says, waving away the gesture. "Just get me back to your house. I need to see my kids."

Julian places his hands on her shoulders. The warmth of the officer's grip reflects in his caring eyes.

"Give me ten seconds to finish my paperwork."

"Sure."

The weight of the unending day slides off her body when she falls into his chair. Her eyelids battle to stay open, and the corner of her eye twitches from sleeplessness. Looking younger than she noticed before, Julian leans over his desk, tongue pushing at the inside of his cheek as he scans the reports fanned out before him. She's about to drift off when an officer crosses the bullpen toward the break room. Officer Wolpert.

Shock pops her out of the chair. Who's watching Hunter and Jennifer?

# CHAPTER TWENTY-FOUR

As Darcy glares at Officer Wolpert, her stomach sick with the knowledge he betrayed their trust, Julian glances up in question. When he follows her gaze toward the break room, where Wolpert sifts through the refrigerator, Julian crosses the bullpen. He isn't quick enough. Darcy beats him across the room and blocks Wolpert from leaving the break room with his sandwich.

"What are you doing here? You're supposed to be guarding Hunter and Jennifer."

Wolpert's face freezes. He looks between Julian and Darcy.

"Dispatch radioed me a half-hour ago. Said we were a man short on the overnight shift, and I needed to get back to the office. From what I was told, you were on your way to the house—"

Darcy turns and rushes for the door, the blood draining from her face. After she passes the front desk, Julian grabs her arm.

"Slow down, Darcy. Let's call their phones. They're probably watching TV and waiting for you to come back."

But neither child answers Darcy's calls. A hastily

constructed message goes unanswered. Alarm lighting his face, Julian peers across the bullpen floor. Darcy doesn't need an explanation. Wolpert disappeared.

"It's a setup, Julian. Officer Wolpert—"

"No...no. I know Wolpert. He's an excellent cop. He wouldn't..."

Julian can't finish the sentence. His eyes swing across the room. Speaking on the phone, the gray-haired officer working the front desk watches Julian and Darcy. Wolpert couldn't have slipped past them. He must be inside the building.

Officer Faust pushes through two rookies crowding the bullpen entryway. Julian puffs air through his lips and waves the female officer over.

"We've got a problem. Have you seen Officer Wolpert?"

Faust spins on her heels and enters the bullpen. Two officers man desks. Nobody in the break room. Ames's door remains closed.

"I passed him five minutes ago."

"Where?"

"He was heading for the refrigerator. Said something about a roast beef sandwich from Nell's."

"He's working with Rivers," Darcy says, drawing both of their glares.

Pulling the keys from his pocket, Julian shakes his head.

"No. There has to be a logical explanation."

Darcy clutches Julian's shirt.

"Wolpert was outside the entire time Vescio broke into my house. How did Wolpert not see him? And he missed the glass cutter inside Vescio's boot. You don't find that suspicious?"

Julian wipes the sweat off his forehead.

"Faust, take Darcy back to my house and put the word out that her kids might be missing."

"Where are you going?" Darcy asks.

"To find out why dispatch called him back to the station." Julian checks his gun and slides it onto his hip. "Then I'm going after Wolpert."

Not waiting another moment, Darcy shoves the door open and stumbles into the dark humidity. A flash of purple light ignites massing clouds over the western horizon, followed by rolling thunder.

"There's a severe thunderstorm watch in effect," Faust says, eyeing the approaching weather. "Let's hope it breaks this damn heat. I wouldn't worry, Ms. Gellar. I'm sure your kids are in good hands."

Ignoring Faust's placation, Darcy sprints toward the first cruiser she sees. The officer catches her from behind.

"Keep your cool, Darcy. I'll get you to Julian's. Follow me. I'm parked in the side lot."

Though Faust never breaks into a run, her strides are smooth, purposeful. Darcy keeps up as the officer angles through a maze of cruisers and civilian vehicles. Every lost second steals a year off Darcy's life. As she walks, Darcy dials Hunter's phone again. Her heart leaps at the sound of his voice, but it's only his voice-mail. A call to Jennifer's phone yields the same result.

She almost runs into Faust when the officer stops beside a cruiser with a paint-chipped dent on the trunk.

"Here we are, Ms. Gellar. Sorry to ask, but do you mind sitting in the back?"

A quick glance inside the vehicle reveals a zipped bag taking up the passenger seat.

"It's fine," Darcy says. "Just get us there."

As Faust fumbles with her keys, Darcy bounces on her toes, the stone and brick police department building pulling her gaze. A flurry of officers rush through the interior. By now, they must know Officer Wolpert works for the Full Moon Killer.

The front door pops open. Faust rounds the vehicle and pulls the back door open.

"My apologies again, Ms. Gellar."

Faust holds the door while Darcy shoves her bag across the seat. When she leans inside the vehicle, Faust's forearms snake under her chin and around her neck.

Then she's dragged down into the shadows between the cruiser and a large SUV. Her legs kick out and strike the SUV's doors, eliciting the vehicle's alarm. Darcy grabs Faust's forearms and fights to pry them apart, but the female officer's arms constrict and squeeze. She's too strong.

With a grunt, Darcy pushes her legs off the SUV and drives Faust back-first against the cruiser. The officer moans as the impact forces the air from her lungs. But as Darcy struggles to her feet, Faust's nightstick smashes against her temple.

Darcy's vision fails. Her legs buckle a moment before her head strikes the pavement. Blood trickles off her lips and pools in the moonlight. Footsteps approach. When she pulls her head up, a black shape stands between the vehicles.

"There you are. I've been waiting a long time to see you again, Darcy."

# CHAPTER TWENTY-FIVE

The shrill of cricket songs force Hunter's eyes open. His body twitches in alarm. He doesn't recognize where he is. Hunter lies on his side, his arms wrenched behind his back and roped around a wooden beam. Confused and groggy, he believes he's inside Julian's house, bound in a room he hasn't visited before. Did Julian have a basement? But the night sounds are too loud for the village, the darkness blanketing the dusty windows too sharp.

Twisting his head around, he finds Jennifer on the other side of the beam. She's roped and bound, her neck lolled at an unnatural angle. Is she breathing?

"Jennifer?"

She doesn't answer. Hunter fights to turn himself over, but the ropes stop him. Jennifer hasn't moved since Hunter awoke.

The night's events seem shrouded in fog. One moment they sat on Julian's couch, a reality show Hunter had never seen before on the television, the house thick with the scent of popcorn as Jennifer carried the overflowing bowl out of the kitchen. A minute before, Officer Wolpert had emerged from the bathroom when his

phone rang. There had been an argument. Something
about a staffing problem at the police station, and Wolpert
needed to leave. On his way out the door, he stressed they
needn't worry. Another officer would take his place if
Julian and his mother failed to return within the hour. The
reason behind Wolpert leaving never sat right in Hunter's
gut. It scuttled like a centipede outgrowing its
subterranean lair. For the next half-hour, they sat together
on the couch and watched the banal reality show, Jennifer
giggling at the awkward parts while Hunter kept checking
his phone for a message from Mom.

Then a knock on the door.

Hunter held Jennifer in place with a warning glance.
Hunter checked the peephole, one nervous hand poised
over the lock. He sighed, recognizing the police uniform on
the other side of the door, the officer facing the street as if
scanning for danger, his face hidden.

But Julian had a back door as well. Before the officer
turned, the kitchen floor creaked. Someone was inside the
house. He spun as the fist thundered down on the back of
his neck. His legs gave way, the room spun. As his legs
spasmed on the floor, Jennifer screamed. The boot to his
head knocked him unconscious.

His memory is blank from that point forward, though
he holds a vague recollection of suffocating darkness and
the rumble of a car motor, his sister's body pressed against
his. Someone kidnapped Hunter and Jennifer and tossed
them inside a trunk. Where are they? Judging by the rustic
wooden interior and lack of furniture, they appear to be in
an abandoned cabin. He can't twist his neck to find the
door, but it must stand behind him.

Scuffs and scratches mark where previous owners
dragged furniture across the floor. Black dots littering the

floor and the stench of urine tell Hunter vermin have the run of the cabin. There's a compact kitchen in the far corner. No refrigerator or table. A loaf of bread lies on the counter beside a dripping faucet. Lunar light bathes the interior, the eerie glow of a full moon.

He pulls at his bindings and calls out to Jennifer again. She lies immobile. It occurs to Hunter their kidnapper might be inside the cabin, but no response comes. That's one shred of hope. If he slips out of the knots and frees Jennifer, they can escape before the kidnapper returns. Or are there two kidnappers? Yes, two people are involved. He's confident the officer outside the door, if it was a genuine police officer to begin with, provided a distraction for the man who attacked him inside Julian's house.

With Leo Vescio locked up inside the Genoa Cove Police Department, only one person can be responsible. Michael Rivers, the Full Moon Killer.

A hand drops on his shoulders. He jolts and twists his neck. Inside the mottled strips of blue light and oily blacks, Jennifer stares back at him. Relief floods his body. She's alive, though her fluttering eyelids suggest she's on the brink of falling unconscious again.

"Where are we?"

With her wrists bound to the beam, Jennifer's fingers scrape across his shoulder and touch his cheek.

"Looks like an old hunting cabin," Hunter says, craning his neck to get a better look at their surroundings.

She takes in the vermin droppings and wretches at the stench. A shadow shoots across the window. Jennifer stifles a shout. When the silhouette repeats itself, Hunter realizes it isn't a human form, but the black claws of tree limbs shadowing the windowpanes.

"This doesn't look like Genoa Cove."

Hunter shakes his head.

"No. We're in the woods somewhere."

"Oh, God."

Jennifer's lips tremble, a tear pushing out of the corner of her eye. She's remembering the abduction in Georgia. Hunter can't imagine her panic, the constant fear that it could happen again coming to fruition and bursting out of the darkness like an unspeakable beast.

"I'll get us out of here, Jennifer, I swear to you."

"But we don't know where we are. We might not even be in North Carolina anymore."

Hunter shakes his head.

"It's still dark out. We couldn't have gone far."

Lightning strobes and fills the cabin with unearthly light. Ten seconds later, thunder echoes the flash and rattles the windows.

"Didn't it thunder at Julian's house?"

Hunter thinks for a moment and nods.

"Yeah, after Officer Wolpert left for the station."

"That's a good sign," Jennifer says, pulling her legs toward her chest when something scurries past her feet.

"How do you mean?"

"If it's the same storm, we must be close to Julian's house."

It might be a different thunderstorm, but Jennifer's theory makes sense. Though he can't remember much after the attack, intuition convinces him only an hour or two passed.

"Who kidnapped us, Hunter?"

He searches the walls and windows for a way out, or a sign civilization lies nearby. Jennifer's question brings his head around. He knows who kidnapped them, and so does

Jennifer judging by the terror in her eyes.

"You know who," Hunter says.

"So the police are behind this."

"At least one of them, yes."

"You think Officer Wolpert did this to us?"

Hunter purses his lips. After the police ignored Aaron's attacks and pinned the Darkwater Cove murders on Hunter, he stopped trusting anyone associated with the GCPD. Bronson Severson retired from the department before he aided Michael Rivers and infiltrated their family. No, he didn't trust any cop. Not even Julian Haines, though the officer's kindness had begun to win Hunter over.

But Officer Wolpert doesn't strike Hunter as a man who'd aid a serial killer, even if the murderer offered Wolpert a substantial bribe. Hunter considers himself a good judge of character. Wolpert never set off alarms inside Hunter's head during their brief encounters, and the officer appeared distraught after dispatch ordered him to return to the office.

"No, I don't think he's involved."

"Then who? Julian?"

Maybe. Julian's relationship with his mother materialized without warning. It all seemed rather sudden and forced. He doesn't want to believe Julian orchestrated the attack. If he did, Mom is in danger.

"Hunter." Jennifer pulls Hunter out of his trance. "If Julian helped the Full Moon Killer, we need to tell Mom. Remember the knock on the door? Was it a police officer?"

"Yeah, but I didn't see a face, just the uniform." Gathering his thoughts, Hunter shakes his head. "It couldn't have been Julian. The officer outside the door looked too small."

"Then it might have been Officer Wolpert. Let's say he faked the phone call. He had time to circle back to the house."

"It doesn't add up. Why return to the house to kidnap us when he'd been inside the whole evening? He had opportunities." Hunter sifts through the officers who visited their house over the last year and the ones he encountered inside the station. Who fits the build of the officer outside Julian's door? "Oh, no."

"What's wrong? Do you know who it is?"

Why hadn't he seen it until now? He'd spent too long matching men to the size of the officer outside the door. But it wasn't a man who betrayed them.

"Officer Faust. It has to be her."

Jennifer's gaze moves to the ceiling. She blinks twice, clearing her thoughts.

"Faust came inside our house multiple times. And since she worked with Julian, she must have seen his house at some point and known the layout. This is bad. We need to get out of here."

"What I don't get is why they kidnapped us and left us alone here."

"You know why, Hunter. This is about Mom. Rivers wants her to watch when he…"

The implication hangs heavy over the room before a blast of lightning ignites the cabin interior. Thunder rolls through Hunter's bones and causes the cabin to tremble. That was close. Summers in Virginia and North Carolina taught Hunter when to worry. This is no ordinary storm. Outside, the wind whistles and shrieks, droplets of rain pattering the windowpane. Worry over the storm smashing the old cabin to splinters gets Hunter working on the bindings again.

Jennifer catches the concern on his face and props her feet against the beam. Pushing off, she bridges and twists her body until her neck and shoulders rest on the dirty floorboards. But when she tries to flip herself onto her knees, the sneaker treads lose their grip. Jennifer tumbles onto her side with enough force to drive the air from her lungs. She curses until Hunter's fingertips slide across her wrists. By sheer luck, her failed escape attempt landed her bindings in reach of his fingers.

"Don't move," he says, biting his tongue as he prays she doesn't slip and tumble away. "If you hold still, I'll try to untie your wrists."

The cabin ignites with alien sunlight when lightning strikes the forest. He braces himself, but the thunder steals his confidence. If only his wrists had another inch of wiggle room, he could get a better grip on the ropes. Sweat pours down his back and slicks his shirt against his skin. The inside of the cabin is a brick oven, the air stagnant.

Now rain pelts the side of the cabin in sheets as though an angry god hurls the ocean across the woods. Straining, Hunter turns his hands until he's afraid he'll dislocate his wrists, guaranteeing they'll never escape. A popping sound accompanies white hot pain.

"Are you all right?"

He doesn't answer. If he stops to consider how much his wrists hurt, he won't be able to fight through the pain. Fingers slick, he loops his pinkie inside a knot and pulls up. To his shock, the rope eases half an inch.

"I've almost got it."

"Hurry, Hunter."

Invigorated, he works faster, his fingers flying over the bindings and searching for a weak point. When the ropes loosen, he extends his fingers inside the loop and pulls.

"You've gotta free your hands, Jennifer. I can't hold the ropes any longer."

Hunter's hands scream with exhaustion. His body trembles when Jennifer's hands pop free.

Releasing his grip, Hunter falls flat on his back and stares at the ceiling, his chest heaving. Jennifer kneels beside him now, fighting to slip her hands inside the ropes holding Hunter's wrists against the beam. It's easier for Jennifer. Her smaller fingers prod the bindings, and it takes less than a minute for her to unravel the ropes.

His hands numb and tingling with pins-and-needles, Hunter crawls up to a sitting position with Jennifer's aid. The back of his neck aches where the Full Moon Killer struck him, and his stomach turns over as the floor gyrates. His sister loops his arm over her shoulders and pulls him to his feet.

For the first time, he sees the entire layout of the cabin. A bedroom sits off to their left with the door cracked open. Darkness oozes through the opening. Until this point, he assumed Michael Rivers and Faust left them while they went after Mom. His gaze held by the open door, he can't shake the feeling they're not alone.

When Jennifer throws the front door open, a gale drives the humid night into the cabin. Lightning strobes over the forest. Though it's no longer raining, the roar beyond the trees warns him the brunt of the storm is close. Spotting a dirt road descending through the woods, Hunter shouts at Jennifer to run.

# CHAPTER TWENTY-SIX

"What the hell are you looking at? Call an ambulance!"

Julian supports Officer Wolpert's head in his hands. The gash across the back of the policeman's head oozes blood. Ames stares with disbelief in the doorway, frozen with indecision until Julian's shout gets him moving. Wolpert's legs lie akimbo on the bathroom floor, the drip of the faucet like a ticking bomb. A rookie officer named Kepler kneels beside Wolpert.

"Who hit you, Officer?"

Wolpert doesn't answer. His eyes roll like marbles, the lids fluttering open and closed as he struggles to focus on the surrounding faces. Julian can feel the lump rising off the back of the injured officer's head. Blood slicks Julian's palms and stains the tiled floor.

"Press the washcloth against the back of his head," Julian tells Kepler, supporting Wolpert's head until the rookie slides his hands beneath.

Trading positions, Julian works the feeling into his legs after kneeling for too long. A group of officers stand in the doorway.

"Someone followed Officer Wolpert into the restroom. Did anyone see who it was?" Nobody answers. "Can someone explain to me how a stranger came inside the department and assaulted one of our officers without anyone noticing?"

Detective Ames skids to a stop in the doorway, short of breath.

"I called. The paramedics should be here any second."

Not concerned by his place in the chain of command, Julian glares at Ames.

"Have you contacted the chief?"

Chief Winston's shift ended at four o'clock. He should be sound asleep at this time of night.

"He's coming in."

"Nobody enters or leaves the station until we know who did this. Why did dispatch call Wolpert back to the station when he should have been watching Darcy Gellar's children? I want an explanation."

Thinking about Darcy's family tightens Julian's chest and sends a shard of panic through his body. At least Darcy will be safe with Faust. He hears the ambulance siren and glances down at Wolpert.

"You'll be fine, my friend. Lie still. The paramedics are on the way."

The glaze across Wolpert's eyes tells Julian the officer didn't comprehend the words, but the color of Wolpert's face improves as the officers talk to him. He hopes Wolpert saw the man who assaulted him, but they're out of luck if his attacker struck him from behind.

Unless the cameras caught the assailant following Wolpert into the restroom.

Julian and Ames scramble toward the front desk,

passing two female paramedics rushing in the opposite direction. One security camera covers the hallway, angling down from the doorway outside the bullpen.

The recording system rests inside a cubicle in the dispatcher's office. Ames interrogates Catherine, the woman working the dispatch desk, while Julian scans the footage. No luck. As he feared, the camera doesn't cover the entire hallway, leaving a blind spot at the door to the men's bathroom. Interesting. It's as if the man who assaulted Wolpert knew about the blind spot. Is one of their officers behind the attack?

"No, I never called Officer Wolpert back to the station," Catherine says. An overweight woman with bottle glasses, Catherine drums her legs as Ames leans over her. The dispatcher's eyes glass over with tears.

Ames places his hands on his hips and marches in a circle. When he spins around, Catherine leans backward. Instead of yelling, Ames stares at the ceiling in resignation.

"Somebody is lying. Either you called Officer Wolpert, or he abandoned the Gellar family on his own."

"That doesn't make sense," Julian says. "He didn't bludgeon himself. Officer Wolpert is the victim here."

"He knows Catherine's voice. He would have questioned the order, if he didn't recognize the person on the radio."

Catherine swings her eyes between Julian and Ames, relieved she isn't the focus of their interrogation. She's a new grandmother, six months from her retirement date. Julian doubts Catherine has a malicious bone in her body. He tenses with a new thought.

"We assumed a man attacked Officer Wolpert. What if it was a woman?"

Ames rolls his eyes at the accusation, then stops. Yes,

the GCPD employs two female police officers, one of which worked inside the office when the attack occurred.

"You don't think Faust..."

The implications hurtle at Julian. Faust's voice sounds similar to Catherine's. In person, he can discern subtle differences in tonality and inflection. But over the phone, the differences wouldn't be obvious if Faust impersonated the dispatcher. Julian left Darcy in Faust's charge. If Faust works for Michael Rivers, Darcy's life is in danger. Julian calls Darcy's phone. When the message dumps him into her voice-mail, he fires off a text, demanding she write back to him.

"Catherine," Ames says. "Get Faust on the phone. I want to know where she is."

Julian knows Faust won't answer.

"Hey, we need to get the FBI in here," Julian says.

"I'm on it. There's a sheriff's vehicle two miles from your place. The deputy will check the house, and I'll trace the GPS on Faust's cruiser."

It won't work. Faust knows about the tracker and will remove the radio antenna, rendering the vehicle invisible to their tracking software.

Spurred into action, Ames turns out of the cubicle and places a call to Agent Hensel. There has to be something more Julian can do. He wants to abandon the search efforts at the station and drive back to his house. It's the wrong move. If Faust abducted Darcy and handed her over to Rivers, they're no longer inside the village.

When Ames gets off the phone, Julian snaps his fingers.

"We can trace their phones. Get the cell company on the line and have them locate the devices."

"I'll take care of it."

Julian raps his knuckles on the desk. Are they really going forward on the assumption Faust is guilty? He's known Faust for three years. She's quiet, reserved, but he always considered her dependable. What does he know about her personal life other than she lives alone in an apartment on Washington Street and keeps to herself? It takes three precious minutes for the cell company to start the trace. When the call ends, Ames returns from the hallway with intensity in his eyes.

"Wolpert is sitting up and talking."

Julian shoves the rolling chair away from the desk and races down the hall. Leaving the flustered dispatcher behind, Ames follows. A debate takes place outside the restroom where Officer Wolpert fights to stand while the two paramedics urge him into a sitting position. The first paramedic, a dark haired female who looks no more than a year out of college, presses her lips together and glares at Julian.

"Would you please tell the officer he needs to go to the hospital? He likely suffered a concussion, and he shouldn't be on his feet."

"I don't have a goddamn concussion," Wolpert growls. "And I can stand on my own, if the two of you get out of my way."

"It's better if you sit," Julian says, winning an approving nod from the paramedic. "Save your strength."

Wolpert's eyes continue to loll as though he came out on the losing end of a heavyweight boxing match. Desperate for information, Julian kneels beside the injured officer.

"What happened, Officer?"

"Did you see who hit you?" Ames asks from behind Julian.

Wolpert closes his eyes and rubs the back of his head. A gauze pad stopped the bleeding, but the lump beneath the bandage protrudes larger than a golf ball.

"I don't even remember anyone hitting me."

"Was anyone in the restroom when you came inside?"

"No, I had the place to myself."

Julian holds Wolpert's eyes and says, "Okay, think back to before the attack. Can you trace your steps?"

Wolpert pinches between his eyes.

"I ran into you outside the break room when I grabbed my food. That Gellar woman was pretty pissed off...shit, her kids. Did something happen to Gellar's kids?"

"After the encounter with Ms. Gellar, what happened next?"

"Well, I took the sandwich back to my desk and checked my messages. But then I needed to take a leak."

"When you headed for the restroom, did you see anyone in the hallway who didn't belong?"

Wolpert fixes Julian with a *you-have-to-be-kidding-me* glare.

"You think I wouldn't say something if a civilian was walking around without a visitor's badge?"

"What about other officers? Anyone hanging out in the hallway?"

Wolpert lifts a shoulder and stares at the wall.

"Just Faust."

Julian's hands turn cold.

"Go on."

"Not much to say, man. She was lingering between the women's and men's restrooms. Asked her if she was considering a sex change. Usually something like that gets a laugh out of her, but she just kinda looked at me. I figured she was having a hard shift and let it go." Wolpert squints his eyes for several seconds, then shakes his head. "Then I went inside the bathroom, and that's the last thing I remember."

Ames moves beside Julian and drops to a knee before the injured officer.

"The dispatcher on the phone. Are you sure it was Catherine who ordered you back to the station?"

Wolpert glances at Julian for an explanation before returning to Ames.

"What kind of a question is that?"

"This is important. Is it possible the voice on the radio belonged to Officer Faust?"

"Why would Faust tell me to return to the station?" When Ames doesn't blink, Wolpert touches behind his head again. "I suppose it could have been her. Are you saying—"

Ames springs to his feet. Julian nods to the paramedics, indicating Wolpert is theirs to take, and runs for the parking lot. Faust attacked Wolpert. What did she do with Darcy?

# CHAPTER TWENTY-SEVEN

Where am I?

Darkness presses on Darcy. Can't move. The enclosure restricts her from rising off the floor. It feels like she's inside a coffin, but the motor's rumble proves she's in the trunk of a moving vehicle.

Darcy's body leaps when the police cruiser strikes a hole in the road. Her head strikes the trunk door, drawing stars over her eyes.

Her instincts take over. She lashes out with her legs and drives her heels against the trunk wall. A memory rushes back to her. The warm macadam scraping at her face, her head throbbing from where Officer Faust struck her. Then footsteps as another figure approached between the vehicles. This wasn't an officer coming to her aid. Though the man stood inside the shadows, she sensed the Full Moon Killer amid the darkness before she recognized his voice. Two powerful hands gripped her by the waist and shirt collar and hauled her off the blacktop. He carried her behind Faust's cruiser, her body limp and powerless. A trunk popped open, and she landed hard when he tossed her inside. Another blow to the head, and she blacked out.

The rhythm of the tires rolling over the road carries a false tranquility, like the flap of a butterfly's wings against a black widow's web. The sharp edge of a zip tie cuts into her wrists, her hands bound behind her back. Ignoring pain and nausea, she twists her head and searches the trunk. Pitch black. Anxiety floods her body, rendering her limbs stiff and useless.

And she doesn't know what fate befell her children.

Officer Faust was supposed to drive Darcy to Julian's house. Darcy plunges into hysterics. Did the Full Moon Killer take Hunter and Jennifer? She rolls onto her back, her hands trapped beneath her spine as she pulls her knees to her chest and drives the heels of her sneakers against the trunk door. The hollow explosion deafens her ears. But the door doesn't budge.

The cruiser careens over another bump. The force drives Darcy's shoulder against the floor. How long has she been inside the trunk? It's impossible to know if the sun has risen, but the dull ache in her bones suggests she's lain inside the trunk for less than an hour. They couldn't have gone far. Vescio believed Rivers had holed up in the forest outside Smith Town. Rivers needs privacy, a place where no one will hear Darcy's screams.

Instead of smoothing out, the ride roughens. Gravel pings the undercarriage as the sedan jounces. Bracing her legs against the wall, Darcy lies on her side. She winces with each impact against her ribs and hips.

It's a battle to stay grounded, to focus on the sounds outside the cruiser—frogs and crickets?—and the lack of other vehicles on the road. But she must. It's too dark inside the trunk, the walls too close. Converging. Stealing her breath.

I can breathe, she mutters to herself.

Except she's breathing too fast, consuming air as she hyperventilates. She needs to slow down and think. There's always the possibility of escape. She just needs to think this through.

The cruiser banks around a sharp curve and rolls her against the trunk wall. A sharp object jabs into her back. Crying out, Darcy slides away and plants her feet against the wall to keep from rolling when the cruiser turns again. Her fingers reach out and search the dark for the object that bit her. With the zip tie clamping her wrists behind her back, she searches for something to defend herself with. Her fingers move over the gritty floor and stop on a device with a hard shell split into multiple pieces.

Can't tell what the hell it is.

It's a series of rectangular pieces and cord. A radar gun. A thought occurs to her. She might be able to snap the tie on the radar gun.

The cruiser slows to a stop. Any second now, the Full Moon Killer will throw the trunk open and drag Darcy into the moonlight. Panicking, she fears she's out of time. The vehicle crawls over an obstruction. The front end tilts upward, then pitches down, engaging the shocks. There must have been a tree across the road, small enough for the cruiser to maneuver over.

Darcy releases her breath when the vehicle picks up speed. They're still moving slow, but the pace is steady, further evidence they've left the highway and turned into the wilderness. There's still time.

This is her fault. Darcy never should have let her guard down and trusted the GCPD. For all she knows, Rivers bribed Faust a year ago and used the officer to throw Ames off Richard Chaney's trail. It explains why the female cop seems so cold in Darcy's presence, as though Darcy and her children are pieces of meat to throw to a wolf.

Squirming across the trunk, her fingers grope until they close over the radar gun. She isn't confident she'll be able to snap the tie against the device. There's an equal chance she'll snap her wrists and render them useless. The housing seems solid, the edges and corners sharp enough to break her binding if she provides sufficient momentum. But the trunk confines Darcy. Makes it impossible to raise herself off the floor without hitting the top.

Planting her sneakers against the floor, she bridges her hips and slides her body over the radar gun. This is going to hurt. Gritting her teeth, she thrusts downward. Her spine hits the shell, shooting a shock of pain up her back. No luck. Eyes watering, she rolls to her side and catches her breath. Darcy gives herself two breaths to recover before she angles her body over the equipment again. This time she reaches out until her fingertips brush the parts beneath her. Sweat pours down her forehead, the interior of the trunk stifling. She clamps her eyelids shut and drops down. The shell chews into the tie, the force ripping at her wrists.

Darcy falls beside the radar gun. Tears wet her face. The zip tie didn't break. She can't generate enough force inside the close confines of the trunk. Below the cruiser, the tires bounce over another rut. Shocks squeal. Darcy's head whips down and cracks against the floor when she falls backward. Before the pain registers, the cruiser whips to the left. They're on a different road now, still in the countryside outside Genoa Cove and Smith Town. She senses they're close to their destination as the vehicle slows.

Desperation drives her. Ignoring the bruises on her spine and the zip tie slicing divots into her flesh, she locates the pieces of the radar gun and lifts her body over the equipment. She battles exhaustion, her thighs trembling as she holds her weight aloft. With a grunt, she drops down against the radar gun and cries when the corner cuts into her back. The zip tie almost broke. She can feel a tear in the plastic as it scrapes her skin. Pushing her feet against the floor, she bridges as high as the trunk allows and falls against the radar gun. The tie snaps in two. Her wrists pop free.

Huddled in a ball, she massages her wrists and works the feeling back into her hands. Blood slicks her fingertips. She searches for the source of the blood and discovers a deep gash on the outside of her left wrist. Darcy pulls her t-shirt over her head and wraps the cloth around her hand. Fortunately, it's a superficial wound, though her blood soaks the shirt as she presses it against the outside of her wrist. Another inch to the side, and the zip tie would have sliced a vein. As she lies prone in jeans and a sports bra, her hair matted to her face, Darcy raises her head when the cruiser jerks to a stop.

The engine purrs. Wind attacks the cruiser and whistles through the cracks. The cruiser rocks as the door opens. It slams shut, footsteps circling around the vehicle toward the trunk. Darcy crawls as far back as the trunk allows, but there's no escape. Her hands search the floor for a weapon. Except for the radar gun, now broken apart and scattered across the trunk, the floor is bare.

A second vehicle pulls up behind the cruiser. She'd assumed Michael Rivers drove the cruiser, but he might be in the unknown vehicle. The smooth growl of the engine tells Darcy it's a larger vehicle, probably the black Lincoln. The new vehicle's beams splash against the rear of the cruiser, bright enough to bleed inside the trunk and illuminate the floor.

That's when Darcy notices the black fabric covering the floor curling up at the edges. Why didn't she think of it before? Shifting forward so she doesn't shake the vehicle and alert Rivers and Faust, she snatches the fabric and pulls back, exposing where the lug wrench is stored.

"I trust the children are inside?"

Darcy freezes hearing the Full Moon Killer's voice. Faust kidnapped Hunter and Jennifer. They're here, wherever *here* is. More footsteps. Shoes scrape against a gravel road or driveway.

"They're inside the cabin," Faust says. "I secured them as you asked."

Thunder claps as Darcy pulls the lug wrench out of its compartment and clutches it to her chest. Eyes wide, she fights to control her breathing as she waits for Faust to unlock the trunk.

She'll only have one chance to strike out against Faust and Rivers before they overwhelm her. Only the element of surprise can save Darcy and the kids.

Keep your eyes down, she tells herself. After being inside the trunk, the sedan's beams will blind her if she looks into the light.

"You did well, Officer. As I promised, I'll make this worth your while."

"Look, I did what you wanted," Faust says, her voice trembling. "Why don't I leave you to it? The sooner I vanish—"

"You'll leave when I say you can."

"The police know I'm involved by now. They'll come looking for me."

"You removed the antenna, so they can't track the vehicle. It will be a long time before they figure out where

219

we are. I'll help you disappear, Officer. When I'm finished, no one will find you."

Faust pauses. Darcy heard the threat in Rivers' voice, and Faust must have too.

"I'll pull Gellar out of the trunk, if you want to check the cabin."

"Keep her locked up for now. I want to see the children, have some fun for a bit. After, Darcy will watch me butcher Hunter and Jennifer. As will you."

Faust kills the engine. Keys jangle as she pulls them from the ignition. When Faust returns to the back of the cruiser, Darcy crawls onto one knee, her torso bent forward beneath the trunk's low ceiling. She holds the lug wrench the ways she would a baseball bat, pulling the makeshift weapon back and ready to smash it against Faust's face when the trunk opens.

She hears the Full Moon Killer walk away. Silently, she prays Faust comes to her senses and flees while she can. Rivers will murder Faust as soon as he's done with Darcy. Faust must recognize this. But the officer guards the trunk as though paralyzed by fear. The cruiser rocks when a gust of wind pounds the frame. She can't hear Rivers anymore.

Darcy wills Faust to open the trunk. The officer got the best of her in the parking lot, but Darcy hadn't prepared for the sneak attack. With the lug wrench as a weapon, she'll take her chances against Faust, but she won't survive Faust and Rivers attacking her at-once. When the keys rattle at the back of the cruiser, she's sure Faust is about to open the trunk. Or flee in the cruiser and deal with Darcy later.

The madman's scream cuts through the approaching storm.

"You fool, they're not inside the cabin!"

Darcy almost fumbles the weapon. Jennifer and Hunter escaped. As long as her children survive, she'll accept whatever becomes of her.

"That's impossible." Faust's voice cracks. "I knotted them to the beam."

"Either you're incompetent, or someone let them out. In which case you were wrong about the cabin being a safe location. Is Gellar subdued in the trunk, or did you botch that too?"

"You know she's inside the trunk, you dropped her in."

"Officer, you won't let me down again," Rivers says, a warning in his tone.

The desperate officer drops her keys.

"I'll show you. Gellar hasn't made a sound since we locked her inside."

When the key scrapes inside the locking mechanism, Rivers shouts for Faust to wait. Too late. The trunk pops open, flooding the interior with the glare of the headlights. Before Faust realizes what's happening, Darcy leaps out of her crouch and swings the lug wrench. Iron meets flesh, the wrench bashing against Faust's cheek. Blood spurts out of the officer's mouth as her head whips around.

Darcy jumps from the trunk and hits the ground running before the Full Moon Killer can react. He shouts in fury behind her as she wills her legs to run. Her thighs cramp from her confinement. She powers through brush and bramble. Darcy tries to block out Faust's screams as Rivers tears her to pieces.

Then the officer goes quiet. The Full Moon Killer is coming for Darcy.

# CHAPTER TWENTY-EIGHT

Against Ames' protests, Julian slides into the last cruiser in the parking lot and turns on the siren and lights. Tires screech as he whips the vehicle around and stomps the gas pedal. He's dressed for a casual stroll on the beach, not for a manhunt. Driven by Agent Hensel, the FBI's SUV trails him. Ames rides with Hensel inside the SUV, as does Agent Fisher.

Hensel's voice booms out of the radio speaker as lightning tears a hole through the black clouds boiling overhead.

"We got nothing from the cell phone company."

Julian grits his teeth to keep from cursing.

"That's because Rivers removed the batteries or destroyed the phones. What do you have on the forest north of Smith Town?"

Julian hears Hensel lower the radio and speak into his phone. After a brief conversation with a technician at the Behavior Analysis Unit, Hensel returns to the radio.

"We narrowed the search to three hunting cabins in the vicinity which fit his needs—isolation and vacancy."

"Have you prioritized which one we're going after?"

"The most likely candidate is a small cabin on a dirt road, four miles off County Route 164. It hasn't been occupied in four years. Rivers would need someplace private to hide out while he went after Darcy and her kids."

And remote enough for him to murder three people without drawing attention. The wind hammers the vehicle and throws branches across the highway. Forcing himself to ease off the accelerator before he loses control of the cruiser, Julian pictures the road map. They're ten minutes from County Route 164, and the drive will be slow once they turn onto the dirt and gravel road leading through the forest. He's running out of time. The Full Moon Killer always stays two steps ahead of the police.

"I know the area, Agent Hensel. The drive will be rough going after we leave the highway."

"You been out that way, Officer?"

"Hunted during deer season last year. I'm sure there are cabins in the forest, but I never came across one. The woods grow thick once you get outside Smith Town. If the cabin is off the beaten path, I wouldn't have seen it from the road."

"Officer Haines, the second we turn off the main road, I want your lights and siren off. No point in announcing our presence."

"We're on the same page, Agent Hensel. Listen, there's a creek that cuts toward the coast paralleling the ridge line. It usually runs dry this time of year." Julian peeks at the black clouds overhead. They dip, spin, and churn, as though the gates of hell are about to open. "But when this storm hits, you don't want to be anywhere near the creek."

"Noted. I'll keep it in mind, Officer Haines."

When the radio goes silent, Julian loses himself in thought. He's at the mercy of regrets and self-doubt. Why did he allow Faust to drive Darcy home? He couldn't have predicted the betrayal, yet he should have protected Darcy as soon as he realized someone inside the department was working against them. He slams his hand against the steering wheel and catches his reflection in the window. The dashboard lights wash the features off his face and color it with pallor. The projection is a bizarre preview of his future, where the decades of facing the wicked side of humanity drain his life away.

A sudden gale rips the cruiser onto the shoulder. Gripping the wheel with both hands, he steers the vehicle into the lane and takes a deep breath. Sweat dots his brow, his stomach tumbling over the near crash.

"You okay up there, Officer?"

"I didn't see that coming, Agent Hensel. This storm is gonna be nasty."

"I've got the National Weather Service running decision support for us. They're worried about tornadoes. A funnel touched down outside Rocky Mount and leveled a gas station, and the system is gaining strength as it moves east."

"Wonderful. How much time do we have before the worst of the line hits?"

"Twenty minutes."

Julian lowers the radio and focuses on the road, surprised when the turn appears around a bend. Pumping the breaks, he tugs the cruiser onto the dirt road. With Agent Hensel's beams in his mirrors, Julian squints at the narrow, shadow-cloaked road. They're in God's country. No more than a handful of people live in this stretch of wilderness. The wind whips the forest into a frenzy. Limbs slap at the windshield as trees bend over the road, straining against the approaching storm. He jumps when a bolt of lightning strikes the earth a hundred feet ahead. Deafening thunder booms as he tries to clear the white imprint from his eyes.

A mile ahead, he slows when he spots a tree across the road. It's a young tree, the green, wilting leaves marking it as recently fallen. Snapped branches tell him another vehicle came this way. Faust?

"Tree across the road," Julian warns the FBI team. "Take it slow."

The deep treads of the new tires pull the cruiser over the tree. A branch latches on the undercarriage. He drags the branch until it breaks off. After Julian checks the mirrors, he urges Hensel to hurry as the black SUV bucks over the tree and jounces.

The storm hurls a curtain of rain across the windshield. Julian engages the wipers, worrying these trees won't stand up to one-hundred mph winds. Inside the forest, they won't see the storm until it's on top of them. The rain stops as quickly as it had begun, the thunderstorm holding back its fury for now.

"It's time, Officer Haines. Kill your lights."

Julian follows Hensel's order and turns the beams off. Now he can't see the road. The tree tunnel closes in on them, as if the forest means to claim Julian for its own.

A second turn materializes, and Julian swerves onto the path. The slumbering bulk of the cabin sits in a small clearing. Stopping the cruiser before Faust and Rivers spot him, Julian climbs down from the vehicle and shields his face from the wind. Hensel pulls the SUV behind a tree. A moment later the agent steps onto the path, flanked by Rivers and Detective Ames.

"I don't see a light," Ames says, bracing himself as the storm shoves him around, bullying the slim detective.

Worried they chose the wrong cabin or their theory about Rivers hiding out in the woods turned out to be false, Julian hopes someone comes up with a theory that will help them track down Darcy and her kids before it's too late.

"How do you want to do this?" Julian asks Hensel, deferring to the FBI agent to lead them forward.

"We'll move in pairs along the...what's that?"

Shielded by a stand of trees, a long shadow pokes into the driveway near the cabin. A flash of lightning illuminates the reflectors.

"That's Faust's cruiser," Julian says, dropping beside Hensel, who looks through binoculars as he kneels on the path.

Realizing they're at the right location, Julian's body tenses with pent up energy. He wants to storm the cabin now. Waiting becomes torture as his mind drifts to dark places, picturing what Rivers is doing to Darcy's family.

"There's something on the ground," Hensel says, pointing toward the back of the cruiser.

Long and athletic, Agent Fisher lifts his own binoculars as Ames squints over his shoulder.

"That's a body," Fisher says, his lips pulled back and grim.

Julian bounds forward, but Fisher grabs his arm.

"Not so fast, Officer. We go in slow. That's our best chance to rescue the family."

But whose body lies sprawled beside the cruiser? He'll never forgive himself if Darcy is already dead. Hensel hands him the binoculars, and Julian focuses on the leg sticking out from behind the cruiser. Darcy wore bluejeans. The prone figure wears black pants issued by the GCPD. He releases a held breath and hands the binoculars back to Hensel.

"Christ. I think that's Faust."

Fisher scans the cabin. He shakes his head.

"I can't see past the windows. Too dark."

"I'm going in," Julian says, checking his gun. "I'm not waiting to find out if Darcy's family is still alive."

Hensel reaches for Julian when a banshee scream rips through the forest. Recognizing the danger, Julian grabs Ames and throws him to the ground as Hensel and Fisher dive for cover. Julian covers his head a moment before the killer wind explodes through the forest.

# CHAPTER TWENTY-NINE

Climbing over fallen brush, Hunter looks over his shoulder and slows so his sister can catch up. Jennifer grabs hold of a tree and leans over to catch her breath.

"I can't keep up," Jennifer says. "You're running too fast."

Hunter studies the shadowed wilderness behind Jennifer and nods. They kept to a frantic pace, alternating between sprints and jogs as they put distance between them and the cabin. He knows they need to rest before one of them, certainly Jennifer, collapses from exhaustion. But they can't rest long. The Full Moon Killer could be anywhere in the dark, and Hunter doesn't trust the police.

"Where do you think we are?" Jennifer asks, gulping air.

Hunter rises out of his crouch and scans the forest. The trees stretch in all directions, confusing him. Then his eyes stop on a glimmer below a steep grade. He can't discern the gurgle over the gusting wind, but he recognizes the creek.

"We're north of Smith Town."

"How can you tell?"

He points to the flowing water.

"See the stream? It follows the terrain and leads to the ocean. We can't be more than ten miles from the shore. If we follow the creek, we'll pass through Smith Town."

Jennifer gives him a nod before a branch snaps behind them. Hunter grabs Jennifer and ducks beside the tree.

"There's somebody out there," Jennifer says, pressing her back against the trunk.

Wishing he had a weapon, Hunter searches the forest floor. Branches lie strewn about his feet. His eyes settle on a stout branch with a sharp point on one end, a limb which broke off the tree towering over their heads. The bough won't stand up to a larger foe, but he can use the point to stab and disable an attacker. He hauls the branch to his chest. Then he waits and listens. The growing wind trails through the forest with unbidden hunger, making it difficult to discern their pursuer's footsteps.

Hunter swings his head around the trunk and sees the shadow stomping through the brush and making a beeline toward their position. The Full Moon Killer. Jennifer's eyes meet Hunter's. No chance he can keep Jennifer calm once she sees the alarm on his face.

"Oh, God. It's him."

Hunter doesn't answer. Just closes his eyes and sends a prayer to anyone listening. He'll die fighting so long as Jennifer escapes. Nothing else matters but his sister's safety.

"Hunter, I'm scared."

He presses a finger to his lips. The footsteps go silent. Knowing the killer must have seen them, he searches for an escape route. He'll take his chances in a footrace with Michael Rivers so long as Jennifer keeps up. The creek. Leaping the water gives Hunter and Jennifer the best chance for escape provided neither falls and twists an ankle. Or worse. Though the storm hasn't hit yet, the water continues to rise. That tells Hunter the storm struck the higher terrain to the west and fed the creek. If they make it past the water, Hunter feels confident they can climb the ridge faster than the Full Moon Killer.

Fixing Jennifer with a glare, Hunter tilts his head toward the creek and urges his sister to run. Eyes wide, she shakes her head and grabs hold of Hunter's shirt. She won't leave without him.

Then the hairs stand on the back of Hunter's neck. Rivers is right behind them.

Hunter spins his body around the trunk, the tree limb raised above his head. Standing a full head taller than Hunter, the Full Moon Killer leers down at him, a lunatic grin painted to his face.

As the maniac lunges for his throat, Hunter swings the branch and strikes Michael Rivers's head. Taken by surprise, the Full Moon Killer's eyes roll back. He stumbles and catches himself on the tree as Jennifer circles around the other side with a rock in her hand. She bashes Rivers in the face at the same time Hunter jabs the jagged point of the branch into the killer's ribs.

Enraged but hurt, Michael Rivers bellows and swings at Hunter. The fist clips the boy's temple and sends him reeling. Clutching his ribcage, his hands stained red with blood, Michael Rivers staggers toward Hunter. A boot to the face snaps Hunter's head backward. The woodlands spin as he crashes against the forest floor.

As Hunter crawls toward cover, Rivers pulls the knife from its sheath. Even in the night, the wicked blade appears to glimmer. Hunter covers his face. The Full Moon Killer sweeps the blade toward Hunter's neck a moment before Jennifer slams the fist-sized rock against the maniac's skull. Though the blow only grazes Rivers, the impact is enough to divert the knife and drop the killer to his knees.

"Go!" Jennifer screams, racing around Rivers as he reaches for her.

He catches hold of her ankle, but she kicks free and hauls Hunter to his feet. His head cloudy from the attack, Hunter stumbles. Jennifer steadies him, but there's no time for Hunter to regain his senses. His hand cupping the back of his skull, Michael Rivers stands. Blood soaks his shirt over the stab wound.

Jennifer pulls Hunter toward the creek. He totters beside her until his legs stop shaking, and his head clears. The killer crashes through the brush, closing the distance. Hunter pictures the killer's hands inches from his neck as he races up from behind. He underestimated the man's speed and stamina. Hunter can't outrun him.

The Full Moon Killer is on top of them when the roar of a thousand freight trains tears through the forest. Hunter doesn't have time to process the sound before the wind strikes them from behind.

As though the heavens swung a hammer across the forest, the storm slams the trees and drives Hunter to the ground. Rain and hail pound his body, the water choking his lungs. He swings his head around and yells for Jennifer. Can't find her. The storm rages around him. Full trees topple and slam to the earth. Then he can't hear the falling trees anymore, only feels the ground shake from their impact. Visibility drops to zero, the woods enveloped by rain and an inhuman wind that lifts Hunter and smashes him down.

Lightning strokes and incinerates a pine tree. After

the blast, Hunter clutches his ears, unable to hear. Digging his hands into the sodden ground, averting his face as tree branches and debris rocket past his face, he crawls through the forest. Then he sees her. Jennifer lies against a swaying tree, her arms wrapped around the trunk. At any second the tree will fall, but it's all Jennifer can do to prevent the storm from lifting her to the clouds.

Another branch rips past Hunter and clips his brow. Blood rushes from the wound, but he won't stop until he reaches his sister. He's five feet from Jennifer when the storm's fury reaches another level. The forest flattens around them as the wind hauls Hunter out of the mud and throws him through the wind and rain. He lands against the creek bank. Can't breathe, can't see past the whirling rain and hail.

The muddy bank churns beneath him. He reaches out for a sapling, still searching for Jennifer, when the bank gives way to the flooded creek. Icy water grips his body and pulls him into its depths.

# CHAPTER THIRTY

The storm's inhuman roar fills Julian's ears as the wind snatches him off the ground and tosses him like a toy. His back smashes through brush, flesh tearing from his shoulders to his thighs. As he shields his face, he watches in awe and terror as the forest comes alive and arrows toward him. A boulder at the top of a ridge juts out of the ground. Fortunate he didn't land against the rock, Julian scrapes at the earth, keeping his head low as he ducks behind the boulder. He searches for the two federal agents and Detective Ames. One second they crouched beside him, the next the storm crushed the forest and whipped them into the air.

The screech of nails ripping from wood brings his head around. The cabin explodes and launches skyward. A funnel-shaped cloud touches down, swallows a chunk of earth, and whips the cabin's debris into a whirling frenzy. Julian ducks before the roof slices the air and crashes against the ridge. Behind the twister, hail the size of golf balls pelt Julian. Soaked to the bone, he covers his head from flying debris.

Then the storm abates. He can still hear the wind

tearing down the hillside, flattening every tree in its path. An eerie, dead calm settles over the wreckage that was once a forest. To his shock, the sky turns crystal clear. Off to the east lightning ignites green and purple clouds.

When he crawls from behind the rock, sharp pain brings his hand to his thigh. He winces, feeling the branch piercing his leg. His hand comes away slick and red. Twisting his head so he gets a better look at the wound, Julian spots the dagger-like branch sticking out of his thigh. He realizes pulling the stick out of his leg will increase the blood flow, but he can't move until he does. Pulling the stick proves futile. It's wedged deep into flesh and muscle.

"Ames!"

His voice echoes across the forest and returns to him. When the detective doesn't answer, he calls out to Fisher and Hensel. No replies come.

Patting his hip, he's relieved to find the holster and gun attached. But the radio is nowhere to be found.

Julian wrestles the sodden shirt off his back and winds it into a rope. Placing the cloth between his teeth, he bites down and tugs the stick. After loosening the branch, it pops free with white-hot agony, the sharp end tainted red as if he'd stabbed a vampire with a stake. He bends over and wretches when the pain overwhelms him. Dizzy, he staggers to his feet and clutches the bubbling wound. Unwinding the shirt, he wraps it around the puncture wound and limps across what was once a property line. Except for a few broken planks and glass shards, there's no sign a cabin ever existed.

Cupping his hands around his mouth, he shouts for the others. Still nothing. Dread turns his stomach. He can't believe he's alive as he stumbles amid the wreckage. Darcy and her kids were in the forest when the storm hit. Desperation pushes him to walk faster. With most of the trees flattened, he's disoriented and can't decide which way to walk. Peering over his shoulder, he scans the wreckage for Faust's cruiser and sees it a hundred yards from where she'd parked, chewed up and deformed into an accordion shape. There's no sign of Faust's body.

Each step causes Julian's leg to throb. He'd hoped the thigh would loosen as he walked, but moving only makes the pain worse. Turning in a circle, he tries to remember where they'd parked. Fallen trees cover the road, making it difficult to retrace his path. Stepping over an elm tree, he spies his cruiser lying on its side, a huge limb puncturing the windshield. The FBI SUV survived the storm. Julian recalls tales of tornadoes destroying entire neighborhoods but leaving a backyard swing set untouched. Perhaps the same unexplainable fate spared the SUV. The wind blew the side windows out, but the windshield appears intact. Driving out of here won't be easy with half the forest across the road, and the SUV will be useless to him unless he locates Hensel, who had the keys.

Unless he hot wires the SUV.

Either way, he's not leaving the woods until he finds Darcy, Jennifer, and Hunter. Faith they survived pulls him forward, keeps him moving. Debris trips him, and he lands on his palms. With a start, Julian realizes he narrowly missed impaling his hand on a nail sticking up from a plank. Pushing himself up to his knees, wary of hidden dangers, he clutches his thigh and follows the terrain downhill. Knowledge of the terrain proves invaluable. Though he doesn't recognize landmarks, following the slope will take him into Smith Town. Would Darcy use the same logic? She's resourceful. Yes, Darcy would head toward Smith Town and civilization.

He's halfway down the slope when he hears the water. The warning he gave Hensel about thunderstorms flooding the creek proves to be an understatement. He's seen the stage high before, but nothing like this. Beyond the snapped and leveled trees, the water surges through the creek bed, turning an ugly brown as it scours mud and chews the banks. Large enough to kill, debris rockets down the stream. How will he cross the water? He'll need a stroke of luck — a stout tree bridging the creek.

Before he moves too far down the slope, he spins and calls out to Ames and the agents again. He gives them a full minute to reply before he resumes walking, grief squeezing his chest.

He approaches the stream and stands fifty feet back. The water laps over the banks now, moving in a blur. Chunks of earth break free and plunge into the water. Studying the creek, he searches for a way across. No luck. With no other choice, he follows the racing waters, keeping a healthy distance. One wrong step beside the bank, and the creek will sweep him to his grave. The creek weaves snake-like through the woods. And it keeps growing wider. Smaller streams branch off the main creek and form new waterways through the forest. He gives them a wide berth as they expand with frightening speed.

As he rounds a bend, he hears a high-pitched sound from downstream. At this distance he can't discern the origin, but he's certain it was a human cry. Darcy? Limping faster, Julian pushes through a tangle of brush and plunges ankle-deep into a newly formed stream. The cold shocks him. Even this far from the creek, the water tugs and rips at his leg, striving to pull him under. Spray wets his face and beads on his bare chest.

Julian spares a glance at the shirt around his leg. Blood soaks the cloth. He needs a proper bandage to clot the wound. He'll require stitches. Many of them. He forgets his leg when the sound comes again. This time he's certain it's a female calling for help.

I'm coming, Darcy.

# CHAPTER THIRTY-ONE

Moments before the storm struck the forest, Darcy heard a yell ring out over the next ridge. She'd been running for too long, clothes soaked with sweat as she searched for a recognizable landmark. She'd raced toward the sound, recognizing her children's voices. Her heart pounded with relief that she'd found them alive, but the scream told her Michael Rivers had discovered her children first.

Now she sprawls beneath a pine, the surrounding trees bending earthward. The storm's roar is unlike anything she's heard in her life. Monstrous trunks snap in half, while others lurch off the ground like the dead rising.

As fast as the thunderstorm struck, it races east and leaves Darcy in a pit of mud. One pant leg is torn to the knee and hanging by a flap. Bits of stone and tree bark impale the exposed flesh, her hair soiled and matted to her face. She struggles to her knees and tumbles face first into the mud. Coughing, she spits the muck from her mouth and hisses. Pain envelopes her body. Thankful the wounds seem to be superficial, she struggles to her feet and leans against one of the few trees left standing.

The banshee wind lashes at the coast now. Darcy pictures the mayhem in Genoa Cove and Smith Town. All around her, the forest lies ravaged. Nobody could have lived through the storm.

Yet she had. Somehow.

And she needs to believe Hunter and Jennifer found a way to survive too.

She presses the heel of her hand against her forehead. It comes away slicked with dirt and blood. Her head wants to explode.

Remembering the Full Moon Killer gets Darcy moving. She limps through the war torn woods, angling toward the source of the scream. The problem is everything looks the same. Snapped pines. The deciduous trees stripped of their leaves and razed. Water flows over shattered stumps, through new divots sliced into the earth, and over rock, following the slope toward the creek. Her sneakers make squishing noises as the mud engulfs her ankles. The effort required to walk leaves her breathless, lungs heavy, as she searches for any sign that her children lived through the storm.

She turns in a circle with no idea where she is. Before she doubles back, a distant yell brings her head around. There—down the slope. That sounded like Jennifer.

Darcy half-limps, half-runs across the broken landscape, worried she imagined the voice. Then it comes again, and this time she's sure it's Jennifer's voice calling, "Mom!"

"I'm coming, baby!"

She huffs and wipes blood from her eyes, wondering where it came from. Gashes mar her scalp and face from where the devil winds peppered her face with bits of forest. Her legs want to give out, but the yells force her to soldier on. When she descends a ridge, the creek opens up to her at the bottom. Choked with water sloshing over the banks, the raging creek throws huge limbs and saplings downstream. She swivels her head back and forth, looking for her daughter, until Jennifer calls again.

Darcy spots Jennifer. Her daughter lies flat on her stomach, her arms extended over the water. Darcy's heart stops. Hunter clutches a fallen tree bridging the banks. The creek barrels over his shoulders and neck, close to choking off his air supply. But the greater danger is the water will rip Hunter away. Though Hunter is a powerful swimmer, only divine intervention will save her son if he loses his grip.

"I can't reach him!"

Jennifer's eyes brim with tears as she yells back at Darcy. Her face holds a mask of determination Darcy has never seen. To Darcy's horror, her daughter slides forward and puts her hand out for Hunter. She's too close to the water. Another foot and the creek will drag her into its depths.

"No, Jennifer! Get away from the water."

But Jennifer doesn't listen. She inches toward the flood, the level rising with each heartbeat. When Darcy reaches Jennifer, she grabs her daughter by the ankles and pulls her back. Jennifer protests and tries to scramble back, but Darcy keeps hold of her until she stops fighting.

Darcy looks down the bank and spots a long tree limb impaled in the mud. It's stout enough that it stands a chance of supporting Hunter's weight. Jennifer follows Darcy's vision and rushes to the limb. Together, they try to yank the branch free of the mud. It's stuck. With no other choice, Darcy navigates the treacherous bank and stomps on the end of the branch, breaking it free. In doing so she lost two feet of length, but the limb still might be long enough to reach Hunter.

"Hold on, Hunter! When the branch is close enough, grab hold and I'll drag you in."

The roar of the water smothers her voice. Hunter, his eyes drooping in exhaustion, nods in understanding. Darcy edges down the bank and slips in the mud. Her legs fly out from under her. The air rushes from her chest when she lands on her back. As though it senses her vulnerability, the water surges up the bank and swallows her up to her thighs. Even with the bulk of her weight out of the water, the creek gropes her, tugging hungrily at her shins and ankles. The frigid water sets her teeth to chattering as Jennifer leans over the bank and grabs Darcy's wrist. As Jennifer struggles to pull her mother out of the water, Darcy digs her sneakers into the mud and walks backward.

Darcy feels winded and shaken when Jennifer hauls her out of danger. But there's no time to rest, not with Hunter's grip beginning to fail. Snatching up the broken limb, Darcy descends the bank where dozens of new saplings sprout from the mud. The small trees give Darcy enough purchase to dig her sneakers into the bank and approach the water's edge. Spray coats her sodden body.

She reaches the tree bridging the two banks. Though it's wide enough to support her weight if she crawls over the water, she's not strong enough to pull Hunter out of the creek from the angle. There's a better chance he'll tug her over the side, and they'll both shoot downstream. Instead, she uses the tree for leverage and wraps one arm around the trunk, the other extending the branch toward Hunter.

His eyes close. Then his head bobs underwater.

"Hunter, no!"

The water's chill jolts Hunter awake. In his panic, he almost loses his grip on the tree. As he calls out to Darcy, the creek gushes over his face and chokes the words away. The water continues to rise. A glance up the creek stops Darcy's heart. A coffin-sized trunk tumbles into the water and rockets downstream, large enough the crush bone.

When Darcy feels a tug on the branch, she pulls her attention back to the water. Hunter has one hand on the branch, the other on the tree as the water rips him from one side to the other. If he lets go of the tree to grab the branch, the creek will claim Hunter, and Darcy will lose her son. With time running out for Hunter, Darcy risks another step forward. Her leg plunges shin-deep into the creek. Jennifer descends the bank and wraps her arms around Darcy's hips. But the broken trunk is hurtling down the creek, heading for Hunter. The jagged end pierces a dam formed by fallen limbs and mud and bursts through the obstruction, clearing the stream and propelling a wave toward Darcy and Hunter.

"There's no time! Grab the branch and let me pull you in!"

Hunter spares a look at the massive stump shooting at him. Letting go of the tree, he swipes at the branch, misses, and goes under again. Darcy leaps forward, now knee-deep in the creek. Hunter's bodyweight pulls at the limb. Good. He hasn't let go. But his body is underwater now, legs arrowed downstream with his hands wrapped around the branch. The stump blasts through another obstruction, now a mere hundred feet from them and coming fast. The creek tries to swallow Darcy as well. Jennifer's strength is the only thing preventing Darcy from losing her balance and going under.

Hunter's head rises out of the water. Still holding the

tree limb, he turns his face so the water doesn't choke off his breathing. With a heave, Darcy drags Hunter toward the creek bed. From the corner of her eye, she spots the stump bulleting toward Hunter. Another tug and Darcy pulls Hunter onto the bank a split-second before the stump roars past and explodes against the tree.

The jolt knocks Darcy backward. She slips on the bank, but Jennifer is there to grab her shoulders before the creek sucks her in. Face down in the mud, Hunter sprawls beside her. His chest heaves as he coughs up brown water. Darcy worries about bacteria, but they'll cross that road when they reach it. Darcy requires Jennifer's assistance as she yanks Hunter away from the water. Now they both lie at the base of the ridge. She stares up at the sky, the water's roar deafening. Thunder growls over the ocean while the clouds scatter overhead. A diamond mine of stars glitter, casting silver light on the war torn forest. Darcy's eyes stop on the full moon.

Branches snap underfoot. Michael Rivers is coming.

# CHAPTER THIRTY-TWO

Darcy and Jennifer urge Hunter to his feet. Michael Rivers stumbles into the moonlight, his face a horror mask of bloody gashes, eyes flared with hatred. A tear in his jeans reveals another laceration as he limps forward, his shirt hanging in tatters. The knife dangles from his hand.

Throwing herself in front of her children, Darcy shields them with her body. The Full Moon Killer's lips curl into a grin.

"Darccccyyyyy…tonight is the night."

Michael Rivers lifts the knife. The steel reflects his face.

"Stay away from my children, Michael."

"Or what? You're in no position to stop me. I'll gut your children first, and you'll watch. I owe you so much."

The Full Moon Killer drags himself a step closer as Darcy retreats up the ridge. The creek traps her to the right and promises swift death should she attempt to cross. She backs up another step when Rivers closes in. Run up the ridge? Even in their exhausted states, she doubts the Full Moon Killer can keep pace with Darcy and Jennifer. Hunter is the problem. Her son can barely stand, and neither Darcy nor Jennifer has the strength to carry Hunter.

Wobbling on his feet, Hunter moves around Darcy to defend his family. She shifts her body to block him.

"Oh, let him through. Hunter and I were having so much fun earlier."

The blade slices the air and draws a thin ribbon into Darcy's shoulder. A taunt. Had he wanted to kill her, Rivers would have done so. He jabs the knife tip at Darcy's chest and backs her into Hunter.

Before Darcy can stop her daughter, Jennifer darts past her mother. When the Full Moon Killer turns on her, Jennifer grabs a handful of mud and stone and whips it into his eyes. Blinded, Rivers doubles over and tries to clear his vision. Grabbing Jennifer's arm, Darcy pulls her children up the ridge. As Darcy feared, they can only run as fast as Hunter, who lags. He needs a doctor's care. Darcy worries about his history of concussions and the head injuries he suffered tonight at the hands of the Full Moon Killer and the flood.

Shooting a look over her shoulder, Darcy watches as Michael Rivers wipes the grit from his eyes and peers up the ridge. The moonlight catches his grinning face a moment before he limps after them.

"Run, Hunter."

Darcy's son summons the strength to quicken his pace, but he'll sap his strength reserves soon, climbing the ridge. On one good leg, Rivers closes in on them. Jennifer throws Hunter's arm over her shoulder and supports her struggling brother. Darcy does the same, but Hunter's legs give out. As Hunter collapses, the Full Moon Killer's footsteps race up behind them.

Screaming, Darcy turns and thrusts her shoulder into

Rivers' belly. The Full Moon Killer's eyes widen, not expecting Darcy's attack. She drives the air from his chest and snaps his head back. Gravity does the rest. The killer tumbles down the hillside. Darcy's shoulder throbs as she pushes herself to her feet. Pain shooting down her arm tells Darcy she separated the shoulder, yet she bought Jennifer enough time to haul Hunter to his feet.

Before Darcy scrambles to her children, moonlight shimmers off steel and reveals the maniac's blade strewn against the ridge. She eyes the knife and calculates the distance between Rivers and the weapon. He's closer, but Rivers hasn't regained his senses yet.

Darcy crawls after the knife. His eyes scrambled, Rivers reads Darcy's intention. Her hand closes over the hilt a split-second before he grabs her wrist. Cursing, she swipes the knife at his face. The tip scrapes his cheek and carves through flesh. Still grasping her wrist, Rivers twists her hand back. She refuses to drop the knife until her wrist cracks. With a cry, she releases the blade. It lands against the weedy ridge. Her eyes return to the killer. An insane smile on his face, Rivers whips his head forward and crushes her skull. Her vision goes black. She loses her balance.

Then she's on her back, the stars and moon swirling overhead as the hillside tilts. Jennifer yells at Darcy to get away. Her body refuses to obey her foggy brain. A black silhouette against the sky, the Full Moon Killer rises up and blots out the light. When the maniac crouches for the knife, a man's voice echoes off the top of the ridge.

"Freeze, Rivers! Step away from the knife!"

She knows that voice. It's Julian. He's alive.

Footsteps descend the ridge as Julian edges down the hillside. He moves sideways to keep his balance, the gun trained on the Full Moon Killer. But where are the others? Darcy's heart clenches with the knowledge Julian would never leave Hensel, Fisher, and Ames, if they were still alive. Clearing her head, Darcy twists to her side and scrambles toward her children. Hunter stands beside Jennifer, but it's clear his legs won't support his weight without Jennifer's help.

The killer chuckles, a sound like fire lapping at parchment paper.

"What a surprise. Your cop hero tries to save the day. I wonder what his true intentions are, Darcy. He worked for Bronson Severson, you know? The same man I employed. Are you sure you trust Julian Haines?"

Darcy inches toward Hunter and Jennifer, never taking her eyes off Michael Rivers.

"I said 'step away from the knife.' Put your hands in the air where I can see them, Rivers."

The Full Moon Killer grins at Julian as the police officer moves down the hill. Debris trips him, and Julian fights to keep his balance. Seeing his opportunity, Rivers lunges for the knife. He stops when Julian rights himself and trains the gun at his head. Rivers retreats a step, his head tilted as he glares at the officer. After Julian descends the hillside, he places himself in front of Darcy's children.

"It's over, Rivers. Take one step back from the knife and keep your hands in the air."

"Do you really think he'll keep you safe?" Rivers leers at Darcy. "Officer Faust served me, as did Bronson Severson. I purchased two officers this time. Isn't that right, Julian?"

As Darcy pushes herself off the ground, Julian shifts his body to keep a sight line on Rivers. Trepidation tugs behind Darcy's ear. Yes, Julian volunteered at Bronson's gymnasium. And he partnered with Faust. That's two of Julian's acquaintances who sold their souls to the devil. Why not Julian too?

No, he's different. Julian Haines hasn't left Darcy's side since the nightmare began. If the killer's attempts to bribe Julian had been successful, the officer wouldn't hold the him at gunpoint. Rivers is bluffing and desperate.

"I've heard enough of your lies," Darcy says. She stands halfway between Julian and Rivers, angled to the side so Julian can keep the serial killer in his sights. "You're not fooling me tonight."

The murderer's grin contorts to a scowl.

"None of you will live to see sunrise."

Digging into his pocket with a free hand, Julian brings out a zip tie.

"Michael Rivers, you're under arrest for the murder of Lindsey Doler. You have the right to remain silent and refuse to answer questions…"

As Julian reads the serial killer his Miranda rights, Rivers lifts his chin and howls with laughter. At that moment, Darcy sees the mass murderer as a demon walking the earth. Immortal. She'll never be free of the Full Moon Killer. The law is on his side. After Julian clasps the zip tie around the killer's wrists and leads them out of the wilderness, Rivers will return to prison. The nightmare will never end.

It won't be long before Michael Rivers uses his vast, hidden wealth to hire another serial killer. Darcy will forever look over her shoulder, waiting for the knife that will end her life. And she'll accept death over a lifetime of fear.

But she won't allow another night to pass with Hunter and Jennifer not feeling safe. What sort of life awaits them? Even behind bars, Michael Rivers will destroy any chances Jennifer and Hunter have at happiness.

It ends now.

When Julian maneuvers toward Rivers with the zip tie in his hand, Darcy elbows her way in front of him.

"What are you doing? Darcy, you need to move."

Someone cries out behind her. It's Hunter yelling at Darcy to step away. Michael Rivers narrows his eyes. His lips peel back and reveal red-stained teeth. Does he know what she intends?

Ignoring Julian's pleas, Darcy shakes off Julian's hand and lunges for the knife. But the Full Moon Killer stands closer to the weapon. He beats her to the knife and clasps his hand over the hilt. Lunging at Darcy, he's stunned when he realizes she never meant to grab the weapon. His eyes widen as she rolls out of harms way, every mud-crusted cut on her body screaming as her flesh stretches. Rivers slices the blade through empty air, missing his target. Three shots to the chest stop the serial killer in his tracks.

Michael Rivers locks his gaze on Darcy as he staggers backward. She fooled him, suckered him in. He took the bait and attacked, leaving Julian no choice but to defend Darcy. The Full Moon Killer drops to one knee. He touches his chest and examines the blood on his hand, confused. Then his strength gives out. Rivers falls to his back. He stares up at the glowering moon as though it betrayed him. He blinks rapidly, his breaths ragged as lifeblood soaks his tattered shirt.

The killer's eyes flutter when Julian kneels beside him, the gun trained on Rivers.

"Move back, Darcy."

"I need to be sure he's dead."

"Give it a few minutes and he will be."

Cautiously, Jennifer and Hunter move toward Darcy and Julian. Cricket songs grow louder among the ravaged forest. Below the ridge, the creek recedes inside its banks, the torrent having broken through a dam of tree limbs and debris left behind by the storm.

"Shoot him again," Darcy says, studying the killer's wounds.

"He's dying. Leave him be."

"I've seen too many horror movies where the hero should have fired one more shot."

Julian raises his eyebrow and turns his attention back to Rivers. The killer's breath rattles through his chest. He can't hold his eyes open.

Then the breathing stops, and there's only the night sounds and the surging creek. Still supporting her brother, Jennifer leans into Julian. The officer drapes his arms over Darcy and Jennifer.

"Let's find our way out of here."

# CHAPTER THIRTY-THREE

The emergency room doctor slides the curtain shut, the snick drawing Darcy awake. She grabs her neck and focuses her eyes, searching for the departed doctor, then she shifts the uncomfortable chair beside the cot to face Julian. Embarrassed she fell asleep while the doctor patched Julian back together, she rubs the damp chill off her arms, the dry blanket over her shoulders doing little to eliminate the chilling memories of last night. While she dozed, she kept picturing Hunter in the creek—the water rising past his neck, the boy's pale flesh, and the look of panic in his eyes as his grip on the tree failed.

Julian sprawls on the cot, impatiently awaiting discharge. It took twelve stitches to close his wound, but he'd minimized blood loss by wrapping the shirt around his thigh. His foot sticks out from beneath the blanket. Darcy pulls the blanket down.

"Stop mothering me. I'll live."

Unlike Hensel. Darcy can't conceal the hurt in her eyes. Julian stumbles toward an apology, but her eyes tell him she needs silence.

A search team uncovered the bodies of the two FBI

agents a quarter mile from the cabin. Swept into the cyclone, Hensel and Fisher never stood a chance. The debris probably killed the agents before the storm tossed them into the forest.

Hensel. A tear follows the contours of her face and burns against scrapes and puncture wounds. Four years ago, Darcy and her partner began their investigation of the Full Moon Killer. Hensel never got to see the conclusion to the story. Michael Rivers forever altered the lives of Darcy and her family, and cost Hensel his.

She rubs her eyes. Agent Fisher had a wife and three children.

"I can't believe Ames survived," Julian says, looking out the window. The first orange glow bubbles up from the east, portending a sunny day and an end to the brutal heatwave. "Someone upstairs must have looked after him."

"Someone looked after all of us. Did the weather service declare the storm a tornado?"

"I saw the funnel. Half the forest vanished. Don't think I'll ever forget that nightmare."

A search team of GCPD and Smith Town officers rescued Ames. The storm had launched the detective over the SUV and into the woods. Sheer luck saved him. Two massive oaks toppled, and Ames landed in the shadow of the fallen trees, shielded from the storm. But he sustained a broken arm and a gash down his back. Blood loss prompted the doctors to give Ames a transfusion. Last Hensel had heard, Ames was upstairs and recovering, but it would be days before the hospital released him.

When the curtain parts, Darcy glances up. Hunter peeks his head inside.

"Is it safe to come in?"

Julian motions Hunter into the room, and Jennifer

follows on her brother's heels. The grin on Julian's face warms Darcy's heart. He's great with the kids.

A bandage circles Hunter's head and covers a cut which required two stitches to close. Thankfully, her son didn't sustain another concussion. How he avoided a brain injury, she doesn't understand. For the first time since last fall, Darcy didn't feel trepidation over her kids waiting in the hallway while the doctor worked on Julian. Darcy and her family are finally safe, the Full Moon Killer gone from their lives.

Hunter wobbles as he sits down, his energy spent after surviving the flood, another miracle Darcy gives thanks for.

"Are you guys almost ready to go home?" Darcy asks.

Jennifer shares a look with her brother.

"Home-home?"

"Why not? We don't have anything to be afraid of anymore, unless you count our nosy neighbors."

"So that means you aren't moving us to Charlotte?"

Darcy shakes her head. Though she has every reason to leave Genoa Cove and put the village behind her, memories of the last year will follow them wherever they land. Jennifer requires additional therapy, and it won't hurt Hunter to talk to someone too. The worst thing Darcy can do is uproot her children and steal them from their friends. But after Jennifer graduates high school in a few years, all bets are off. By then Darcy will relish a fresh start with neighbors who accept her as one of their own.

"But all of my stuff is at Julian's." Hunter says. "We just packed. Perhaps it would be better if we stayed a few more days. You know, to rest up before we move again."

Darcy swings her head to Julian, who displays the same smile he's worn since the kids joined them.

"My home is your home," says Julian, flinching when he shifts his leg. "You're welcome to stay as long as you like. Besides, I had my heart set on ordering pizzas again tonight and watching a movie."

"What do you think?" Hunter asks Jennifer.

She shrugs, but the curl of her lips belies her indifference.

"Fine with me. I don't plan to do anything but sleep for the next week. I'm in no rush to get back."

Fat chance, Darcy thinks. She gives Jennifer until Kaitlyn's next text arrives, spurring a miraculous recovery. Then Jennifer will beg to attend some party her friend threw together. Darcy's head swims with worries about underage drinking, boys, and the GCPD raiding their party. And she's fine with that. She welcomes normal parental worries.

On queue, Hunter dips his hands into his pockets. He wears a pair of blue jeans one of the officers retrieved from the kids' room at Julian's house. The officer also grabbed two pairs of sweat pants for Darcy and Julian. Julian's sweat pants hang loose on Darcy. The scent of his laundry detergent wafts off the cloth. She's already learned to associate the pleasing smells of the officer's soaps and colognes with his beautiful face. Feeling her cheeks bloom, Darcy clears her throat.

"What am I going to do about getting another phone?" Hunter asks, slumping in his chair.

While Jennifer's phone is still on the coffee table in Julian's living room, Hunter had his phone in his pocket when Faust and Rivers abducted them. Unless the police discover where Rivers disposed of their belongings, Hunter will need a new phone.

"We don't have the money right now." Darcy raises

her hand when Hunter opens his mouth. "But there's still a chance the police will locate your phone. And if they don't, maybe we can work something out. Call it an early birthday gift?"

Hunter winks at his sister.

"Sounds like a deal, Mom."

When the orderly returns with Julian's discharge papers, Hunter helps the police officer off the cot. It takes Julian several ginger steps before he can put weight on the leg without hissing. Darcy winces, imagining the stitches tugging under Julian's sweat pants.

The drive back to Julian's house feels different. Darcy doesn't sense hatred when pedestrians' eyes follow them down the road, and the shadows don't prickle her skin with goosebumps. Inside Julian's little home, the sun cascades through the windows, the warmth comforting rather than suffocating. Julian even cranks open a casement window in the kitchen to let the breeze inside, and nobody bats an eyelash.

Julian's mail lies scattered on the living room floor, and one of the end tables is on its side, the glass cracked down the center. While Julian gathers the letters into a pile and sets them beside the television, Hunter hoists the broken end table and carries it to the foyer where Jennifer holds the door open. After setting the table curbside, Hunter returns to the house and instinctively turns the deadbolt on the door.

"No, don't," Julian says. He glances at Darcy for confirmation, and she nods back at him. "Go ahead and slide it open to the screen. I can't remember the last time I let natural light inside."

Julian's phone rings before he can sit down. He frowns at the screen, and Darcy moves beside him on the couch.

"It's the sheriff's department," Julian says.

"Do you want privacy? I can take the kids into the kitchen."

"Don't worry," Jennifer says. "We're gonna crash for a few hours, if that's okay."

As Hunter and Jennifer turn out of the living room, Julian answers and puts the phone on speaker.

"This is Julian."

"Officer Haines, this is Deputy Mahorn at the County Sheriff's Department. Not sure if you remember me, but we worked the Kirkwood case together last summer."

"Sure, I remember you, Deputy. You do exemplary work. Just so you know, I've got you on speaker phone. Darcy Gellar is in the room with me."

Mahorn pauses before he continues.

"I guess that's fine, provided you're okay with me sharing details about Officer Faust. I understand Ms. Gellar profiled Michael Rivers for the FBI, so she'll want to hear this too."

At the mention of his former partner's name, Julian sits forward. Moving too fast, he grabs the back of his thigh.

"No secrets here, Deputy."

"How are you holding up, Officer? I heard you spent the morning in the emergency room."

"Just a few stitches. It seems all the king's men really could put Humpty Dumpty back together again."

Mahorn chuckles. A passing car in the background tells Darcy Mahorn is outside, possibly at Faust's residence.

"With three members of your department

incapacitated, the GCPD called us in to handle the investigation. I'm running point on the Faust case."

Julian wipes his hand across his mouth.

"What have you learned?"

"Does the name Dawn Chambers mean anything to you?"

Julian squints his eyes.

"No. Should it?"

"We found a driver's license and passport inside Faust's bedroom dresser. It appears she intended to change her name and disappear soon. We traced Dawn Chambers and discovered a recent home purchase on the Oregon coast. No mortgage. She paid cash."

Darcy sets her hand on Julian's and squeezes.

"So we were correct about Rivers funneling money to Faust. What else?"

"Well, you might want to sit down for this one."

Julian shares a look with Darcy.

"I'm already seated. After last night, it's gonna take a lot to shake me, Deputy."

"As you might imagine, we're working closely with the FBI. As far as they're concerned, Officer Faust got two of their agents killed, and they want a conclusion to this case just as bad as we do."

"Go on."

"The FBI discovered an oddity in Clarice Faust's time line. Eight years ago, she dropped out of college during her junior semester. Records from Pace University indicate Faust was on the Dean's list every semester and active in campus groups, including the Future Police Officer's Club. Then she quit school without warning and didn't return until a year later to finish her degree."

"Could be she ran out of funds. Faust never struck

me as someone who came from money."

"That's a logical conclusion, and her family ranked on the lower third of middle class, but we think there's more to the story. Beginning in her sophomore year, Faust started dating a graduate student named Everett Banks. The university expelled Banks after two females came forward and accused Banks of stalking."

Darcy's stomach flutters. She rests her elbows on her knees and leans over the phone.

"Strange as that is, the FBI searched its data bank and couldn't find any record of an Everett Banks. It's as if his life began and ended at Pace. But we contacted one of the girls Banks stalked. Turns out she lived in the same residence hall as Faust. The girls became friends. Officer Haines, she had a picture of Banks. I believe you'll recognize the boy."

Julian's temple twitches.

"Can you send the picture to me, Deputy?"

"It's on the way. Check your email."

"Hold on, Deputy. I'm loading it now."

Julian pauses the conversation and opens his email. Finding the message from Mahorn, Julian clicks on the attachment. It takes a long time for the scanned photograph to load, then it fills the screen. Swiping at his phone, Julian zooms in on the photograph. Darcy immediately recognizes a younger Faust from the picture. The girl wears her hair longer than she had as a police officer, and a handful of pimples dot her forehead.

But it's the shark's grin of the man beside Faust that stops Darcy's heart. It's Michael Rivers.

"Jesus," Julian says, pushing the hair out of his eyes. "She knew him all this time."

"Not only that, but the girl who shared the picture

contends Faust never would have dropped out of school on a whim. Faust wanted to be a cop. She had the grades and recommendations to push her as far as she wanted to go."

"So why did she drop out?"

"The friend believed Banks...or Rivers...raped her. When Faust returned to school the next year, she'd changed. She became distant and had a hard edge to her nobody could understand. Even her parents couldn't figure out what caused the change. Officer Haines, do you think Clarice Faust was the Full Moon Killer's first victim?"

The question dangles in the air and never gets answered.

Darcy leans back and closes her eyes. It makes sense now. Like many serial killers, it took time for Rivers to develop a taste for murder. He'd begun with abduction, control, and rape. Rivers altered Faust, just as he did Amy Yang, Darcy, and every woman he touched. Something about the FBI investigation of Rivers never sat right with Darcy. Studying Rivers's childhood, she never uncovered the telltale signs of a budding serial killer—violent outbursts, cruelty to animals. The expected tendencies should have manifested before his high school and college years, yet records indicated Rivers never attended college before he became an electrician and began kidnapping girls in his van. His metamorphosis into a psychopath occurred organically, as if he was the Grand Guignol's version of an autodidact. Or simply the devil's hand.

Did he change his name to Everett Banks at Pace to cover a criminal past?

Darcy touches Julian's shoulder. Worry creases his brow. How many lives did Rivers ruin?

# CHAPTER THIRTY-FOUR

"There's something important I want to tell you after we get to Harpy's."

Standing in the doorway of her house near the cove, Darcy slips her heels on and checks her hair in the mirror. Julian twirls the key ring around his finger. There's a bounce to Julian's demeanor that Darcy hasn't seen since that fatal night in the forest two weeks ago. He still limps whenever the leg wound tightens, but he's back to his old self, and Darcy finds his enthusiasm infectious. She worries the hem of her skirt and wonders, as she had the first time Julian took her to Harpy's, if the skirt shows too much leg. They're eating at an upscale seafood restaurant on the Genoa Cove pier, not hitting the clubs.

"Stop fretting," Julian says. "You look beautiful."

Darcy doesn't feel beautiful. She's a jumbled mess of nerves.

"I'm heading out with Julian for a few hours," Darcy calls down the hall. Hunter grunts in acknowledgment from behind his bedroom door, a surefire sign he's immersed in a multi-player Xbox game. Jennifer is at Kaitlyn's, another source of Darcy's consternation. She can smell a teenager party from a mile away. She swings her gaze back to the gorgeous man leaning in the entryway. "So what's so important that you have to tell me at Harpy's?"

"Patience, grasshopper. We'll talk over dinner."

Julian's car speeds out of the neighborhood. Darcy had caught her neighbors peeking through their windows while Julian helped her into the passenger seat, but Genoa Cove turned quiet after the Michael Rivers nightmare ended.

Late afternoon sun sparkles off the water when Julian pulls his car into Harpy's parking lot. Breakers slosh against the bordering beach, sunbathers dotting the sand as children leap through waves. The wind carries the scents of salt and tanning lotion, the breeze a friendly hand that pulls the hair back from her eyes.

In a stroke of luck, they score a coveted outdoor table on the deck. An umbrella shields Darcy and Julian from the North Carolina sun, and the sea breeze keeps the temperature comfortable. Julian wears a knowing grin as he orders appetizers. What's the big secret? Darcy does her best not to notice and spends a long time deciding between the crab cakes and scallops. When she can't handle waiting anymore, she drops the menu and rests her chin on her fists.

"This is making me crazy. What's so important that you had to wait until we ordered dinner?"

Julian sips his water. Holding up a finger, he dabs his face with his napkin.

"First off, guess who Medlock and Isaacs arrested this afternoon?"

"Who?"

"Your best friend, Harold Gibbons."

Darcy tries to picture Gibbons breaking the law and fails miserably. The man is pushing sixty-five and only curses when he's out of weed killer.

"Arrested?"

"Gibbons walked into Severino's on Hill Street after lunch. Know the place?"

"The bar, right?"

"That's Severino's, but they serve a mean burger. Anyhow, Gibbons started an argument with two men at the bar about Darcy Gellar and Michael Rivers."

Darcy's water goes down the wrong pipe. She coughs into her hand.

"This doesn't sound good."

"It was the usual Gibbons. He went on about how you're a scourge to his fine village, and if it hadn't been for you, Rivers never would have come to Genoa Cove. Yada, yada, yada."

"Well, he's not wrong."

"The two men at the bar took your side and called you a hero. Basically said Genoa Cove needs more people with your backbone, and anyone who wanted to speak ill of Darcy Gellar shouldn't let the door hit them in the ass on the way out."

"You're taking poetic license."

Julian's grin displays his teeth.

"Am I?"

"At the very least, you're exaggerating."

"This came from Medlock and Isaacs. So as you might imagine, Gibbons didn't take kindly to anyone arguing on your behalf and tossed his scotch in the first man's face. Somehow it ended up with Gibbons taking a swing and getting knocked cold. No charges against the men in the bar. Self-defense. On the other hand, Gibbons is spending the night in our finest cell. Two complementary meals on the village of Genoa Cove."

Darcy's jaw unhinges and clips the table.

"That's insane. On one hand, I want to laugh. On the other, Gibbons isn't young enough to start bar fights. I hope he isn't injured."

Julian puffs derision through his lips.

"The only injury was to his colossal ego. Everyone in Severino's shouted Gibbons down. There's a swell of support for Darcy Gellar in Genoa Cove."

The waiter sets the appetizers on the table. Darcy dunks a fried shrimp into a spicy cocktail sauce.

"I'll believe it when I see it."

She shakes her head.

"What?" Julian asks, creasing the corners of his eyes.

"I can't believe you brought me to Harpy's just to tell me Harold Gibbons had his lights punched out today."

Julian swallows a bite of shrimp and winks.

"That's not the reason."

"There's more?"

"Detective Ames came into the office today. First time since the storm."

The cocktail sauce lights Darcy's mouth on fire. She chases the heat with water.

"Oh? How's he doing?"

"He says the pain is way down, and he's able to take short walks now."

"Thank goodness. It's a wonder any of us survived the tornado. Detective Ames is no spring chicken. Well, I'm glad he's doing better. That made my day."

"Darcy, Ames is retiring."

Darcy wipes her hands on the napkin.

"Did you know this was coming?"

"He reached eligibility last year but kept working. I think the storm, the Rivers case, and watching his mom fight dementia changed his perspective. He wants to enjoy his remaining years and be around the people he loves."

Darcy recalls meeting the detective's mother last year at the police department. The woman fretted over Jennifer. It broke Darcy's heart that Ames's mother sneaked out of the senior home to see her son.

"We should all live by those rules. Please thank him for looking out for my family, and congratulate him on his decision. He must be thrilled to never deal with Darcy Gellar again."

Julian lowers his voice and leans forward.

"The chief called me into his office after Ames turned in his papers. He wants me to move up to detective."

Darcy's eyes light with surprise.

"Are you serious? That's great news."

"Technically, he has to advertise the position to all the eligible officers. But neither Medlock nor Isaacs want it. Wolpert only has two years on the force, and Faust... well..."

"Right. So are you going to do it? That would be a nice bump in pay, right?"

Julian pops another shrimp into his mouth and squints when the fire hits him.

"Damn, these are spicy. Yeah, it's a bigger paycheck. The problem is the chief is closing in on retirement too, and he planted another bug in my ear. The mayor likes me. His approval rating shot up five points after we took down Rivers."

"Are you suggesting you could be Chief of Police in a few years? That's incredible. Julian, you should go for it."

Darcy sets her plate aside, not wanting to spoil her appetite for dinner. She frowns when Julian doesn't mirror her smile. "But you're not happy. What am I missing?"

Julian shrugs and sits back in his chair.

"You remember that talk we had about getting out of Genoa Cove and away from the village gossip? I'm worried if I stay another two years, I'll never leave. Don't get me wrong. It's beautiful here, and gossip aside, the people mean well."

"But?"

"I don't want this to be my final chapter."

Adjusting the strap on her dress, Darcy wonders if she made the right decision when she dropped out of the bidding for the house in Charlotte. She wants her children to finish their teenage years with their friends in Genoa Cove, but how easy will it be to move three years down the line? Roots have a funny way of grabbing a foothold beneath the surface. Once they're established, digging them out becomes a battle not worth fighting.

"Have you considered working your way up to chief, then lateraling to a similar position in a larger city? You'd have the advantage of already holding the position."

"Outsiders get consideration, but generally the local officials choose from a pool of existing candidates inside the department. I'd have to walk on water to beat out anyone with a pulse."

"Well," Darcy says, holding up her glass in toast. "You are the officer who shot the Full Moon Killer."

Julian pushes his hand through his hair in indecision. The waiter removes the appetizer plates and sets down their entrees.

"We'll cross that bridge when we come to it. Let's eat."

Darcy smiles back at Julian. How did she get this

lucky? He's strong and beautiful, and he proved he'd give his life for her kids. Already, Darcy feels her life bonding to his. After Jennifer graduates high school, Darcy's next move might depend on Julian's career. Will she have the courage to make the right decision for herself and her family?

Stop it, she chides. You're getting ahead of yourself. Just enjoy your time together and let the story unfold.

Her heart warms as she sneaks looks at him across the table. He's everything she's ever wanted. Maybe she's already decided.

\*\*\*

Want to find out what happens next with Darcy and Julian? In the next book in the Darkwater Cove series, Julian's niece goes missing from college. The local authorities don't take the disappearance seriously, and Darcy senses something dark stalking the shadows. Is a serial killer loose on campus?

Ready to read the heart-stopping sequel, The Vanishing Girl?

Find out what happens to Darcy and Julian by ordering The Vanishing Girl on Amazon.

Whispers in the Dark

## Let the Party Begin!

I'm a pretty nice guy once you look past the grisly images in my head. Most of all, I love connecting with kickass readers like you.

Join the party and be part of my exclusive VIP Readers Group at:

WWW.DANPADAVONA.COM

# Whispers in the Dark

## Support Indie Thriller Authors

Did you enjoy this book? If so, please let other thriller fans know by leaving a short review. Positive reviews help spread the word about independent authors and their novels. Thank you.

## *About the Author*

Dan Padavona is the author of the The Darkwater Cove series, The Scarlett Bell thriller series, Severity, The Dark Vanishings series, Camp Slasher, Quilt, Crawlspace, The Face of Midnight, Storberry, Shadow Witch, and the horror anthology, The Island. He lives in upstate New York with his beautiful wife, Terri, and their children, Joe, and Julia. Dan is a meteorologist with NOAA's National Weather Service. Besides writing, he enjoys visiting amusement parks, beach vacations, Renaissance fairs, gardening, playing with the family dogs, and eating ice cream.

Visit Dan at: www.danpadavona.com

Whispers in the Dark

Made in the USA
Middletown, DE
21 July 2020